THEIRS TO RANSOM

A Marriage Raffle Novel

STASIA BLACK

Copyright © 2019 Stasia Black

ISBN-13: 978-1950097227
ISBN-10: 1950097226

All rights reserved. No part of this publication may be reproduced, distributed, or transmitted in any form or by any means, including photocopying, recording, or other electronic or mechanical methods, without the prior written permission of the publisher, except in the case of brief quotations embodied in critical reviews and certain other noncommercial uses permitted by copyright law.

This is a work of fiction. Similarities to real people, places, or events are entirely coincidental.

In the not too distant future, a genetically engineered virus is released by an eco-terrorist in major metropolitan areas all over the globe. Within five years, almost 90% of the world's female population is decimated.

In an attempt to stop the spread of the virus and quarantine those left, a nuclear war was triggered. It's still unclear who began attacking who, but bombs were dropped on all major US cities, coordinated with massive EMP attacks.

These catastrophes and the end of life as people knew it was collectively known as *The Fall*.

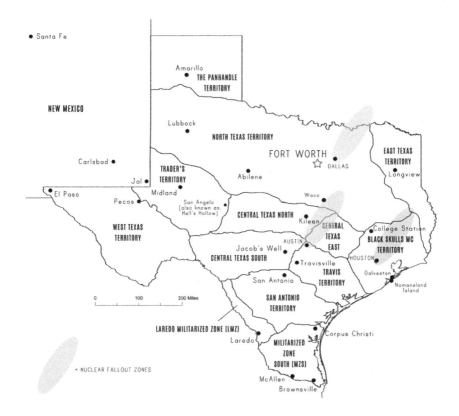

CHAPTER ONE

SOPHIA

Sophia held her purse up on her lap and let out an irritated huff at Finn who'd pulled their truck over to check his compass for the ten *millionth* time.

"Oh my God, Finnigan, we're going west. The sun just came up, so guess what? If we go in the opposite direction, we're heading the right way!"

"Oh wow, please do edjumacate me some more, Miss Sophia. Me big dumb boy. Don't know my ups from my downs," Finn quipped as he snapped the compass shut and pulled the truck back on to the road to head—you guessed it—exactly where Sophia had pointed out they should go five minutes ago. "It's not like I'm the one with all the tracking experience who's been out on about a hundred Scrapper runs. How many have you been on again? How many trips have you taken out of Jacob's Well, in point of fact?"

Oh, how she wanted to smack her purse in his superior face. Instead, she smiled sweetly. "You mean the *diplomatic missions* I've been on? Seven. Compared to your... how many was that again?" She held a hand to her ear. "Oh, zero? Hmm. How about that."

"And to think, we're only a day into this little adventure. I thought it'd take at least five before you turned into a harpy fish wife."

"Harpy f—" Sophia cut off in a huff, turning her face fastidiously away from Finn. Finnigan Knight was absolutely, positively *the* most annoying boy on the entire planet.

She wished she could go back in time and uninvite him from her little diplomatic trek over to New Mexico.

Except... well, she most likely did need the big, dumb oaf.

When they'd received the call from the Governor of Santa Fe in New Mexico, she couldn't have been more excited.

New Mexico! No one had heard anything from them in years other than the occasional trader who claimed to have passed through on treks from farther lands. They said it was all but abandoned apart from roving herds of bandits.

There'd been rumors that there was some sort of war between the southwestern states like New Mexico and Arizona around the same time as Texas's war with the Southern Alliance States. No one had any real concrete information, though. Which was in itself odd and not a little spooky. An entire states' citizens didn't just *disappear*.

Well, the person who'd called Jacob's Well's sat phone had answers.

There *had* been a war, which they'd lost to Colorado. Apparently Colorado was the state they'd all been fighting, just like the Southern States had all been ganging up on Texas. And like Texas, Colorado also won—and when they did, they apparently took *all* the women from the losing states.

Sophia hadn't been able to stop herself from gasping at that.

No women left? At all?

None, said the Governor. At least none that hadn't been hidden extremely well. But that was difficult to manage for long since New Mexico wasn't the most forgiving land.

New Mexico was finally starting to rebuild, though. At least in Santa Fe. They'd gotten Jacob's Well's number from President Goddard's trade secretary, the man said. And not only was Santa Fe a thriving community that had restored a portion of the power grid there, but they were eager to establish trade relations with The New Republic of Texas.

They'd give the Texans anything they wanted—in exchange for brides.

Brides.

That was the term they'd used. If they'd said *women*, like they were trying to sell women or barter them like cattle, Sophia might have hung up right there.

But no, apparently they'd heard of Jacob's Well's lottery system. They wanted in. And they'd pay big for the privilege.

"It's the future of our nation-state at stake, you understand, Miss Wolford?" the man on the phone had pleaded. "Without you, we'll disappear in a generation."

How could she say no to that?

But she wasn't going to just rush in. She had to make sure they were who they said and that they could offer what they promised.

And she wanted to show them good faith that they could deliver the goods as well.

So she was going.

To offer herself as the first bride.

She'd show Dad she could be more than just a pretty face who could throw wedding parties and work at the soup kitchen. She could be just as brave as any of them and serve her country too.

Dad needed troops to fight General Travis and take back the Republic. New Mexico had men. Plenty, it sounded like. And Texas had women. There were all the ones Drea had just freed and even more once they liberated San Antonio.

Plus, Sophia was sure Daddy wouldn't let some other jerk take the Presidency. Not another President Goddard. Maybe Daddy himself would be President. He'd done such a good job with Jacob's Well. Imagine what he could do with the whole New Republic! He'd definitely honor whatever agreement Sophia made.

Then she frowned. He hadn't exactly been thrilled with her the last time they'd talked over the phone. And they'd gotten cut off so abruptly and then the battery on her sat phone had run out and she hadn't wanted to go back to the caves to get another. Nope, she didn't want to run into Dad again until her mission was a success.

Besides, she could use the sat phone they had in New Mexico. Or better yet, just show back up with her new army behind her, like a modern day Joan of Arc.

Sophia sighed happily.

"Do I even want to know what it is you're plotting over there?"

Sophia glared Finn's way, her good mood immediately souring again. Right. Finn. The unfortunate tag-along she'd been forced to ask to help her.

Because while she might like to pretend she was a warrior-diplomat, yeah... the warrior part might be a stretch. She felt confident of her diplomatic abilities—hadn't she watched her dad at work for years and welcomed every new girl to Jacob's Well since she'd turned seventeen?

But if some bandit or smuggler came after her while she was traveling, she'd have little idea what to do. Dad was so protective of her, he'd taught her basic self-defense moves even though he swore she'd never have to use them in Jacob's Well. And she practiced them over and over at night in her room after he was asleep.

But practicing against an invisible opponent and coming up against the real thing? In spite of what everyone thought of her, she wasn't that naïve.

So she'd thought carefully about all the people she might approach to help her. Maybe Nix or one of Shay's husbands... Or maybe Vanessa would lend her those big, burly twins of hers...?

But talking to Dad had put the kabosh on that. Any of those people would only side with her dad. They'd tell her she should wait. That she should take more people. Or more likely, that *she* shouldn't go at all. That was *definitely* what Dad would say.

So she had to go before he got back. And take someone with her who was totally reckless with little appreciation for authority or doing things the proper way: Finnigan Knight, *ding ding ding ding!*

Because no matter what Drea or anyone else thought, she was more than just Daddy's little girl. She cared about the future of the

Republic as much as anyone else. She loved her country. She'd fight for it. She'd... she'd *die* for it, if it ever came to that.

A shudder ran down her spine at the thought, but she only stiffened and sat taller. But it was true. Those courageous boys out with General Cruz fighting in San Antonio weren't the only ones who could be brave.

Maybe most people wouldn't think much of a couple of days travel and then throwing an elaborate wedding... but there was still something to be said for a feminine form of warfare.

Sophia had dreamed of her wedding for as long as she could remember.

And obsessed about her lottery so many times she'd about crawled out of her skin waiting for the day to finally come.

Well, here it was. She turned nineteen next week. And maybe the wedding wouldn't be exactly as she'd always imagined, in the old Catholic church in Jacob's Well, with the big bell that rang out over the town and echoed in the hills. And maybe her dad wouldn't be there standing beside her to give her away. And maybe she wouldn't be surrounded by the faces she'd known since she was a little girl.

But she'd be married and finally get a start on her lifetime of loving someone, several someones, and learning what it felt like to be loved back.

And that was all she'd ever wanted.

She let out another happy sigh, imagining her future husbands. Would they be big men with lots of muscles? Or sleek and refined? Maybe one of each? Would another be musical and sing her to sleep at night? Ooo, or a poet! She'd love to be married to a poet.

Sophia, how I do love thee, let me count the ways...

She couldn't help the happy sigh that escaped.

"Are you like, constipated over there?"

"*What?*" Sophia jumped in her seat and glared again at Finn even as she felt her face heat. "No I am not— Why would you even say—"

"I don't know," he said, one hand casually on the wheel as he glanced her way before looking forward again. "You just keep making these little noises. *Hmmmm. Ooooohhh*," he mimicked.

She crossed her arms over her chest and huffed, turning her back to Finn and looking firmly out the window.

"Oh come on, Soph," Finn laughed. "I'm just joshin'. You're just so pretty when your cheeks get all pink like that."

So— *Pretty?* Did he just—

She swung her head back around to look at him but he was watching the road again. He did glance her way, though, and caught her looking at him. He shot her a quick wink, then went back to looking at the road like nothing was out of the ordinary.

Sophia let out an infuriated huff and swore to herself that as soon as she was married, she would have *nothing* to do with Finnigan Knight ever again so long as she *lived*.

CHAPTER TWO

FINNIGAN

"Finn, I need to go," Sophia said, that little breathy whine in her voice that drove Finn crazy. "I need to go. *Bad.*"

Finn clenched his hands on the steering wheel and repeated what he had the last million times. "It's not safe to stop around here."

They were close to the border with New Mexico and this whole area was notoriously dangerous. There was a reason there wasn't open trade with Texas and whatever the hell was left of New Mexico.

And a reason people considered everything past the Texas border to be wildlands where only fools or the insane dared tread.

So naturally Sophia had come into his cavern two days ago declaring she was going not just over the border, but deep into the wildlands. All the way to fucking Santa Fe.

She wasn't normally a fool but when it came to the real world outside Jacob's Well, the girl didn't have the good sense God gave her. Or shoulda gave her.

So if she was gonna survive the trip, he was going to have to go with her. Get the girl to Santa Fe. Come hell or high water, he'd get her there. And get her there in one piece.

"You said it wasn't safe to stop around Fort Stockton." Sophia threw her hands up. "And then it wasn't safe to stop around Pecos. But we passed Pecos twenty minutes ago. I'm seriously gonna pee my pants if we don't stop soon!"

Finn glanced her way. By the way she was twisting on her seat, it looked like she wasn't just being dramatic.

He looked back at the road. "I told you not to drink that whole bottle." Any Scrapper worth his salt knew you rationed your water intake so you weren't forced to stop somewhere you didn't want to. Either that or you got real familiar with pissing into a bottle.

Sophia let out a little exasperated huff and Finn shook his head. After thirty hours in a car together, he was becoming more than familiar with all her little noises. For the most part, they were damn cute.

Not that he'd ever tell her that.

"Look, Soph, it's just another three hours till we get there—"

"Three *hours!* No way. Finnigan Knight, you will pull this truck over right this instant."

He glanced her way again. "It's cute that you think you're the one in control here."

Her mouth dropped open for just a moment before she clapped it shut and ground her teeth together. "This is *my* mission. You just happen to be along for the ride."

"Oh is that so?" Finn laughed. "How do you figure it? This is my truck. And you're depending on navigational expertise. Seems to me like if it's anyone's, it's *my* mission. So we'll go by *my* rules. Which means no stopping on the most dangerous stretch of road we seen yet. Here, if it's that bad…"

He rustled around the seat behind him and then held out an old plastic Big Gulp cup toward her.

"Don't be crude." She yanked the cup out of his hand and threw it back behind the truck seat.

"I was being serious."

She made another huffing noise. "Why are you being so stubborn?

There's nothing to be afraid of. It's flat." She flung an arm out toward the front windshield. "We can see for miles in both directions and There. Is. No. One. We're perfectly safe stopping for five minutes so I can relieve myself. Now stop the damn truck!"

Oh shit. The perfect Sophia Wolford had just cursed. Sure it was just *damn* which was like the most Mary Sue of all curse words but still. She was really upset. Looking at her, he could see she did look almost panicky.

This time it was him huffing out a loud breath. He spent all his time around guys. It was hard to remember that chicks might work different. Sure whipping out your dick and peeing in a bottle was nothing for dudes but Sophia? Prim and proper Sophia? The idea of losing her composure like that? Or worse, actually pissing her pants?

Goddammit. A guy would just laugh it off and Finn would make a joke about having to scrub down his seats but fuck, this truck had seen a lot worse. Johnson almost died on that seat, guts half falling out, blood everywhere. The seats were that fake leather so it mostly came off. Johnson survived too, so wins all around.

But a girl like Sophia? She had a working *shower* in her house for Christ's sake. She cared about, like, dignity and shit. Something most folks he knew had given up on long ago.

Finn checked the rearview mirror for about the tenth time in as many minutes. Like she said, it was clear. Road ahead, too.

"Fine," he said. "But you get *two* minutes, not five."

"Thank you, Finn. Thank you."

Well damn, she really must be desperate if she was actually *thanking* him.

He pulled the truck off to the side of the small country highway and jammed it into park. "Go," he said, reaching under his seat for his rifle.

"Don't look," she said as she pushed open her door and he rolled his eyes and did the same

"Oh yeah, I can't wait to get a view of your backside as you squat and—"

"Don't you dare finish that sentence!"

Finn lined the butt of the shotgun up against his shoulder and looked down the sights back the way they'd come. There was a little bit of dust kicked up from their truck, but other than that, nothing. He swung around to the road ahead and it was clear there, too.

Okay, good.

He listened and didn't hear anything but the sounds of late summer.

"You done?" he called.

"Just give me a second."

"Jesus Christ, I thought you said your bladder was about to burst."

"I'm used to a toilet. You pressuring me isn't helping."

"Jesus Christ," he muttered again, swiveling back to look behind them.

He'd swear he could feel the seconds ticking by. He turned around he didn't know how many times checking to see if anyone was coming.

And still nothing from the other side of the truck. But so help him God, if she didn't start to piss soon, he'd—

Fuck!

Someone was coming from behind. Multiple someones, on motorcycles.

"Done," Sophia called.

"Get in the truck," Finn shouted as he tore his door open.

"What is it?" Sophia asked, door open with one hand over her eyes as she looked behind them.

"Get in the fucking truck, Soph!"

She must have finally seen the bikes because her eyes widened and she scrambled up into the seat, pulling her door shut behind her.

"What do we do?" she asked frantically as she put her seatbelt on.

"We drive." Finn yanked the gearshift into drive and jammed the pedal to the floor. The wheels spun on gravel and then finally got purchase. The truck jerked forward as Finn pulled back onto the road.

The ancient engine whined at being pushed so hard. The truck was close to ninety years old, one of the reasons it had taken them so long to get here. He rarely pushed her above fifteen to twenty miles an hour. Using old vehicles like this meant you spent half the time with them up on blocks in repairs. Most of the Jacob's Well fleet was held together with duct tape and prayers.

The bikes behind them weren't sparing on speed though. Finn glanced in the rearview and counted. One, two, three, four, five, *six*. Shit. Who the hell had that many working bikes, this far out in the middle of nowhere?

He hadn't been stupid enough to take them straight through Pecos, they'd gone in a wide circle around it on back roads, but surely the town that was barely a smear on the map couldn't be that well supplied.

But they were near the border. He'd had a bad feeling in his gut all morning as they got closer. Place might as well be the Bermuda Triangle for as many people came back who ventured over the border.

He should have tried harder to dissuade Sophia from leaving for this damn fool mission. He knew exactly how dangerous the world was. But he'd known the only way to stop her would have been to tie her up, something that had seemed too extreme to him at the time.

Now he was kicking his own ass for not doing it, no matter if she hated him the rest of her life. At least she would have *had* the rest of her life to hate him.

"Finn, they're getting closer!"

He looked in his rearview and goddammit, she was right. They were almost on their tail. And the one in the lead was lifting a machine gun.

"Get down!" Finn shouted only seconds before the back windshield shattered as the truck was peppered with gunfire.

Sophia screamed but bent over and Finn ducked down as much as he could. He hadn't gone another ten feet, though before the inevitable happened.

He'd just clicked his seatbelt into place as the back tire blew out.

Shit.

Sophia.

He threw out an arm to try to hold her in place as the truck spun out off the road and then—

They were rolling. Sophia screamed. Glass shattered. Everything was ass over end—

Fuck!

...

...

Finally the truck settled.

Finn blinked and groaned, trying to get his bearings.

Upside down. They were upside down.

"Soph?" Finn looked frantically in her direction. "Soph, are you okay?"

She groaned in response and put a hand to her head. Fuck, her hand came away bloody.

"I'm fine," she said. "Where are they?"

Oh shit. The bikers. How had he forgotten, even for a second? Some protector he was turning out to be. He reached around for the rifle. Couldn't feel it. Godfuckingdammit. Where was the rifle? He looked this way and that.

And finally spotted it. Out the shattered front windshield. Lying in the grass about five feet away.

He reached for his seatbelt and undid the catch. And promptly fell on his head.

"Shit!" He tried to right himself and climb through the shattered front window at the same time. He could hear the bikes. They were almost on top of them. Then he heard the roar of an engine cut off. Fuck. They were here.

He shoved his body through the windshield and army crawled to the shotgun. "Don't move," he hissed in a whisper to Sophia.

Did she listen?

Of course not. She released the catch on her seatbelt and tumbled down but he couldn't watch her. He moved along the back side of the truck, hidden by the long bed.

He cocked the rifle and then peeked out past the tailgate.

Two motherfuckers approaching, machine guns at their shoulder. Again, what the fuck? The waste of bullets was incomprehensible.

He closed his eyes. One, two...

On three, he swung the rifle around the back of the truck, lined up the shot. *CRACK*. He recocked. *CRACK*.

Two motherfuckers down. Four to go.

He cocked the rifle again. He only had six shots.

That meant he couldn't waste a single one.

No pressure.

He glanced around the back of the truck. He'd given away his position with the fire but that was part of his intention. To draw them away from Sophia back in the cab.

He glanced around the corner of the truck again, yanking back only milliseconds before gunfire erupted. He hunched down against the ground. Thank Christ these old trucks were made so solid.

The gunfire pinged like rocks against the metal but didn't penetrate.

Finn crawled back to the front of the truck. With so many of them, no doubt they'd try circling around from behind—which meant they'd find Sophia. Right as he came back around the front, more gun fire sounded.

It was Sophia. Shooting blindly behind her as she crawled out the front of the truck, looking terrified.

Finn grabbed her arm and pulled her around the side of the truck right as more machine gun fire came.

"Where the hell did you get a gun?"

"Dad gave it to me."

"Do you know how to shoot?"

She nodded shakily.

"Then don't waste any more bullets."

"Here. I have this too."

Finn had his rifle at his shoulder, swinging back and forth trying to prepare for either direction they'd attack from.

"Finn," Sophia said insistently.

He was about to tell her to stop distracting him when he spared a glance her way and grinned. She was holding out a grenade.

He grabbed it and dared to pop up over the back of the truck to gauge their position. He couldn't waste their one advantage.

He ducked right back down, to the predictable gunfire.

They were split up as he'd thought. Two up front, two coming around back.

"Okay," he whispered to Sophia. "Follow me. I take one, you get the other. Got it?"

She nodded. Then he pulled the pin and lobbed the grenade toward the men at the back of the truck. Then he jumped to a crouch and ran toward the front.

There was shouting a moment before the *BOOM*.

Finn didn't waste a second. He ran around the front of the truck and shot a guy still reeling in surprise from the explosion.

The last man standing wasn't so slow. He had his gun up, also a rifle. Sophia had her gun up... but she didn't shoot. Why the fuck wasn't she shooting?

Finn cocked his rifle again so he could take the bastard out himself.

Except it didn't cock right. The pump action was caught on something and didn't eject the last casing.

There was no time to think or try to fix it. The man with the rifle was lifting it to his shoulder. He'd kill Finn and then go for Sophia.

Finn shouted at the top of his lungs and then rushed the guy. Finn grabbed the end of the man's rifle and jerked it upwards right as the guy got his finger on the trigger. The shot went off into the air and Finn jerked the gun out of his grasp, then, grabbing both ends, he smashed it into the man's face.

Finn didn't stop there, either.

He smashed the stock into his face, again and again until the guy's face was bloody and unrecognizable.

Only when he was sure the guy was down did he pull back and look around.

Sophia was crouched against the side of the truck, hands covering her head, her gun on the ground beside her.

What the fuck was she thinking?

He looked to the back of the truck. At least the grenade looked like it had done its work. The two bodies back there weren't moving. Still, if Finn had learned one thing in the years since The Fall, it was to make sure an enemy couldn't come back to bite you in the ass.

Or put a bullet in your head.

He walked over to Sophia, snatched her gun off the ground, and went around, putting a bullet right between the eyes of every man there.

"Sophia. Keep watch behind us while I clean up here."

She jerked at the sound of his voice and he breathed out hard.

"Look, Soph, you can fall apart later. But we're exposed. You gotta keep your shit together right now. You hear me?"

Her head lifted at this, tear tracks staining her pretty cheeks. "I'm sorry if I can't help feeling human emotions when my life was just in danger," her voice cracked, "and human people just *died* in front of me."

Finn shook his head. "Look, Princess. You were the one who thought you could just waltz out here into the big, bad world. Well this is what it's like," he threw his hands up gesturing around them. "Kill or be killed. I learned that lesson when I was thirteen. So just be happy you got to be a kid as long as you did."

Her chest heaved and she opened her mouth like she had a hundred retorts but then she closed her mouth again, into a tight line. She stood up, her back rigid, and swiped angrily at her eyes.

"Fine," she said coldly. "I'll keep watch."

Finn shook his head and grabbed the hunting knife from his belt as he jogged over to the bikes. What the fuck did she think it would be like out here? What did she think her dad created Jacob's Well for? Everything Eric Wolford did to create that little paradise in the center of chaos was to protect his daughter.

But did she appreciate it?

No.

Just like she didn't appreciate Finn.

He'd just risked his life for her.

Jesus Christ did she realize how close they'd both come to dying?

He jammed his knife into the tire of the bike with the lowest gas in the tank and slashed backwards with all his might.

In only helped release a little of his fury. Ten tires later and he was feeling mildly calmer.

He went back to Sophia and she'd gathered the weapons along with a giant hiker's backpack she'd brought along stuffed to the gills with who the hell knew what.

"No way," Finn said, gesturing at the backpack. "We aren't taking that thing. The weapons, yes. But not that."

She set her jaw. "I'm not leaving it. This is a diplomatic mission. You don't show up for a diplomatic mission without gifts."

"You do if you almost die on the way getting attacked by road bandits." He threw an arm out in the general direction of their upended truck.

She ignored him, hiking the backpack up higher on her shoulders and flouncing past him toward the last bike standing.

"I take it this is our transportation?"

"Women," Finn muttered under his breath, picking up the guns and slinging them across his chest. He grabbed a few belongings from the wreckage and then joined Sophia on the road. At least she'd had the good sense to pull a long-sleeved linen shirt out of her backpack so she wouldn't burn under the punishing Texas sun while they drove. But she looked ridiculous with the pack on her back. It dwarfed her small frame.

Whatever. He wouldn't waste his breath arguing with Her Highness.

He climbed on the bike and took a deep breath.

Something he needed, especially when she climbed on behind him and her slim arms slid around his waist, her thighs contouring to his.

Jesus Christ.

He swore he couldn't make up his mind about Sophia. One minute he wanted to strangle her and the next, all he could think about was—

He swallowed hard and gritted his teeth, trying to ignore the tightening in his jeans. Especially since he knew it was about way more than lust when it came to Sophia Wolford.

He'd been a damn goner for her ever since he stumbled into Jacob's Well at fifteen years old and the brown-haired beauty had served him soup and smiled shyly at him his first day in town.

After years scrambling just to keep body and soul together, she was the symbol of everything he'd ever wanted his whole life but never had —she was good, clean, sane. *Innocent.*

She was perfection and he was the shit people tried to scrape off their boots. And now he was dragging her down into his world.

What the hell was he doing?

"Soph." He turned his head to the side, not quite looking her in the eye. "Let's go home. We can turn around right now. This bike could probably get us as far as Central Texas North. I know that land like the back of my hand. I could get us back to San An—"

"No!" Sophia exclaimed. "Finn, no. I'm not giving up just because of this... setback. Look, I'm sorry if I—" He felt her shift behind him which really wasn't helping distract him from the warmth of her against his back. "I'm sorry I didn't shoot when I was supposed to. I had my finger on the trigger and I was standing just like Dad taught me but I just—"

Finn shook his head and put his hand over Sophia's that she still had on his waist. "Don't. It's not a bad thing you don't want to kill a man, Soph. I shoulda never asked it of you."

"What does that mean? Just because I'm a woman?"

Finn rolled his eyes. "Jesus, Soph. You know what I mean. You're you. You should be planning weddings. Long as I've known you all you could talk about was raising babies. There's some things once you do them, you can't ever scrub 'em from your head. Your dad didn't want this kinda life for you and neither do I."

She didn't say anything for several long moments.

"So we turning around?"

Her arms tightened around his waist and he couldn't help the small catch of his breath.

"No. I can do more than have babies. We're at war. Colonel Travis is threatening everything we hold dear. He's enslaving women just like me, Finn. We have to keep going. We have to."

See? It was stuff like this that made Sophia Wolford get under a man's skin. She was more than a pretty face. So much more.

"Hold on," Finn muttered gruffly, then kicked the bike into gear and took off down the road.

CHAPTER THREE

SOPHIA

Sophia had decided while holding on to Finn for dear life as they sped down the deserted highway, weaving in and out of stalled out cars left on the road from a decade ago, that she should be nicer to him.

Because back there? With those bikers?

She would have died. Without Finnigan, she would have died.

When she'd gotten the call from Santa Fe, it had all sounded like such an adventure. She'd charge in. Save the day. Bring home an army to Dad.

Like something she read in one of her novels.

But watching that man's face explode as Finn's rifle shot hit its target?

There was nothing romantic or heroic about that.

She'd been supposed to shoot the other man. She'd felt confident she could. He was the bad guy. He was trying to kill them. She knew how to shoot. Dad practiced with her twice a month ever since they'd gotten to Jacob's Well. It should have been simple.

But after witnessing the gore of Finn's shot, she froze. Even watching the man lift his gun and aim it right at Finn. Even seeing the panic in Finn's eyes when his own rifle got stuck.

Finn didn't freeze, though.

No, he just charged the man about to blow his brains out.

Sophia thought she understood what courage was but she hadn't.

Courage was running straight toward a loaded gun even when you were afraid.

But Sophia? Fear paralyzed her. It always had. Because she was a coward.

Cowards froze. Cowards dropped their guns and put their hands over their heads and waited for all the shooting to be over.

Cowards stayed upstairs hiding in a closet, doing nothing while their mothers were downstairs being brutalized and murdered.

Sophia clenched her eyes shut and pressed her forehead into Finn's back. No. She didn't remember that. She never let herself remember that.

Anyway, none of that mattered. What mattered was keeping positive now. So they didn't have the truck. This bike would get them there faster anyway. If anyone could look at lemons and see lemonade, it was her, dad blam it.

Only seconds after she had the thought, though, there was a loud *POP* noise, followed by sputtering. The bike swerved violently.

Sophia squeaked in terror and clung even tighter to Finn. She felt the flex of all his muscles as he fought to keep the bike upright.

The bike wobbled back and forth and Sophia squeezed her eyes shut. She forced them back open the next second. She would *not* be a coward. Finn couldn't afford for her to be.

They were slowing down but not as quickly as they should. Whatever had happened, it was clear the something had happened to the engine. Were the breaks shot, too?

Oh God, please don't let her come all this way only to die before she'd ever even done anything with her life.

"Are you okay?"

"Fine, I'm fine," she said shakily. In fact she felt like running over to the side of the road and barfing her guts up, but it wouldn't do to be telling Finn that.

He'd managed to bring them to a stop. It had all happened so fast, she could barely even recollect how he'd done it. He put his boots down to the asphalt, all his muscles tense, but he'd kept them steady as they slowed down and finally, finally came to a stop.

"Come on," she said, pushing her hair out of her face. It was a mess, having been whipped all over the place by the wind. She pulled out her ponytail and redid it as best as she could without a comb.

"We should get off the road, shouldn't we?"

Finn stood there watching her another long moment before nodding and gesturing toward the other side of the road.

"We can follow the Pecos River up. Safer than staying on the road and we'll have water."

Sophia nodded, hiking her backpack up on her shoulders. Finn must have noticed because he held out a hand.

"Give me the pack."

"Oh it's fine. I've got it—"

"Sophia, don't be a brat. Give me the backpack. You look like you're about to tip over backwards any second."

She shot him a glare. She was really making an effort to be nice to him but did he have to make it so dang difficult?

She slung the backpack down off her shoulders. "I totally could have handled it. It's not very heavy." She threw it towards him.

He caught it and staggered back a step. "Damn, girl. You're stronger than you look."

She rolled her eyes. "All right, jackass. Which way to the river?"

"I wasn't kidding. This thing is heavy. What the hell you got in here? A few bricks you just couldn't bear to leave behind?"

She frowned, looking over at him as he readjusted the straps and slung it over his shoulders. She couldn't tell if he was joking or not about the weight and her being strong. Sometimes she thought she was strong from constantly carrying huge cornmeal bags and soup pots here and there between the kitchens and the serving window in the soup kitchen but it wasn't like she had many people to compare herself to.

"How far is the river?" she asked, lifting a hand over her eyes in the direction Finn had pointed.

Even though it was late autumn, the day was sweltering. She'd already sweat through her linen shirt but knew she couldn't take it off no matter how hot she got. Finn must have been thinking along similar lines because he came over and pulled a baseball cap from his back pocket. He settled it on her head.

"River's probaby about twelve miles."

"Twelve..." Sophia's mouth went dry even at the thought. "How much water do we have left?"

"Two bottles were all we could carry. But I also grabbed a pot so we can boil the river water and drink all we want once we get there." He turned slightly and she saw both the bottles and the pot tied on to his belt. With that and the pack on his back, he looked ridiculous. But efficient.

Still. Only *two bottles*?

"Here, have a swallow now and then not again for a while, all right?"

He untied one of the bottles and held it out to her.

She took a swallow, feeling panicky at the thought of how tightly they'd have to ration the water. As soon as she handed the water back, she realized just how much she'd drank and felt embarrassed and guilty.

"We'll be okay, Soph. I been in worse situations, believe me."

She nodded and smiled brightly in spite of her anxiety. "I'm not worried. Get to the river, follow the river up to Santa Fe. No problem."

Finn just stood there looking at her.

"What?"

"Soph, you gotta know that's not realistic. You think we're just going to walk across New Mexico? Santa Fe's clear on the other side of the state. We don't know what's going on in this territory. It was one thing when we had a vehicle. Gas was gonna be an issue but we maybe could have figured our way around it. But without something to drive—"

"We'll make it," Sophia said determinately. "We have to."

"I'm sure your dad and Drea and General Cruz have it under contr—"

"But they don't," she said, unable to help her exasperation showing through. "Don't you get it? Dad never expected Jacob's Well to get attacked. I overheard General Cruz talking about how outnumbered his men were. It's two to one against Travis's forces. No one saw this coming. No one prepared for the President getting assassinated or Travis making his power grab, and—"

"Soph, don't you think taking on the world's problems all on your own shoulders is a little much, though?"

"Drea never did. She saw something that needed doing so she did it. She never waited around for someone else to do it."

"Why are you bringing her into this? I thought you hated her."

"What? I don't hate her! Sometimes I may have thought she lacked a certain... grace. But I admire her. She went into that MC compound and singlehandedly freed all those women." Sophia shook her head.

She couldn't even fathom the courage something like that would take. And she was finally mature enough to say that all her attitude toward Drea over the months might have been partially driven out of envy.

Drea was everything Sophia wasn't. Cool, calm, collected, and a total badass. When Drea stepped into a room, people took a step back, either in reverence, fear, or dislike. Some people didn't like so much confidence and drive in a woman.

When Sophia stepped into a room, there were smiles all around. For a long time, she'd thought that meant she was doing everything right. But maybe that just meant people thought of her like they did pretty pictures on the wall. Nice enough to look at but basically useless when it came to anything else.

"Come on." Finn looked around. "I don't like being on the road."

"Not that it will make much difference." In spite of how hot it was, Sophia shivered when she looked out. And out. And out and out and out.

There was nothing.

Not even trees.

It was just flat. With the barest of scrub brush.

She knew in theory that east Texas was basically a desert but seeing it up close like this. Being *stranded* here...

Finn didn't seem bothered though. He'd just started walking and several paces later turned back around, frowning.

"You coming?"

Sophia nodded because all the sudden, her throat felt incredibly dry and she wasn't quite sure she'd be able to get any words out.

They continued on like that for half an hour, Sophia just focusing on putting one foot in front of another on the dry, cracked earth, avoiding the occasional shrubs. She'd never seen earth so scorched. She'd just taken water for granted, living in the hill country like she had all her life. Before The Fall water came out the tap and afterwards, she'd thought she'd suffered learning to adapt to walking two houses down to the well to get water most of the time.

She knew in a sort of esoteric way that she was privileged. Good Lord, twice a month Daddy even let her use the solar panels on the roof to run a bath or shower and have hot water in the house.

But God... What did people out *here* do?

Then again, she didn't see any people.

She knew there were people. Finn had driven wide circles around towns so she hadn't seen any close up but there *were* towns. She supposed they had wells too. Aquifers ran underneath all of Texas, even out here if she wasn't wrong.

But what did they do for food? This ground couldn't be good for farming. Maybe ranching, but how fat could cows get, eating this scrub?

"Whatcha thinking about so quiet over there, Sophia pizzeria?"

She shot Finn a look. "Pizzaria?"

"It was either that or tortilla. Not that many words that rhyme with Sophia. I've been thinking on it the past, like, fifteen minutes. I got pizzeria, tortilla, and diarrh—"

"I get the idea," she cut him off.

He smiled. "I figured I like pizza better than tortillas."

"Tortilla rhymes better."

"But I like Pizza."

She shook her head. "I think you just like being contrary."

His smile turned to a grin. "I wouldn't say that."

"Only proving my point."

They were quiet for awhile after that. Finn tried engaging her in conversation a few more times but Sophia couldn't give him much in return.

She was too busy trying to ignore the growing pain in her feet.

The hiking boots she was wearing?

Well, she hadn't exactly had much time to break them in. And they were chafing something awful.

She hadn't expected she'd have to *walk* so much in them. She thought they'd be driving the whole way.

She'd just grin and bear it, then give her feet a nice long soak in the cool river tonight.

At least that had been her plan, but after walking a couple hours, it was too much. She stumbled and fell.

And landed on a cactus. Because oh yeah, in addition to the scrub brush, the only other thing that grew in abundance? Friggin' prickly pear cacti.

"Son of a *witch*!" she shouted, not daring to move and get even more cactus spines in her butt. She'd at least twisted as she fell so she had a butt full of cactus spines rather than a face full. Something that was little comfort at the moment.

"Shit, Soph!"

Finn hurried over to her, took her hands, and helped her up off the cactus. But standing just hurt worse, her feet were in so much pain.

"Turn around, hon. I gotta pull the spines out."

If there was anything more humiliating than bending over in the middle of nowhere so Finnigan Knight could pull cactus spines out of her behind, Sophia didn't know what it was.

He was at it a good twenty minutes. Sophia finally had to get on the ground on hands and knees because she just couldn't handle standing another second.

"All right, I got all the ones I can see. If you got another pair of jeans in the backpack, I think you should put them on cause if I didn't, you don't want to accidently sit down and get an unpleasant surprise later."

Sophia nodded as she turned around and crawled toward the pack.

"Hey, Soph. You crying?"

Sophia shook her head back and forth rapidly, turning her head away from him. God. Of course she was crying. She'd been crying ever since she fell into the damn patch of cactus. But crying silently was a skill she'd perfected a long time ago.

"I'm fine," she said and her voice didn't even break.

She unzipped the backpack and her cheeks colored. She hadn't anticipated having to open it in front of Finn.

"Can you turn around? While I change."

"Sophia. You're hurt. Let me help."

"I said turn around," she spat.

"Jesus. Fine."

She swallowed but her throat felt as dry as the desert around them even though Finn had insisted she take a long drink of water right after she'd fallen.

She unzipped the backpack and pulled out the bag that took up the largest portion of the big camping pack.

She reverently touched the plastic as she set the huge bag on the dirt beside her.

Her mother's wedding dress.

The fact that she still had it after all these years was something of a miracle.

She'd insisted they take it that horrific night so long ago. She and mom had talked about it so many times.

Some day you'll find your Prince Charming who sweeps you off your feet.

Just like Daddy did you?

Just like Daddy did me.

And I'll wear your dress, Mama.

And your daddy will walk you down the aisle. I'll be in the front row bawling my eyes out at seeing my baby all grown up.

Not much would be like her mother envisioned all those years ago. Mama died. Daddy was off fighting a war.

But she still had Mama's dress and by God, she'd be married in it. No matter if she had to carry it all the way across New Mexico.

Except… she wasn't sure she could walk ten more steps, let alone across an entire state.

More tears slipped down her cheeks and she sniffled and swallowed again.

She'd figure it out. Somehow. She had to. Daddy needed—

"What the hell is that?"

Sophia swung around, mortified. And then furious.

Finn was walking toward her, eyes locked on the wedding dress in the plastic bag beside her. She grabbed it before he could grab for it, clutching it to her chest.

"Nothing that concerns you."

Finn had tied a handkerchief over his nose and mouth to protect his face from the sun but she could still see his eyes and he looked furious.

"Sophia Wolford, tell me that is not a fucking wedding dress."

Sophia pursed her lips. She was having the worst day of her life and he was going to yell at her? Screw him.

"I told you this was a diplomatic mission. They want to start instituting the Marriage Raffle. I'm going to offer myself as a sign of good faith."

"That's the stupidest fucking thing I've ever heard." He tried to snatch the dress away from her but she just held on tighter.

"Don't you dare! Let go, Finn! I'm not kidding. Let go!"

"What the fuck are you thinking?" he shouted, finally letting go and standing up, running his hands through his hair and turning away from her, but only for a second.

"Jesus Christ, Sophia! Your dad spent his whole life making the Raffle safe for *you*." He threw his hands toward her. "Why do you think there's such a careful vetting process that men who want to enter as potential husbands have to go through? You have to live in town for two years and have regular meetings with an elder before you're even qualified for the outer tier of eligibility. And now you're just going to go throw yourself like a sheep among wolves. They'll tear you afucking part! No. I won't let you. We're going back home."

"You do *not* get to say what I do and don't do," she cried, painfully getting to her feet. She could ignore it. She was so furious, she could ignore anything. "You're not my father. And even if you were, I'm nineteen. I'm a grown woman. I can make my own choices. I can do my part!"

She shoved Finn hard in the chest but he didn't even stumble backwards. She shoved him again.

She shouted in fury and when she went to shove him again, he pulled her into his arms.

She fought him at first. She was furious at him. She hated him. Stupid Finn. Stupid men. Stupid feet.

Why was everything going wrong?

If only those bikers hadn't come after them and wrecked the truck.

If only the bike hadn't malfunctioned.

If only she'd packed better shoes.

If only she weren't so goddamned weak.

She buried her face in Finn's chest and wept. He pulled her close and then his strong arms wrapped around her.

She didn't know how long he held her like that. She was the one who finally pulled back, feeling stupid and panicky at the thought of how much water she was wasting by crying. And because her feet still hurt like all hell.

"My feet," she said, feeling her face crumple.

Finn's features were awash with concern but he cupped her face and forced her to look at him when she tried to avert her eyes.

"You are going to let me help you. Without giving me any lip. We'll figure this shit out. But we'll do it together, okay? No more secrets."

Sophia hiccupped but nodded. And staring into Finn's eyes... How had she never noticed the fact that he had green eyes before? Green with little flecks of gold.

God, maybe she was getting loopy with dehydration in all this heat. Because she let Finn help her. With everything.

Her legs felt shaky as he tugged her jeans down. He unbuttoned the long-sleeved denim shirt he was wearing and laid it out on the dirt for her to sit down while he took a look at her feet.

And she couldn't help looking at *him*. It was so ridiculous to even be looking or thinking anything like *that*.

But his back was broad and his shoulders were muscled. Since when had Finnigan Knight gone and grown into a man?

She quickly averted her eyes when he turned back toward her, pulling off her first boot.

"Jesus, Soph, why didn't you say something earlier?"

She winced with pain as he tugged down her sock. The back of her heel was bleeding and the outer side of her foot looked worn raw, too.

"I thought if we could just get to the river…"

She thought he'd yell at her again but he just looked pained as he gently lifted her ankle and looked at her foot from all sides.

He was so gentle with her it just made her want to cry again.

"How are we going to get to the river now?" she whispered, more stupid tears seeping down her cheeks.

Finn gave her calf a squeeze and looked her in the eye. "We'll make it there, Soph. I promise, I'll take care of you. Okay? I swear."

His voice and gaze were so intense as he said it, it made Sophia's insides quiver. She bit her lip and nodded, just barely stopping herself from asking, *why?*

Why, Finn? Why did you agree to come in the first place? Why are you looking at me like that?

But she just bit her lip harder as Finn pulled off the other boot, giving that foot just as thorough an examination.

"You got a first aid kit in the bag?"

She nodded and he rooted around for it. But even while he did, he kept one hand on her leg. It was presumptuous but she liked the contact. Maybe he felt like he needed to stay tethered to her as much as she suddenly needed to be to him.

She could have told him that she could put on the ointment and bandages herself. She should have.

But she didn't.

She let him do it. Marveling the whole time at how gentle his big, clumsy fingers were at the task.

All she'd ever seen Finn do was haul around Scrapper junk and do construction. Oh and she'd seen him going in to visit Ana Martinez, one of the few single women in Jacob's Well who shared her favors widely, about six months after he turned 18. One of the many men who did.

That was when she'd seen Finn for what he really was. Just another man. Not special or romantic or any of the other hundreds of stupid little fantasies she'd woven around him since he'd first strutted into town like a prize peacock the handful of years before like he was God's gift.

But now here he was, bending over in the dirt to patch up her *feet*.

"It's okay, I think they're good now," she said, putting out a hand on Finn's as he looked over his work, again examining her right foot from all sides.

She withdrew her feet away from him, bending her legs as modestly as she could. "Can you get me another pair of socks?"

Those hazel eyes of his flicked back up to hers again. She felt snagged by his gaze. Like suddenly her lungs felt too big in her chest.

"Sure," Finn said, suddenly looking away like he was embarrassed to have been caught staring. Didn't he realize she'd been staring too?

She put a hand up to her cheeks. They didn't feel any warmer than they had all day but she'd swear they were flaming.

He rummaged through the backpack and pulled several items. He handed her socks and another pair of jeans.

She gingerly pulled on the socks first and he turned his back as she leaned on her elbows and lifted her bum to wiggle into the jeans.

She was sweating more than ever when she sat back up with the jeans on. Putting stifling denim back on made her feel like she was suffocating but the only other things she brought were skirts and dresses.

Still, looking around and then back at her boots, she had no idea how she'd be able to keep going.

"Here," Finn said, "put these on."

"Those are house slippers."

He kept holding out the fuzzy slippers. He flipped them over. "They've got soles. And there's no way your feet are getting stuffed back in those boots. I think these are our best option."

Sophia looked doubtfully at the thin soles that were little better than cardboard. But she took them because really, they were her *only* option if she didn't want to walk through the desert in her socks.

And she'd decided that maybe Finn *did* know what he was talking about when it came to surviving in this outside world. All she'd ever known of it was life before The Fall and then that one last horrific day—

She put it out of her head and pulled the slippers on, wincing even at the slight pressure they put on her sore feet.

Finn stood up and held down his hands to her. The sight of him standing above her, shirtless, his silhouette surrounded by golden sunlight... well, it was sure a sight to behold.

Sophia swallowed again before grabbing hold of his hands and letting him pull her to her feet. He shook out his shirt and then pulled it back on. He fastened the buttons quickly and then without a word, put all their supplies back into the backpack.

Including the wedding dress. Though Sophia didn't miss his sharp, jerky motions as he shoved the wedding bag to fit into the backpack. Or the hard line of his mouth as he slung it across his shoulders.

Still, when he next looked her direction, his features softened again. "How does standing feel?"

"It's— It's okay," she stuttered.

He frowned. "Here, take another drink of water."

He reached around to the side pocket of the backpack and pulled out a water bottle. It was almost empty and he'd barely drunk any.

Sophia took a small sip and then held out the rest to him. He just shook his head and went to put the bottle away when she stopped him.

"Don't be stubborn, Finnigan. You're no use to me passed out in the desert because you wouldn't take care of yourself."

He arched an eyebrow but finally nodded and took the last swallow of water from the bottle. Then they headed out.

Sophia's feet did feel much better but she'd already done so much damage to them that it was still rough going. Not to mention that she was much more cautious about where she stepped now. She was also aware the whole time about how much she was slowing Finn down.

She tried suggesting he go on ahead of her but he shut her down every time she brought it up.

"Jesus, stop talking like that. I'm never gonna leave you alone out here in the middle of nowhere. Not in a million years so just stop saying it, okay?"

She bit her lip and they went on in silence for another long while. Maybe even an hour. The sun was punishing and it took more concentration than Sophia would have thought to stay upright and trudging ahead.

Finn paused every once and awhile for them to take sips from the water bottle and Sophia was far more careful about how much she drank. Still, with as much as the both of them were sweating, she couldn't imagine the little they were drinking was enough to keep them hydrated.

"What we *should* talk about is what I'm carrying around in this backpack," he said sometime later, as if picking up their conversation right where they'd left it.

"I don't want to get in another argument," she sighed. She was already *so* tired. She couldn't handle arguing with Finn on top of everything else. Her feet felt battered and her legs like jelly. How long had they been walking? Hours. But how far had they come and how many more miles was it to the river?

"I don't want to argue. Hey." Finn reached out and touched her shoulder. "No arguing. Okay?"

The earnestness in his eyes made her pause. She didn't know what to do with earnest Finn. It was kind of freaking her out. She shrugged and then started forward again.

It didn't stop him talking though, as he easily kept up beside her with his long legs. "I worry about you. You look at people and see the best in them. But the world out here isn't like that. You can't just trust people. Everyone out here is only looking out for themselves. They'd betray you as soon as look at you."

Sophia shook her head. "Just because you're a pessimist doesn't mean I have to be. Some people see the glass half full."

"It's not— Jesus, Soph."

"Look, I'm not trying to argue," she said, reaching out and putting a hand on his arm. She pulled it back almost immediately because touching Finn was... weird. It made her feel weird. *Anyway.* "I know the world's a bad place, okay? Dad drummed it into my head. *It's dangerous out there, honey,*" she lowered her voice in an imitation of her dad's. "But regardless of if it's dangerous or not, we still have to live in it. The hard stuff still has to get done. Somebody has to do it. So I don't see the harm in trying to stay positive."

"The harm is that you aren't prepared for when the awful things happen."

He said it so vehemently that Sophia couldn't help turning to look at him again. His jaw was clenched and there were two bright spots of pink high up on his cheekbones. She didn't think they were because of the heat, either.

"What happened to you?" she asked. The question came out almost as a whisper but his head jerked her way violently, but almost as quickly, he looked away again.

"I'll tell you," he said. "And then maybe you'll get what I mean. You can't trust people. Anyone."

Sophia frowned but then he started speaking.

"I was eleven when D-day hit. My mom had split years before, she was a real winner like that, so I still don't know what happened to her, but I guess she probably died. Anyway, Dad was in prison doing a nickel for trying to rob a 7-11—and I was living with my Uncle Murphy."

He shook his head, like he was getting off track. "I was a little shit. Always in trouble at school. I got in fights and stole stuff all the time. So then there's the Fall and the Death Riots and to Uncle Murphy it was like Christmas had come early."

Sophia's mouth dropped open but he just kept going.

"There was so much to loot, you see. And I was small enough to slip in between all the other looters in the riots. So he'd use me and we'd work in pairs, me running into stores and snatching what I could off the shelves and bringing it out to my uncle."

"But you were just a child!"

Finn held up his hands and wiggled his fingers. "Light fingers, heavy pockets. And the other looters were still less likely to beat up a kid to get to the loot. Most of the time."

"They hurt you?" Sophia felt breathless as she asked it, and not just from the exertion from walking for hours under the boiling heat.

Fin shrugged. "It got worse the more time went on when there was less and less to find in the stores."

"And your uncle just kept sending you in there all alone?"

"Oh, that and much worse than that. I was like you once. Well, maybe I always thought the glass was just about empty going on gone. But I still thought, I don't know. No matter how desperate things got, some things still mattered more. Like family. But I was wrong. Really, really wrong."

Sophia felt her stomach go sour. "What's that mean?" She asked it even though she wasn't sure she wanted to know the answer.

"It was a couple years after The Fall and supplies were running low. Uncle Murphy said he'd heard of a trading post where we'd get good trades for the little we did have left. We had some gold and jewelry stashed and I thought that's what he was gonna sell. Instead, after we got to Hell's Hollow, Murphy sold me."

"Finn!" Oh God. Finn just kept on walking though, so she hurried to keep up with him.

"I don't even know how much he got for me. He left me in the outer room while he went in and made the deal. Then he wouldn't look at me while two men dragged me away."

Finn shook his head. "Big fat fuck he sold me to tried to bugger me that night. But I'd got strong in the two years since The Fall. And I'd always been a fighter. So even though I was small..." He shook his head again, like he was trying to shake off the memory. "Anyway, I killed him that night."

Sophia's mouth, already dropped open, fell open even wider. "How?"

"Shard from a vase I broke."

Sophia blinked. She wanted to ask a million more questions but had the sense not to from the look on his face.

He'd said he'd killed a man when he was thirteen. This had to be what he'd meant. God. She couldn't even—

"And you got away?"

Finn nodded, jaw flexing. "I ran."

"But you were fifteen when you came to Jacob's Well, right?" She knew he'd been fifteen but she still asked it as a question. For a short period of her life, she'd made it her business to know everything about Finnigan Knight. But she never wanted him to know that.

"Yeah."

"So what happened in the two years in between."

"I kept running. Went east. Did any work I could. Stole when I couldn't. Fought on the front. They were so short on soldiers they didn't care I was just fourteen. I could hold a gun."

"God, Finn!"

He shrugged and rolled his eyes. "It's okay. I'm okay. I didn't tell you all this so's you'd feel sorry for me. I'm just tryin' to make you see. It's not a nice place out here, Soph. People will use you, abuse you, sell you. Everyone's got an angle. You can't trust anyone."

I trust you, was her immediate thought.

He finally stopped and put a hand on her arm. "And control is just an illusion. You don't have any control out here. There's no steady ground underneath you. The second you think you've got some, it'll shift. Even Jacob's Well. Look what happened. Your dad worked for years to make it a safe place for you. And even he couldn't keep control for long and he's one of the strongest men I've ever met."

"Finn." Sophia wanted to reach up and hold his face. Pull him into a hug. "I'm so sorry for all you've been through. I can see why you see the world the way you do. I might too, having been through all you have."

She searched his green eyes. "But it doesn't have to be that way anymore. That's what Dad's trying to do. What all of us are trying to do. We're going to build a better world. One where you don't have to be afraid all the time. One where you can feel safe."

But Finn only looked frustrated at her response. "Soph, you aren't hearing me. The world's not changing. It caught up with Jacob's Well, that's all. No place is safe."

"Then why are you here?" she asked, exasperated. Her voice was a croak, her throat was so dry.

He just looked at her like she was missing the obvious. "You, Soph. I'm here for *you*."

What?

Sophia's breath caught. Had he just— What did he—

Those damn blue eyes of his were more intense than ever as he moved closer. His head dropped and hers rose like they were magnets attracted to one another.

Sophia's heart was thumping so hard she was sure it was about to beat right out of her chest.

Did Finn— Did he like her? Like her like *that?*

His head dropped and she felt dizzy. Was he about to— Was this her first kiss? Where was she supposed to look? It felt weird looking at his face, he was so close. She'd be cross-eyed. That wasn't sexy. And she suddenly very desperately wanted to look sexy. So should she close her eyes?

But what if he thought that meant she didn't want to?

So she opened her eyes again and looked away from his face which was closer than ever.

And saw a glint in the distance.

"The river!" she exclaimed, pulling back from Finn. She realized a second too late that she'd ruined her own first kiss.

Finn jerked back and looked over his shoulder.

No, she wanted to say. *I mean, yes. The river. After we kiss, we'll go to the river.*

But Finn was hiking the pack higher on his shoulders, clearly focused on the river now. He did hold his hand back for hers, though, so maybe she hadn't ruined everything.

She took his hand.

It was so strong and steady and it made her stomach swoop to hold it.

It was only after she'd held it for several steps, furtively stealing glances at Finn that she asked herself what the hell she was doing.

You're about to get married!

To strangers.

From a strange land.

She clutched Finn's hand even tighter, his warnings swirling in her head. Could she really do it?

She'd been so sure of her path for so long. Did what just happened really change anything? The closer they came to the river, though, she couldn't think about anything else but taking a long, cool drink of water.

She couldn't. She knew they had to boil it first but still. Water. She could soak her feet. Take off all her clothes and soak her whole body.

She couldn't help her eyes inadvertently flicking to Finn at the thought. Her tongue flicked out to wet her dry lips. It didn't help much considering how dry her tongue was, too.

Finn turned to her and grinned. He pulled out the water bottle and handed it to her. "Here, have the last bit. I'll get to boiling some more."

He was always thinking of her needs first. Taking care of her. He was a good man.

You, Soph. I'm here for you.

She took the bottle and drank the water but left some for him. And she didn't take her eyes off his as she held out the bottle.

"You can have it all, Soph."

She shook her head and pressed the bottle into his hands.

He took it and drank, doing the same as her, looking at her the whole time. No, not just looking at her.

She'd never been *looked at* like that before.

She felt like a meal he wanted to devour.

She was about to get that first kiss after all. She stepped close, breathless after he finished the water and tossed the bottle to the ground. He threw the backpack and the guns he had slung over his shoulder to the ground the next second.

He reached for her, eyes full of that devouring hunger and she wanted it just as badly—

When the bank of the river was suddenly full of the sound of stomping hooves.

Finn's eyes jerked up, over Sophia's shoulder. In a single moment, desire was exchanged for terror.

He shoved Sophia behind him, arms out to protect her, but it was too late.

Men on horseback had them surrounded.

CHAPTER FOUR

FINN

Finn didn't even have time to reach for the guns before the men on horseback had them completely surrounded. He tried to duck down for one but the leader, a huge man in black, made his horse stomp forward until Finn and Sophia were forced to take several steps back away from the guns.

Finn moved in front of Sophia, between her and the lead bastard on the biggest horse.

No, was all he could think. Not now.

He had to protect her.

But how?

They were surrounded. Finn didn't have a gun and they were circled by—he did a quick count—six men on horseback.

He pulled the knife he always kept on his belt and brandished it at the man who seemed to be the leader.

"Whatever you think you're going to get here," Finn growled, "we won't be giving it easily. So why don't you just move along and save all of us the trouble?"

But the man wasn't looking at him. He was looking past Finn's shoulder. At Sophia.

Finn was about to snarl at him to get his eyes off her when the man spoke.

"You wouldn't happen to be Sophia Wolford now would you?"

"Yes," said Sophia slowly, peeking out from Finn's back. "How did you know? Who are you?"

"Name's Jagger." Jagger slid one leg over his horse and then jumped down. The guy was huge, tall and barrel-chested, maybe in his late thirties or very early forties.

"Governor Rodriguez from Santa Fe called and told me you'd be coming. I'm the Governor of Carlsbad, just a little bit up the way." He jerked a thumb over his shoulder. "We started riding south as soon as we heard you'd be coming this direction. The border's lousy with thieves and bandits and Governor Rodriguez wanted to make sure you got through safe."

Sophia turned to Finn, her face alight with relief. "Oh thank God. Finn, I told you we'd be all right. See? They're here to guide us safely the rest of the way."

Then she turned back to the man in black. "Thank you, Governor Jagger."

The man smirked. "Just Jagger's fine."

Finn scowled at him, glancing between the man and Sophia's beaming face. This didn't feel right. Finn didn't like this guy.

It all felt just a little too slick, a little too convenient. If they'd really headed out as soon as the Governor of Santa Fe told him about Sophia coming, why hadn't they made it further south?

A man could cover thirty miles on a horse in a day, easy, more if he was determined. But Finn still had the map in his head and if they'd hit the river where he thought they had, then Carlsbad was only about a five-mile walk up the road.

So either this guy was lying or he had a *really* bad sense of direction and had been riding in circles for a day and a half.

"So you have a sat phone," Sophia went on. "Can we use it? I need to talk to my father and let him know I got here safely. I don't want him to worry."

"Damndest thing," Jagger said. "It went on the fritz a couple days ago right after we talked to you. Got our top tech-head on it but he can't figure it. Thing's solar and the battery cell seems all charged up. Just can't get sat signal for shit."

How convenient.

But Sophia was just nodding. "Same thing happened to our sat phone. What on earth?"

Jagger shrugged. "Main thing is to get you to town and settled in for the night. I know a lotta people who'll be mighty happy to see you."

Sophia grinned wider and Finn wanted to punch Jagger in the center of his smug face. His story seemed to add up. How else would he know Sophia's name? But Finn had known too many guys like this growing up with his dad and his uncle—smooth talkers who'd shake your hand with one hand while stealing your wallet with the other.

Beware friendly strangers had long been his motto.

His other? Like he'd told Sophia: *Trust no one.*

When Finn walked into Jacob's Well five years ago, he hadn't believed the rumors that it was a place where law and rule reigned again, set apart from the madness of the rest of the world. He was just as suspicious of it as he was of every other place he'd been, so he kept waiting for the seedy underbelly to show itself.

And then he'd seen her.

Sophia Wolford.

It was his first night in town and he was so hungry. He'd been on the road for days and the last time he'd eaten was when he'd caught a rabbit in the woods. He'd been in the process of skinning and preparing to roast it when another man came upon him and attacked him over the kill.

The man had a knife and in the surprise of the initial attack, had sliced Finn's shoulder. But the guy was weak from starvation, and other than surprise, he didn't have any more tricks up his sleeve. It hadn't taken much for Finn to get the knife away from him and force him face first into the ground.

Finn hit him over the head with a nearby rock to make sure he was down and then took his rabbit and lit out.

But that was days before and the rabbit had been small in the first place. All he could think about was getting to the front of the soup kitchen line and getting that food.

And then he saw her.

She was brunette with warm, tawny skin and the face of an angel. Her smile hit him straight in the chest.

She looked so genuinely *delighted* to see every person she handed soup and bread to. She was young, too. Maybe around his age or just a little younger.

Too young or maybe just too protected to have developed the layers of deceit and artifice everyone on the outside world had.

That was when he realized the genius of this place. A security officer had explained the Marriage Raffle system to him when he'd signed the papers applying for citizenship, but he hadn't really fully understood it until he saw Sophia Wolford.

This wasn't some utopia where men's base natures suddenly changed as soon as they stepped over the territory line. No, Commander Wolford had just channeled those desires into an orderly system. The same way societies used to.

You wanted the good life? You could have it. Or at least a chance at it, if you worked hard. Two years and you could be entered in the largest pool for the Raffle. That meant no matter who you were, you had a chance at a wife all your own. Regular sex. Affection. A home.

In the meantime, there was nothing saying you couldn't try to charm one of the handful of unattached ladies in town.

But Finn only had eyes for Sophia.

The only reason he went to that stupid school was to be close to her. He knew how to survive on the outside, what did he need more book learning for? No, he went for her. He lived for any glances she shot his way or the sound of her coquettish giggle. Or on the rarest occasions, he might get a word here or there with her.

He got a job afterschool in the stable but was soon volunteering for Scrapper runs. He knew the terrain and how to survive. Plus he knew where there were cashes of old scrap that could be useful. Not always in Central Texas South but the Scrapper Teams didn't mind venturing out of the territory.

And maybe it was just his imagination, but Sophia always looked especially anxious before he left on the runs and relieved when he got back.

Everything he did was to improve his rank in the Marriage Raffle pools and level up so that by the time Sophia was of age, he'd have the best chance for being chosen as one of her husbands.

Stupid probably. Idiotic.

But that was how Jacob's Well got to people. It made you hope. It made you hope for ridiculous things, but even the hope was enough to have the roughest men behaving.

That was Jacob's Well, though. Out here in the lawless West? Without a system in place to protect Sophia?

How the hell was he supposed to keep her safe now?

Jagger held down an arm to Sophia and, as trusting as always, she grabbed it, put her foot in the stirrup, and swung herself up onto the horse behind him.

Finn took a step forward but it was too late. She was already up on the man's horse. At least her hands didn't slide around the man's waist. She was just holding on to the edges of the saddle underneath her thighs.

"Who can Finn ride with?" Sophia asked.

Oh, so at least she remembered he existed.

"We brought an extra mount," Jagger said. "He ain't the steadiest. Ain't been gelded yet so I figured it's safer for you to ride with me. But if your servant man here knows anything about horses, he should be able to handle him for the five miles to—"

"I'm not a servant," Finn grumbled at the same time Sophia piped up. "Oh, he's not—"

Finn would bet the man knew he wasn't a servant and was just trying to get under his skin. Establish his dominance. Well he'd soon find Finn wasn't the kind to go down without a fight.

Finn mounted the horse. Or at least tried to. Every time he put his foot in the stirrup and went to lift himself up and over, the horse took a few steps forward or backward, making him have to jump back down and try again.

"Finn—" Sophia started but Finn just growled out, "I got it."

He grabbed the saddle even harder this time and hiked himself up. When the stallion started it's dance back and forth, he just held on and finally swung his leg around. The stallion didn't like that at all. Finn barely got his hands on the reins before the damn thing started bucking.

"Whoa, boy whoa!" he said, but he didn't have a good enough seat or hold on the reins and the next thing he knew he was flying through the air.

THUMP. He landed on his ass.

Owwwwwwwww.

Jesus *fuck*. Everything hurt.

"Finn!" Sophia cried but he winced and held a hand up.

"Fine," he coughed. "I'm fine."

He didn't miss the outright chuckling from the guy on the horse behind the one Sophia was sitting on. Thanks, asshole.

"Can he just ride double like I am?" Sophia asked but Finn shook his head and said, "No," loud enough so they'd all hear even though he was still struggling to get his breath back.

It wasn't just for his pride's sake, either.

He had more than a sneaking suspicion that the barely broke horse had been brought on purpose. And not just as a test. These men had to know Sophia wouldn't be coming alone. What better way to render her even *more* helpless and dependent on them than if her companion was say, injured? Or even dead?

Trust no one and always suspect the worst. There was a reason he'd survived as long as he did even when he was smaller and weaker as a teenager.

But that didn't mean he'd give up and ride bitch to any of these bastards. Because them writing him off as weak and not a threat wasn't acceptable either.

So he stood up, dusted himself off, and walked back toward the horse, approaching slow so the horse could see him coming. The horse snorted and danced back and forth on his heels, nervous and skittish.

Finn put out his hand and paused. It was several long moments before the horse calmed long enough to investigate, nosing closer to his hand and sniffing him.

Finn slowly reached for the reins, keeping his movements smooth as he gathered the reins and stroked down the horse's neck.

"Don't have all damn day for you to seduce the horse," said the squat man behind the leader. "You wants we leave the two of you alone, that's fine, you can have 'em all to yourself, but only after you get 'em to the stable."

Raucous laughter broke out among the men but Finn didn't take his eye or hand off the horse. No matter how much he wanted to go stab the man for saying something so foul in front of Sophia.

"All right, there we go," Finn murmured in a soothing voice to the horse as he moved around and grasped the saddle again. "Nice and steady."

Really getting to know a horse took a helluva lot more time than he had but maybe the small moment he'd taken would help? Only one way to find out.

He pushed up and swung his leg over the saddle. The mount stayed still. He grabbed the reins up, leaving the smallest bit of slack and he held on with his calves.

"That's a good, good boy," he said soothingly and the horse neighed.

"Fucking finally," said the same man who'd made the crude joke earlier. He turned his horse around and started galloping away.

Finn finally turned his attention from his horse and looked toward Sophia. Her head was swung back toward Finn, eyebrows scrunched in concern.

Finn didn't know if she was going to try to say or communicate something to him, though, because the next second, the horse she was on leapt forward, too. She swung her head back, arms flying around the man in front of her, clinging to him as the horse took off.

Finn knew exactly what it felt like to be that man. She'd held him just as tightly when they'd been on the motorcycle.

And now she was clinging to someone else.

Just like how, in a matter of days, the girl of his dreams would be marrying someone else.

CHAPTER FIVE

SOPHIA

It had been awhile since Sophia had been on a horse and she'd never ridden like this—on the back of a saddle, which forced her body up against the man in front of her, with no control over the reins or how fast they went.

And they were going terrifyingly fast.

It was all terrifying.

Ever since they'd lost the truck, she'd been in a permanent state of fear. The shooting and then losing their supplies and then walking through the desert and now, now being with these *strangers*.

That one man who'd made those terrible jokes was just awful. And some of them smelled bad. Not the man who's back she was all but cemented to, thank God, but a couple others who'd passed by her stank so strongly it had been all she could do not to hold her nose. Holding her breath was hard enough.

And she was going to *marry* men like this?

Stop it, she chastised herself.

She was making snap judgements off of what? How some men

who'd obviously been out riding horses in the heat smelled? Or the off-color jokes of one man among a whole group?

She rarely spent time in the company of men back in Jacob's Well and she'd probably find the same there if she did.

Finn wasn't wrong about the fact that she'd been sheltered.

But she also knew how evil men could be. Though she'd hid from the memories for years, she was ready to confront the world again.

Maybe there weren't a lot of good people out here in the world. But didn't that mean that people like her father and Drea were more important than ever. Good people of strong, unswerving character were needed now more than ever if good was going to win the day.

Besides, a man could be taught to bathe more regularly. Love could transform people. Hadn't she always grown up hearing about what a slob her dad had been before he met Mom? But her mom didn't put up with that and soon he was cleaning dishes with the best of them and their house was always spotless. Of course the military might have helped with that some, too.

Still, her mom had always talked about how a good marriage was about communication and give and take. Partners made compromises because they loved the other person and wanted their happiness more than they wanted to continue a particular habit.

That was the kind of marriage Sophia wanted. And she knew she could have it, no matter whether it was arranged by a raffle or not. It was all about your willingness to bend and the love you poured into the partnerships.

Sophia was ready.

So she held on, closed her eyes apart from the times she looked back to make sure Finn was still with them, and tried to be brave in spite of the terrifying ride that seemed like it would never end.

And finally, *finally*, they rode into the town of Carlsbad.

It was... well, it was a town.

It didn't have the homey character of Jacob's Well. There weren't trees everywhere or a town square or anything.

There were streets and sidewalks and buildings. Evidence of the riots and looting were still obvious everywhere. Blackened burned out buildings stood half-falling in among abandoned ones with all the glass shattered.

No matter where Sophia looked, it was just all so... *grim*. Everything was covered in a layer of dirt or soot so that even the buildings that were in better shape all had a brownish gray quality to them.

People bandied about the word *apocalypse*, but here it looked like it had actually happened. The end of the world.

Where were the children running around and laughing? Or the people chatting and gossiping in the streets?

The streets were abandoned on the outskirts of town. It was only as they got further in town that she saw some activity. Tarps had been set up, no doubt to shield from the burning sunlight, and men lounged underneath them along the sides of buildings.

A *lot* of men.

Sophia's breath caught at the sight of them. So many men. For a second, she froze, then her hands around the waist of the stranger started to shake. What if these men were like the kind that had chased them down by the border?

But no. No. These men were civilized.

She frowned and took a better look. Most of the men weren't wearing shirts and even from the distance of the road, she could see they were filthy.

Did they just... *live* out here? On the sidewalk, under their tarps?

Sophia shuddered.

And then immediately felt guilty for how judgmental she was being.

She should be *glad* there were so many men here.

Men meant bodies who could fight in a war. The more the merrier. This was the whole reason she was here. She could give these men purpose and resources if they'd come to Texas to fight for the right side.

She took a deep breath and sat up straighter.

The deep breath was a mistake, though.

The whole town... well it stank.

She grimaced and then immediately tried to train her features.

Because all those men on the side of the street? They'd all sat up, too, and were watching them like they were a parade.

Which, come to think of it, maybe they were.

When was the last time these men had seen a woman?

Much less, a clean—or relatively clean—well put together, respectable woman? Sophia swallowed hard at the thought. Because the men scrambled and shoved one another out of the way to get a look at her.

Yet none stepped one toe off the sidewalk. They pushed right up to the edge but no further.

And though she could hear the hum of excited chatter, no one called out anything rude. So see? That meant they *were* civilized after all. They were just poor and there was no shame in that.

Hard times had fallen on them all. And if she could bring them hope of a future, then—

BANG.

Sophia screeched at the gunshot. The man on the horse in front of them had whipped out his gun so quickly, Sophia could only watch in horror as a man who'd stepped off the sidewalk fell dead.

She didn't know if she felt more or less horrified when she saw that he was naked and that he'd had his hand on his— on his exposed *manhood*—

"Oh my God," she whispered.

"Don't look," Jagger said. "These kind are an unfortunate reality of any settlement these days. Desensitized by the mobbing and violence. We deal with them the only way we can. In the only language they understand."

Even though he'd told her to look away, she couldn't. Her eyes were fixed on the man in the street and the pool of blood growing around his head. He was so skinny she could have counted his ribs if she'd wanted.

She only looked away when her vision was blocked by Finn coming up to ride beside her. She breathed out in relief at the sight of him. Finn, so familiar and steady. She might be in over her head, but he'd lived for years in this world. She wanted to reach out for his hand but

Jagger clicked his teeth and their horse jumped forward again, forcing Sophia to fling her arms around his waist.

When they next slowed and came to a stop, it was in front of the only trees she'd seen in miles. Though the large lawn was brown, the trees studded throughout were green and flourishing. Sophia could have cried at seeing the greenery. Which was stupid, completely stupid. But everything else was dead and grim and so depressing and here was finally some little bit of home. Because the lawn and trees were in front of a courtyard.

And even though it wasn't exactly a town square and the courthouse wasn't nearly as picturesque as the one in Jacob's Well, it was enough to at least *remind* her of home and she'd take anything she could get at this point.

Maybe it was a sign that things were finally getting back on track.

"So explain again how it works?" Jagger asked. "Everyone writes their name on a slip of paper and it goes into a hat?"

"Well, we have an official box. That's tamper proof," Sophia added quickly, alarmed at how casually Jagger had recapped the process of the Marriage Raffle. They'd been in the courthouse for about half an hour. Jagger had treated her and Finn to water and let them wash up.

And then he dropped the bomb that Sophia's Marriage Raffle would be held here in Carlsbad instead of in Santa Fe.

Jagger said he'd okay'd it with the Governor of Santa Fe before coms went out. Sophia was smiling and putting up a good face but Finn's words kept ringing through her ears.

Trust no one.

Glass half full interpretation of their situation: it was just as Jagger said and the Governor of Santa Fe thought that having a Raffle in one of the outer cities would be just as effective as having one in the capital, proof of concept wise. More so, even, because it proved that even the common man would have access to the brides if he volunteered to fight for Texas.

Glass half empty interpretation: Jagger was lying and something hinky was going on, though Sophia couldn't imagine what. He hadn't hurt them and was treating them respectfully.

Still, it was clear Finn was going with a glass half empty view, judging by his closed off features and the alarmed looks he kept sending her when no one else was looking. Not that she had a moment to talk to him about it. Everywhere they went, Jagger's men escorted them, ostensibly for their protection.

But even if something nefarious was going on, what could they do?

Finn had been right beside her on the way into town. He'd seen the same hordes of desperate men she had.

They were surrounded. So surrounded it took her breath away if she stopped too long to think about it.

When Jagger declared they'd be doing the Marriage Raffle here, Sophia had seen Finn's hackles go up and knew he was about to start arguing. She'd also seen the man behind Jagger drop his hand to the knife on his belt, a cruel look on his face.

So Sophia had interrupted and started talking logistics about the Raffle itself.

She'd dragged Finn into this—whatever *this* was. She couldn't get him hurt or killed because of her.

The man behind Jagger had backed off immediately once she started discussing the Raffle. So she barreled on ahead, pretending confidence.

Fake it till you make it?

Oh God, what if she'd made a mistake in coming here? If these men weren't what they seemed, then she'd dragged Finn out here for nothing. *All* of this had been for nothing... But no, freaking out like this was probably just a normal reaction when everything was so nuts and she was used to a calm, quiet life. This was all probably just how things were done out here in the real world, right? *Right?* Plans changed and you rolled with the punches. Considering everything that had happened, it was all but miraculous they'd made it here in one piece. That had to be a sign? Maybe things were finally starting to go their way and all this was completely legit?

"Do you have anything secure like that?" Sophia asked, trying to focus back in on the moment. "A hat really isn't quite... official.

Because it's important for the public to have trust in the impartiality of the process."

"And then men who enter should be vetted," Finn broke in. "It can't be just any asshole off the street. In Jacob's Well, they put them into pools according to their years of service to the town."

They were all sitting around a long table set up in the large open lobby of the courthouse where light poured in from the tall windows that surrounded the building.

Jagger nodded. "Wise."

Sophia watched him. He had strong features and a square jaw. He wasn't conventionally handsome but she liked the look of him. Not that that meant anything. "So how quickly do you think you'll be able to put everything together?"

Jagger lifted a hand to his chin thoughtfully. "About half an hour."

Sophia choked. "Half an—"

She'd meant how many *days* did he need to put it together. To conduct vetting interviews for applicants or at least to construct the *box*—

"Isn't that a little too fast?" Finn snapped. "How can you possibly vet the men who will enter in just half an hour."

Jagger never turned his attention from Sophia. "I'll immediately begin a larger vetting process but like you said, it takes time. Years even to truly know a man. So for the other women, it will take longer. But for you, we'll just have a small pool for this first lottery, made up of men I know and trust."

Okay. That was something, at least. Sophia shot a glance over at Finn. He was still glaring darkly at Jagger.

It turned out Jagger's estimation was correct.

It was little more than a half an hour later when Jagger led her back out to the front of the courtyard.

Sophia's mouth dropped open the second she stepped out the door. The lawn that had previously been empty was now positively *packed* with people.

No, not people.

Men.

The lawn was packed with *men*. Talk about surrounded.

And they were all looking at her like she was something to eat. Oh crap. What the hell was she doing?

But it wasn't like she had a choice at this point. She was in too deep. She shot panicked eyes around the steps of the courthouse and saw Finn's concerned look.

Then Sophia grabbed Jagger's arm. "Wait a second." Her voice came out an octave higher than normal.

Jagger raised a dark eyebrow.

Sophia swallowed hard before talking again. "I forgot to tell you something."

"Well the crowd's all here. If it can wait—"

"It can't."

"What is it, Soph?" Finn asked, stepping up and glaring at Jagger. "If you're having second thoughts, that's fine. You don't have to do this."

Jagger looked like he was about to argue and that squatty man who was always at his back took another step forward so Sophia hurried to cut him off. "No, it's not that. But please, can we go back in. Just for five minutes. Less. Three minutes. Please, Jagger."

She grabbed his arm in supplication. God, if she had any feminine wiles, now was the time to use them. Everyone always talked about how innocent looking she was, so she flitted her eyelashes. Men liked that, right?

Jagger looked put out but he glanced down at her clinging to his arm and his gaze softened just the slightest bit.

"Of course," he said. "Whatever makes you the most comfortable." He signaled to one of his men and then led her back inside.

"So?" he asked once they were all standing in the lobby, eyebrows lifting again.

"I forgot to tell you that one of my husbands is already spoken for. It happens sometimes in Jacob's Well—when a woman already has a man going into the lottery."

Sophia thought of Shay and stood taller even as internally she cringed at what was about to come out of her mouth. "Finn will be one of my husbands because we're already engaged. We have been for a while now. So the lottery will be for four more, not five."

She heard Finn suck in a breath but she couldn't bring herself to look at him. *Please, please don't contradict me*, she begged silently. It was completely unfair to just spring this on him. Everything she'd asked of him on this trip was unfair but this most of all. He hadn't wanted any of this. She'd dragged him out here and hadn't gone back when he said they should, time and time again. She'd been stubborn and naïve and refused to listen and—

And now she was demanding even more of him. A greater sacrifice than any yet, an entire life bound to her.

She was selfish and horrible.

But she didn't take it back. Because the truth was, no matter how rosy a picture she tried to paint about all of this... she was absolutely terrified.

Stepping out there and seeing all those men and realizing that, God, oh God, she was about to be married to complete *strangers*, that tonight, she'd be expected to have *sex* with men she'd never even *met*, with no one to help if they were rough or cruel or—

Panic all but choked her as she stared at Jagger, not able to glance at Finn, praying that one or both of them wouldn't call her on her lie.

The touch of Finn's fingers intertwining with hers was so startling, she almost jumped out of her skin.

"That's right," Finn said confidently. "It's better you know now. I didn't want to say anything before Sophia did."

Her eyes shot to his. He was— He didn't look mad. His eyes were full of warmth. Sophia was so confused, but grateful so she squeezed his hand back.

"I know how important this mission is to you," he continued. "But I also know you need me by your side." Then he looked back to Jagger. "So if it's a dealbreaker, better you know now. You get me as one of the five husbands, or you don't get her."

Jagger's mouth hardened into a line but he gave one short cutting nod. Then he took Sophia's arm, and before she even had a chance to thank Finn, to tell him all the things she needed to, to apologize for—

She was thrust back out into the sunshine, and Jagger was announcing in his booming voice that the first ever New Mexico Marriage Raffle had begun.

There was no box.

It was a hat after all.

A *hat*.

And it was one of Jagger's men who'd ridden with them pulling the names out.

The first indication that something suspect was going on came with the second name. The first name called had been Leo Navarro.

The second was Mario *Navarro*.

As the two men stepped forward, it was clear they were related. Brothers, most likely. What were the chances that the first two names called were *brothers*?

Then came the third name: Toby Ross.

Sophia's stomach soured when she recognized him as another of Jagger's men—the squat one who always stood behind him, the same who'd made the crude jokes and laughed when Finn fell off the horse. She stepped closer to Finn as Toby grinned and men around him slapped him on the back.

Then came the last paper pulled from the hat and the final name called:

"Jagger Kincaid."

Jagger smiled and came forward, putting his hand to the small of Sophia's back. She could only blink in shock as the crowd cheered, whistled, and some boos broke out.

What were the chances that Jagger's name got called?

Had they even *put* names in the hat or had Jagger just told the man what names he wanted him to call out?

Oh God, this man was *nothing* like her father. He'd cheated.

She'd barely wrapped her head around the thought before Jagger gave a significant nod to one of his men standing in front of the crowd and more guards entered the courtyard.

Jagger held up his hands to quiet the crowd. "Friends and fellow citizens, by the power vested in me as the Governor of Carlsbad, New Mexico, I now pronounce this woman, Sophia Wolford, the lawfully wedded wife of myself, Jagger Kincaid, as well as Toby Ross, Leo Navarro, Mario Navarro, and..." He paused, turning to look at Finn. "What's your name again."

"Finnigan Knight. But this isn't how—"

"And Finnigan Knight! We are now united in holy matrimony. It is witnessed and so it will be recorded in the city records."

Then he dropped his arms and turned to usher Sophia back inside the courthouse. She was still in shock.

Wait. *WHAT?* Was that the wedding? Ridiculously, all she could think was: *What about her mother's dress? She was supposed to wear her mother's dress when she got married. Not—Not dirty* house slippers*!*

"But I—" she started to say.

"Back inside, darling," Jagger said, ushering her back inside the courthouse doors. "Time to eat, wash up, and then get this marriage consummated."

CHAPTER SIX

JAGGER

The woman wasn't a fool. It was clear she realized the raffle was fixed. Not that Jagger really even bothered trying to hide it. She'd learn the score soon enough. Might as well start easing her into it right off the bat.

Jagger had plans for her, and he didn't want any fucking idiots in the marriage with him. The Navarro brothers were benign and easily controlled. And Toby, well, Toby was a pain in the ass but he would've made trouble if Jagger didn't make him a 'winner,' too. As much as he annoyed the fuck out of Jagger at times, he couldn't say the man didn't get the job done at the end of the day.

And really, that was all Jagger cared about. The bottom line.

Sophia's pretty green eyes were wide and dazed as the man with her, Finnigan, took her arm and led her quickly back inside the courthouse as the crowd started growing rowdy again. Jagger eyed Sergio and gave a sharp nod. Sergio then sent a signal along to his men to keep watch over the crowd.

They kept an iron fist of control over this little city of theirs. He who controlled the water was king. Jagger had fought mercilessly to be king and the men respected him for it. Or at least Jagger made damn sure they feared him. He'd rather be feared than loved any day of the week and it was something his Captain of the Guard knew better than anyone. He had the lashes on his back to prove it.

Toby shoved the brothers, Mario and Leo, to the side as he tried to follow Sophia into the building.

Jagger clapped a hand in front of his chest to stop him. "Not so fast."

Toby's dark glare landed on him in response but Jagger ignored it. "Don't forget the bigger picture. She's a payday. Don't fuck this up."

Toby shoved Jagger's hand off him. "If you think you're gonna keep me from getting my dick wet tonight you got another thing coming. I ain't had any ass in months and I aim to take that little cunt as hard as I please."

Jagger's jaw flexed.

Of course, another way to deal with Toby would be to put him six feet under.

If it was just Toby, Jagger would have taken that option a long time ago. But it wasn't. Toby had friends. The fucker had a crude charisma to him. He could whip people up, get them energized. It was as useful as it was dangerous. Which was why Jagger had decided to keep him close.

But he'd never let Toby forget who was in charge so he stepped in front of Toby, blocking the door.

"We do this my way or you're free to leave right the fuck now."

Jagger could see Toby's hackles rise but he didn't give a fuck. He just rose to his full six-foot-four height and glared down at the man. "Still got the hat out. I can walk right back out there and tell them you gave up your spot."

The vein in Toby's neck twitched at that but he sneered a forced smile. "Whatever you say, *boss*."

So it was looking like the Toby problem might have to be dealt with sooner rather than later. But not tonight.

Jagger stepped to the side. "Well let's go enjoy our fucking wedding feast."

Toby relaxed and his smile grew more genuine at that. "You gonna bust out the moonshine?"

The homemade whiskey, like everything else in town, was rationed. Granted, Jagger's men got more than most, but even they had their limits or it'd all be gone in a matter of weeks.

But Jagger only smiled at Toby. "As much as you can drink, it's all yours. It's our fucking wedding day. No rationing tonight."

Toby's eyes lit up at this. "Fuck yeah no rationing tonight!"

And this, ultimately, was why Toby would never be the leader Jagger was. The man was intemperate. He let his passions rule him.

People called Jagger cold and unfeeling but they were wrong. He felt things and he liked pleasures as much as anyone else. He sought them out, even.

He just knew that life was ultimately meaningless so he saw pleasures for what they were—distractions to fill the time until that grim and probably gruesome end came for him just like it did for everybody.

Jagger nodded Sergio over.

"Yes, boss?"

"Make sure Toby's cup is never empty tonight."

Two hours later, Jagger looked around the table coolly.

Jagger had claimed the top floor of the courthouse as his residence because it was spacious and well-lit by windows, the offices made for good sleeping quarters for him and his men, it was easily defendable, and the solar panels on the roof made electricity that allowed the water pumps to work so the building had running water and a few other electronic comforts.

Right now they were all gathered around a table in the small office kitchen. Toby was passed out in the corner after downing glass after glass of the strongest batch of whiskey Jagger had on hand.

While their new wife had taken a sponge bath in the bathroom, washed her hair, tended to her sore feet, and changed into a pretty sundress after the wedding, she'd barely touched her dinner. And

Jagger'd had his cook go all out for the dinner—wild roasted turkey, potatoes and refried beans.

Meanwhile her companion had shoveled his food in his mouth while eyeing everyone else around the table and looking like he wanted to stab his dinner knife through all of their eyeballs. Pleasant fellow, that one.

Toby had made a usual obnoxious ass of himself, only getting worse with each drink—but without his lackeys around to bolster him, he'd been manageable.

Mario had hulked like a giant bull at the table and eaten silently like always while Leo attempted conversation to smooth over the entirely awkward, manufactured situation.

"So this Travis, he has the whole state under his thumb now?"

"No!" Sophia had been quiet throughout dinner, but as soon as Leo started prodding about the state of things in Texas, her eyes had flashed with fire. "No, my father and the rebels are fighting back. They'll have taken San Antonio by now and have a whole Army. It's only a matter of time before we defeat him. We just need more men."

She looked around the table, her chin notching up ever so slightly. "Which is why we came here. With the New Mexico reinforcements, we'll be able to crush Travis once and for all."

She spoke so passionately. She'd had the looked of a spooked rabbit ever since the Raffle results but she was all avenging angel now.

She was obviously terrified but this cause of hers was important enough to risk her life for.

Jagger tilted his head at her.

Had she really been so sheltered in that town of hers where her father had ruled? How could anyone have that kind of dedication to an ideal? In this day and age and in this post-Fall world?

She'd learn soon enough how foolish she was. That fire in her eyes would die out. The only question was how quickly. Jagger had dispatches about Arnold Travis. It was men like him with ruthless ambition who got ahead in this life.

Men like Jagger himself.

There was a twinge in Jagger's chest, a foreign tug. He frowned. Remorse? He wasn't a man who felt shame or guilt.

Even knowing that he'd be the one to make the fire in his new wife's bright eyes flame out forever.

He shoved his chair back from the table abruptly and threw his cloth napkin on top of his plate. He'd eaten every morsel and soaked up every ounce of dripping gravy with the bread.

The only point to life was avoiding pain and experiencing pleasure to the fullest. And there was a ripe young woman to be enjoyed and by God or the devil, he was going to enjoy her.

"I think it's time for bed."

Sophia's wide, startled eyes shot to him. They were a virgin's eyes, innocent and afraid. It was probably wrong that the thought stirred his cock, but then again, Jagger had given up on right and wrong a long time ago.

Leo stood up without question and like always, Mario followed his brother's lead.

Sophia nodded rapidly and pushed her chair back like she was steeling herself for the firing squad.

Finnigan's head snapped back and forth as his eyes darted around the room. What, was he looking for a weapon to defend his maiden love? If Sophia was an ill-fated innocent, Jagger didn't even know what to think of her companion.

Because Jagger suspected by the wary, suspicious way the man watched them that *he* wasn't as unfamiliar with the way the world really worked. So why had he ever let Sophia venture from her safe cocoon? Granted it sounded like they'd already been uprooted from their little town but from what they'd said, she'd been safely ensconced in a cave somewhere near San Antonio. Did the man believe in the rebellion so vehemently that he was willing to sacrifice not only his own life, but hers as well?

Not that any of it fucking mattered.

None of it ever did.

So Jagger decided to put it all out of his mind.

There were pleasures to be had. That was all that did matter. Feeling good *now*, before the now was snatched away.

"This way." Jagger smiled and held out a hand for Sophia.

She looked up at him uncertainly but it didn't stop her from quickly heading the direction he indicated. Finnigan followed on her heels.

Jagger held out an arm for Sophia and after a moment's hesitation, she took it. Jagger's cock stiffened even further at the mere contact of his skin with hers.

He'd forgotten how goddamned *soft* women were. He was only too happy to lead her down the hallway to the largest office that he'd converted into his sleeping quarters. He'd brought in all the amenities. A huge king-sized bed with the finest linens, two couches and a wall where he'd installed floor to ceiling shelves that he filled with books for his own personal library.

A fan twirled on the ceiling—a waste of the limited amount of power the solar panels on the roof produced, but Jagger had decided impressing their out of town bride might go a long way toward keeping her docile. This was all part of the image they were projecting. At least that was why Jagger had prepared it all this way—the extravagant meal, the electricity displays, the copious amounts of ice in the water he'd had served all during dinner along with the homemade whiskey.

The way Sophia's mouth was dropped open, Jagger thought he'd succeeded. He wasn't sure if it was shock on her face, though, or horror at his gauche displays of wealth. But then he shook his head. He'd never met a female who wasn't dazzled by wealth and status. No doubt this one was the same underneath and this façade was just another part of *her* façade. Maybe she did know something of the world after all. Maybe *he* was the one being played by this innocence act.

All right, little girl. Time to see what she was made of.

Her breath hitched when he shoved the door open, probably a little more vehemently than was necessary.

But he'd wanted her ever since he'd heard her breathy voice over the line almost five days ago and pretended to be the Governor of Santa Fe, enticing her to come to him.

It was an easy enough lie. He'd picked up the sat phone for cheap in Hell's Hollow a couple weeks ago from a fella that apparently used to be the Trade Secretary to the former President. The man was on the run after President Goddard was assassinated and desperate for coin, so Jagger got it for almost nothing. It was a lark to call the numbers programmed on it. They were all labeled nice and neat so he knew who he was calling and had prepared a little script for each.

Sophia Wolford was the only one who fell for the trap, with her soft voice and little sighs that made him hard from hundreds of miles away.

Then when he'd laid eyes on her, fucking Christ, he'd about lost his seat on his horse. He thought for sure his fantasies had been delusions and that some stout and zealous middle-aged woman would show up, if she showed at all.

Instead it was this tiny wisp of a girl, all dark enticing eyes and curves that would tempt the most chaste of men.

While Jagger had never pretended to be chaste, women were few and far between out here in New Mexico. Even when he'd found a willing one, always for a pretty penny, none had been as fresh or sweet-looking as this woman.

So he didn't waste any time in leading her to the bed and then climbing on top of her.

If he thought she'd sounded breathy before, it was nothing to her little startled gasps now as he nudged her legs open with his knee and dropped his head to kiss down her neck.

"Wait," Finnigan said from somewhere behind them. "You can't just—"

"Leo," Jagger growled before continuing his path kissing down her neck. She was flushed and her chest heaved. Christ, his cock was fucking steel and he'd only just begun. Still, he didn't want to pace himself. He needed to touch her. Needed his fucking mouth on her.

He grabbed the front of her sundress and ripped it apart. Sophia gave a little screech of surprise, her ample breasts heaving in a sweet lace pink bra.

"Sophia!" Finnigan shouted. "Get the fuck *off* me! Sophia, I won't let that bastard hurt you. Son of a bitch, let go of—"

"Finn." Sophia struggled underneath Jagger and he let out a growl of frustration, finally swinging his head around to look at the bastard that Leo and his brother were restraining near the door. Finn was fighting like an animal to get to the bed and 'rescue' Sophia.

"Finn, stop it," she said, her voice only trembling a little. "I'm fine. This is my wedding night. Stop making trouble."

Then she laid back down underneath Jagger, taking a deep breath like she was steadying herself. She also closed her eyes and her hands fisted as if she was preparing herself to be violated.

Jagger ground his teeth. That wouldn't do.

He took a breath himself and dropped his forehead to her chest. Okay, so the innocence thing wasn't an act. Somehow, she was actually a damn virgin.

When he glanced back up at her, her eyes were still clenched shut.

Shit. He'd been out in this fucking desert too damn long. Had he really forgotten what it used to be like? He tried to think back but the memories were so vague about the dance between a man and a woman.

Jagger was going to take a lot from Sophia, but he wouldn't take this. Not her first time. But that didn't mean he wouldn't do his damn-dest to see if he couldn't get her willing to give it.

He went up on his knees so he wasn't crushing her and then leaned down. He ran just the tip of his tongue down her plump breast, circling her nipple through the thin lace of her bra.

She gasped and he didn't think it was only in surprise. There was pleasure in the sound, too. Jagger smiled as he teased his tongue back and forth, flicking her nipple before drawing the slip of lace down and sucking her dusky pink nub into his mouth.

The sharp little cry of pleasure was all the permission he needed to continue. He palmed her other breast as he continued suckling. Fuck, was there anything more perfect in the world than a woman's breasts. He rubbed his thumb back and forth across the nipple of the other breast and she squirmed beneath him. She shifted, her legs slightly opening so that the knee he had between them slid further up between her thighs.

That's right, he wanted to croon. That's right. Let me in.

Because he was wrong. There was another part of a woman's body even more perfect than her breasts.

And suddenly he couldn't wait to fucking taste it.

He let go of her breast with a suckering *pop* and then crawled down her body. He had her skirt flipped up before he thought she quite grasped what he was doing.

She had on pink lacy little panties that matched the bra and he about died. He wanted to rip them off but stopped himself, settling for just pulling them down. Sophia lifted up to help him get them off. Good girl. Good, good girl.

But he'd held himself back all he could.

He shoved her thighs open wide, bracing them apart with his forearms and then he leaned down and licked up the world's sweetest fucking slit.

Jesus fucking Christ she smelled so good. He never ate the whores out. Their saggy cunts were just depressing. Good enough to use for an afternoon but nothing you wanted to look too closely at.

But Sophia's? Jesus, Sophia's cunt was firm and fresh and glistening with her arousal and—

He dived in with his entire face, burying himself in her and lapping up her sweetness. He shoved his tongue as far inside her as he could. Even by that, he could feel how tight she was. Jesus fuck, she'd grip his cock so hard. Even the thought all but had him coming on the fucking spot.

No. Fuck. He wouldn't waste this gift. He would relish every goddamned fucking second of this night with her. And if he wanted another, he'd have to ease her into this. She was tight and he was big and if he wanted her to give him access to the sweet eden of her body again, he'd have to take this carefully.

So he tongued up to her little clit that was already swelling and teased gently with his tongue as he lifted a finger and gently massaged all around her opening.

Her breasts arched upwards as the sweetest little noises came out of her throat. *Fuck* but she was responsive. That was another thing you didn't get with whores. Some of them would make a show of coming but they were too hardened to feel much of anything. Half of them were so fucking high the whole time they'd lost the ability to feel anything but craving for their next high.

But Sophia, Jesus Christ, every time he swirled his tongue around her clit, she all but bounced off the bed.

How often did she touch herself? he wondered. Did she stick fingers up inside of herself? Fuck, the thought of that almost did him in and had his teeth near clenching, which was a problem, because he was still sucking on her clit.

But she cried out, a more ecstatic noise than ever at what must have been a somewhat painful bite.

No fucking way.

Did she—

Could she really like—?

He reached up and pinched one of her nipples. Hard.

Her hands balled in the blanket and she screeched as she came, thrusting her hips up into Jagger's face.

Aw fuck, aw *fuck*. He had to have her. He had to fucking have this woman right the fuck now.

He climbed up her body, freeing his cock from his jeans as he went. He shoved them down his ass.

When his cock nestled into her wetness, he about passed the fuck out.

He looked into her wild, startled eyes and smiled.

He'd be the first to ever have her. This moment was one goddamned thing life could never take away from him.

"Relax," he whispered, dropping down to his elbows on either side of her head so all she could see was him. "Let me in."

She closed her eyes again but she didn't go tense.

He kissed her eyelid as he started pushing inside, breeching her most sacred place.

She sucked in a breath and her eyes looked everywhere, like she was confused by all the new sensations assaulting her, but he just whispered, "Shhh, shhhh, I got you, honey." He kissed across to her other eyelid, then down her cheeks. "I got you."

The tip of him was in when he felt her barrier.

He kissed the very edge of her mouth. "I got you, honey. Hold onto me. I got you."

And then he slowly but inexorably, thrust his hips forward.

She cried out in pain but she didn't grab at the blanket again or try to shove him off. Instead she threw her arms around his neck and held on so tight that for a second, Jagger couldn't breathe.

She wasn't squeezing the breath out of him or anything. It was just the fact that she was clinging to him while he was— While he was— He was a stranger to her and she'd opened up to him like a flower, accepting him in, and now embracing him with every part of her body—

With an animal growl he shoved in the rest of the way.

She let out a small scream of pain.

"Sophia!" Finn shouted again but she just shook her head and bit out through gritted teeth, "I'm fine. Stay back."

Jagger immediately hated himself. He'd fucking hurt her. But she only clung to him tighter, her legs coming up to wrap around his waist.

He couldn't understand— How could she—?

He tried to say something, maybe something comforting but nothing would come. His throat was too tight or clogged or some shit.

He bowed his head into the crook between her neck and her shoulder, completely still, his cock buried to the hilt inside her. *Move*. His entire body screamed at him to fucking *move*. To pull out and then shove back in. To push past all that delicious resistance and take and take and fucking take her.

She was his *wife*. It was his *right*.

But he couldn't hurt the sweet, shaking creature clinging to him anymore than he already had. At the same time, he couldn't pull away from her, either.

A better man would. But Jagger was not a better man and he never would be. He'd never wished he was, though, more than in this moment.

"It's okay," she whispered, startling the shit out of him. "You can... you know. It doesn't hurt as much now."

He lifted his head from her shoulder and was surprised to see her eyes open. His throat was still too tight to speak but she must have read the question on his face because her eyes softened and then dropped furtively to his lips.

"Can I... I've always wanted to try..." Awkwardly, she lifted her head up from the pillow, her lips coming toward his.

Jesus Christ. She'd never been kissed. He'd shoved his cock inside her and she'd never even been kissed.

The thought should have made him disgusted with himself. And it did. But it also made him hard as fucking stone again.

He dropped his head, his lips crashing against hers.

It wasn't an elegant first kiss and probably not the kind she'd fantasized about in her girlish dreams.

He took her hungrily, quickly thrusting his tongue in between the seam of her lips to connect with hers.

The second he did, it was like when he'd first latched onto her nipple. She shuddered around him and he'd been wrong earlier. He hadn't been all the way inside her because her body loosened with her arousal and let him in another half inch.

He growled into her mouth and slowly pulled his cock out of the sweetest, tightest pussy on God's green earth and then pushed, just as slowly, back in.

He didn't miss her wince but if she wasn't asking to stop, then neither was he.

He reached down between their bodies, determined for her to feel as fucking amazing as he did.

"You're so fucking beautiful," he whispered between kisses. "The most beautiful woman I've ever fucking seen."

Her brow scrunched. "I'm sure that's not true," she murmured.

He stopped and looked at her incredulously, hand pausing on its way to her sex and briefly lifting to her face. He pushed back her hair and cupped her cheeks.

"Sophia, I mean it. You're beautiful. A fucking goddess. Having you here, with me," he thrust his hips, "fucking *beneath me*, I can barely believe it's happening."

It wasn't even a lie.

Sophia was nothing he'd expected. None of this was—

He swooped down to kiss her again before he could look too closely at any of the rest of what he was feeling or thinking.

The reality of the outside world would be waiting for them tomorrow morning.

But tonight there was only Sophia's body.

Only the pleasure he'd wring out of her.

Over and over and over again if he had his way. He'd bring her to orgasm and teach her to enjoy sex. It would be an even exchange of pleasure. He wouldn't owe her anything come tomorrow morning.

He dropped his hand back down between them, his seeking fingers quickly finding her sweet little bud.

It took several minutes to have her breathy and gasping again. She got there just in time, too, because the way she was milking his cock, he couldn't have lasted much longer.

"Come for me," he demanded, rolling her bud in between his fingers. "Come for me now, wife."

And damn him, but she did.

She came with a keening cry that probably echoed down main street and had every cock in the whole town stiffening. But *he* was the one who got to be buried inside her and feel every spasm around his cock as she clenched and squeezed on him all through her orgasm.

When he came, it was with a roar as he spurted his cum deep inside her.

He collapsed to the side of her, holding her close, eyes closed, just breathing her in.

He was—

That had been—

She was just the most—

Perfect.

For a moment, just a single fucking moment, his mind was quiet. There was stillness in his soul.

...

...

...

But then, with the relentlessness of a crashing wave, it all came rushing back. The world had ended. His twin sister was still dead. None of this had any meaning. It was just another fleeting pleasure, here now and gone tomorrow. Just like everything else.

He untangled himself and rolled away from the woman.

Finnigan rushed to her side in his absence but Jagger was quick to snap, "Leo, Mario, your turn."

CHAPTER SEVEN

SOPHIA

"She's had enough for one night," Finn said vehemently as he put an arm around Sophia and flipped the blanket off the bed to cover her nakedness.

She immediately started shaking her head even as she clung to Finn's forearm. She'd been one hundred percent terrified walking into this room, she wouldn't lie.

But then Jagger had been gentle. And the things he'd done to her body... He couldn't be all bad if he was that considerate in bed, right? He hadn't violated her. He'd gone slow and attended to her so tenderly. He'd given her her first kiss and all of it had been overwhelming, but in a good way.

"It's okay, Finn," she said, giving his arm a squeeze. "This is how it works. It means the wedding is real." And it meant there was a chance this would work out after all. If she could connect to each of her husbands like she had Jagger, maybe everything would be okay. "Everyone sleeps with all their husbands the first night."

Finn swung his head to look at her incredulously. "How the hell do you know?"

Sophia felt her cheeks flame. The other girls talked about touching themselves in the dark, but Sophia had never done it. She'd wanted to know it from her husbands or not at all.

And now she knew. She got to know because she was a woman now. She was a *married* woman and if there was any way she could reclaim this marriage from the sham it felt like earlier this afternoon, then by God she was going to do it. One way or another, these men were her husbands and she would *make* it work if at all possible.

"The women talk," she whispered.

"Well were they all virgins?"

She glared up at Finn. "Yes, in fact. Some of them were. I'm doing this and if you can't handle it, you can leave." She couldn't help her eyes dropping. She hadn't had a chance to even talk to him since roping him into being her husband and she hated to argue now. God, what must he think of her? "And um, I know I sort of forced you into marrying me. It's okay if you don't want to stay and— You don't have to, is all I mean."

She cringed. God, how awkward was this? He'd just watched her have *sex*. Finnigan Knight had just watched her lose her virginity. Her face flamed even at the thought.

He only reached out and took her hand though. "I'm not leaving you tonight, Soph. I promise."

She looked up at him, unable to help the flood of relief she felt at his answer. This was exactly why she'd wanted him with her in this marriage.

The thought of being *alone* with all these strange men... God, it was terrifying enough as it was. But Finn being there, even with all the intimacy that entailed, it made it all better. She reached out and squeezed his hand tight.

Jagger repeated his earlier snapped order. "Leo. Mario. We don't have all night."

Sophia's head turned to Jagger in confusion. He'd been oddly gentle with her only moments before. Where had that man gone? Even his face was different. His eyes. He was distant now. All the warmth was absent and the connection she'd felt with him, gone.

"How should we do this?" she asked, proud when there was only the slightest quaver to her voice.

"Up on your knees," Jagger said. She looked toward him. He'd pulled off his shirt and pants and stood there in his boxers. Her eyes widened when she saw he had his long, thick shaft in his hand. That had been *inside* her? No wonder it had hurt. He stroked it lazily and the sight had her legs shifting and her sex tingling.

She bit her lip. Because while it had hurt at first, she hadn't forgotten how *good* he'd made her feel, either.

"Knees," he snapped.

She scrambled to get to her knees.

"Hey asshole," Finn started. He still hadn't moved from the edge of the bed and she put a hand on his arm.

Which was when she realized she was almost one hundred percent naked. She still had her bra on, but Jagger had pulled her breasts out of the lacy cups, so it barely counted.

And Finn was just sitting there. *Right beside her.* While she was *naked*.

But she didn't have very long to think about it because the two other men in the room were walking her way.

Sophia was shaking, but she forced herself to look at them and offer a wobbly smile.

The brothers. Leo and Mario. She blinked up at Mario first. He was a giant. So huge and tall her neck almost hurt as she craned her head backwards to look up at him.

His face was blank as he stared down at her.

Talk about terrifying.

All Sophia *wanted* to do was to cling to Finn and beg him to take her away from here. Everything with Jagger had been insane enough, but she'd done it.

Now here were two more men. She had to start all over again.

But Audrey had done this. So had Shay and Vanessa and Drea and a hundred other women in Jacob's Well after their lotteries. Was she going to be the first bride to wimp out, especially when it was so diplomatically crucial?

She pushed the blanket Finn had pulled off and climbed up onto her knees like Jagger had ordered.

"Leo, tell your brother to sit at the head of the bed. You get behind her. And take off your clothes. You're fucking your wife, not going to confessional."

"Yes, sir, boss," Leo answered. "Mario, you heard him. Sit in front of her."

Sophia swallowed, eyes dancing nervously around the room and quickly darting away as Leo and his brother disrobed.

And then they were climbing on the bed with her.

Naked men were climbing on the bed with her.

More than one of them.

She'd envisioned this moment so many times. Because while she might have talked about her dream wedding with her girlfriends, it was her wedding *night* that she'd secretly fantasized about in her bedroom at night.

But this was so much... *more* than she ever could have dreamed up.

Especially when Mario sat down in front of her and his... his... *thing* seemed to take up her entire sphere of vision.

Suffice to say, she'd never seen one up close.

Donna at school said she'd touched Alex's when they made out behind the schoolhouse and she'd described it. Like a cucumber with two little garlics attached on the bottom, she'd said with a giggle.

The huge, hard fleshy member in front of Sophia didn't look anything like a cucumber.

And then Jagger's hot breath was on her ear. "Take his cock in your hand."

Sophia sucked in a quick hiss of air through her teeth, head swinging his way only briefly. His dark eyes were glittering and his hand on his own shaft tugged more insistently than ever.

She nodded and swallowed, then reached out for Mario's... Mario's *cock.*

Her fingers closed around the middle of it, mimicking how Jagger held his. Mario's was warm and smooth. The skin was soft and velvety, but underneath, it was so *rigid*. Like rock.

"Fuck, that's hot," Jagger whispered. "Now lick it. Right there at the slit."

Sophia felt her eyes go wide. Of course that was what he meant for her to do. She should have realized. He'd done it to her, after all. Used his mouth to— to—

She bobbed her head down, afraid if she thought about it anymore, she'd wimp out. She stuck her tongue out and tentatively swiped it over the little slit Jagger was talking about.

"Now put your mouth around it." Jagger's voice sounded a bit ragged as he ordered it, and the fact that she knew she was affecting him had Sophia throbbing again between her legs. God, how did he have that power over her already?

She'd heard the whispers and giggles among the married women about bedroom play and what it could be like but never thought—

"Don't make me say it twice. Suck his cock."

She obediently widened her mouth and took the fat head of Mario's cock into her mouth. His huge, hairy thighs tensed as she closed her lips around the crown of his member. Tentatively, she swiveled her tongue around the smooth surface. Again, she felt the odd little slit at the very tip and tried teasing her tongue back and forth across it.

Mario's whole body jumped when she did it and her eyes flew upwards. Was that a good thing or a bad thing?

By the dark, intense gaze Mario directed at her, she hoped... *good?* He was younger than she'd initially thought, looking at him now. He was so huge, he'd seemed like he had to be a lot older but now she wondered if he wasn't only a couple of years older than her. He lifted a hand like he wanted to touch her but then dropped it back down to the bed.

She pulled back off his shaft to murmur shyly, "It's okay. You can touch me."

Mario's eyes flashed back to her, almost like he was astonished she would speak to him.

"Did I say you could stop sucking his cock?" Jagger growled.

Sophia dropped back down to take Mario back into her mouth.

"Who the fuck do you think you are?" Finn asked heatedly. "Stop ordering her around."

Sophia just reached out for Finn and felt down his arm for his hand. She squeezed it. She didn't know how to voice it but... she *liked* it when Jagger did that. It just took all the pressure off. To say she felt in over her head was an understatement. But if he was there telling her what to do and how to do it? Then she didn't have to think or worry.

Especially after the week spent second-guessing this entire mission as a colossal screw up that might have gotten her and Finn both killed—it was more than a relief to hand off the reins to someone else.

Sophia started to experiment with her tongue again. Because she didn't just want to do this right, she wanted to do it the *best*. She wanted each of them to leave this room feeling like the luckiest man on earth to have gotten her for a wife. She wanted them to eventually look at her the way Nix did at Audrey or Charlie did at Shay.

"Now go deeper. Take him to the back of your throat. And Leo, you can start touching her, too. Get her ready for you."

Sophia was concentrating on the first part of what he said so she wasn't quite ready for the touch in her most intimate places.

"*Jesuchristo*, she's so soft," Leo's voice came from behind her as fingers slid between her folds. Just like Jagger, Leo seemed to know exactly where to touch her. His fingers zeroed in on that spot at the top of her slit and he rubbed circles so delicious she couldn't help moaning around Mario's cock.

Mario's hand lifted again when she did, and this time, after a moment's hesitation, he didn't drop it.

She wasn't sure what she expected when he reached for her. Maybe for his big hand to settle on the back of her head? To push and pull her up and down on his cock, in the rhythm he liked best?

It sure wasn't for his thick fingers to ever so gently tuck some stray hair behind her ear. She'd only had time to pull the front part of her hair back into a barrette but after her time with Jagger, she could only imagine how she looked.

He didn't pull his hand away. Instead, he caressed his giant thumb down her cheek. She looked up at him with wide eyes, instinctively knowing even before Jagger commanded it that she was supposed to bob up and down.

She couldn't read the expression on Mario's face. But whereas at dinner he'd only stared at his plate and shoveled food in his mouth without a word to anyone, now his focus was entirely on her.

And when she dipped down, so deep that his cock touched the back of her throat, she saw the way his barrel chest moved up and down.

He cupped her face and his huge hand easily curved around the back of her neck at the same time. He didn't apply pressure though. It was like he just had a need to touch her, to connect in a way beyond his cock in her mouth.

She groaned long and deep when his brother gently breached her from behind, all the while with a hand around her hip strumming her clit.

She was sore after Jagger, there was no doubt. But she was slick too, with her own juices and Jagger's cum, and he'd already stretched her out not that long ago. So Leo slid in without nearly the pain of the first time with Jagger.

And watching the intensity on Mario's face at the same time Leo rubbed and circled her while the fullness of his cock filled her, such a new sensation but one her body was quickly coming to accommodate and enjoy… it all had the pleasure swooping in her stomach climbing and climbing and—

Oh God, really? Again?

Yes, really. It was slower to rise and not as sharp when it hit, but the orgasm soon had her arching back against Leo like a stretching cat as it washed through her.

"Good girl," Jagger murmured. "Now pull off Mario and let him come on your face."

Sophia let go of Mario's cock with a slurping noise and looked up in confusion. On her *face*? What did that—?

But Mario seemed to understand exactly what Jagger meant because he'd grabbed his shaft and was stroking roughly up and down while she watched.

"Face up," Jagger instructed, reaching down a hand underneath her chin to angle her face up to them. Jagger was still pulling on his own cock, too, gripping it hard as he dragged up and down on it, then twisting and squeezing every time he got back up to the head.

"Christ, I love it when you squeeze me like that, *mija*," Leo said from behind her.

She'd barely registered it, though, because right then Mario's cock erupted. She squeaked as his seed shot right toward her face. She shut her eyes as it hit her but didn't miss how Mario groaned in pleasure.

She blinked her eyes open. The... *stuff* had only gotten on the lower half of her face so she could still see just fine, and the look of unguarded pleasure on Mario's face as the last of his seed dribbled from his glistening cock had an aftershock tremoring through her own sex.

"Now show me all that you learned with Mario," Jagger said, and the next thing she knew, he'd pushed Mario out of the way and he was pressing his cock between her lips.

His cock that had been inside her not forty-five minutes ago. Her mouth opened wide as the thick mushroom head popped inside her mouth, salty from Mario's transferred seed.

"That's right," he cooed, his voice once again going soft, just like it did the first time they'd had sex. But his words weren't soft. They were shocking. "I'm going to fuck your face now. Suck on it. Suck his cum and mine. I'm going to cum in your mouth and you're going to swallow every drop."

Sophia blinked rapidly and took in a deep breath through her nose as Jagger pulled his cock out of her mouth and then pushed back in again.

It was overwhelming at first. He was just so *big*. Far thicker than Mario had been. Her mouth barely fit around him.

"Shit," he hissed. "Lips over your teeth!"

She hurried to comply, wrapping her lips over her teeth protectively and he continued pushing in and out. She tried to swipe her tongue over his tip and suck on him but he seemed to like it bobbing in and out just on his tip, especially when she applied pressure with her mouth so that it was a tight fit every time he pushed in.

"Gimme your hand," he breathed out, his voice gravelly. She was affecting him and just the knowledge sent a thrill through her. He might be pretending to be in charge, but she could affect him, this powerful man who commanded an entire city with thousands relying on him.

She did as he asked and lifted her hand towards him.

He placed it around the base of his cock, his around hers to show her how he liked to be stroked. But she'd been watching earlier and she mimicked him, quickly getting the hang of dragging his skin up and down while she took him in and out of her mouth.

"Fuuuuuck, that's good. That's so fuckin' good."

She looked up and saw his stomach flexing in response to her every movement. All the while, Leo was still taking her from behind. She was totally stretched and used to it now so it didn't hurt at all.

From time to time Leo would grab her hips and drive in harder, but then that hand of his would go seeking again for her clitoris and the swoopy feelings would start all over again.

She wasn't Sophia Wolford in this moment. She was a goddess and they were her supplicants worshiping her.

It was nothing like she'd expected but everything she'd wanted.

She wasn't a girl anymore.

She was finally a *woman*.

She sucked even more strenuously at Jagger's cock.

"Fuck, I'm coming. Swallow it down. Swallow it all, baby. Swallow it all for me."

Jagger pushed back in and then her mouth filled with the same salty substance that she'd only had a mere taste of. She choked on it at first, it was such a surprise.

But then she started to swallow, almost convulsively. She swallowed and swallowed and swallowed. Jagger's hand came to the back of her head, his fingers sifting through her hair as his hips thrust again and again into her mouth and she slurped the last of his essence from him.

Finally he collapsed back against the headboard, his stomach and chest heaving. "Fuck," he swore, forearm swiping at his face. "That was fucking incredible."

Sophia glowed.

"I'm close," Leo said. "You're so hot, *mija*. Hottest thing I've ever seen or touched."

Sophia bit her lip and tried to focus on tightening around him. They were muscles she'd never flexed before and it felt strange and wonderful. So did the way Leo cursed every time she did it.

He continued his fingers swirling at her clit and the nice feelings were there. She wasn't sure if she could orgasm again, she was so oversensitive and every thing was just so *much*.

But it felt good, everything he was doing to her, and when he thrust and a stuttered groan came from his throat, she felt so satisfied that even though she was sweaty and exhausted, she kept moving her hips back and forth, grinding back on Leo to help him get the most out of his climax.

But finally, with an intimate massaging caress of her hips and buttocks, he slid out.

The bed dipped as both Jagger and Leo climbed off.

And almost immediately, Sophia was being pulled into another set of arms. Sophia looked over her shoulder as Finn pulled the sheet over her to cover her nakedness, then he pulled her against his body.

She blinked in surprise at the action, and even more so when Finn spoke to Leo. "Leo, go get a damp cloth so she can clean up."

And then Finn's worried voice was in her ear. "Are you okay, Soph?"

He was so familiar but him holding her so tight after... after...

She nodded, not sure she could form words just right now, squeezing her eyes shut. She would not cry. She would *not* cry.

No one had hurt her but it was so *much* all so *quickly*.

She'd thought she was prepared. She thought she was so grown up. Did all brides feel like this on their wedding nights?

She flipped around and buried her face in Finn's chest and his arms came around her tighter than ever.

"Shhh, I've got you, Soph. I've got you, and I'm never letting you go."

CHAPTER EIGHT

FINN

So he'd have to be sneaky if he wanted to kill them and still get him and Sophia out of town alive. He'd have to get Jagger first, followed by that Toby asshole. Leo seemed like a nice enough guy but his brother was a goddamned tank. No way they'd get past him if he decided to be loyal to his boss even after he was dead.

Poison maybe? Take them all out at the same time?

Sophie heaved a sweet little breath and shifted in Finn's arms. He held her tighter, breathing in the sweet scent of her hair. She was using his chest as a pillow. His right arm had long gone numb but he didn't care.

Jesus she was so tiny. And all those bastards had just used her like she was— Like she was a—

Finn gritted his teeth.

Watching them take her, being right there on the same goddamned *bed* while they—

He squeezed his eyes shut, but that didn't help. Everything was on constant replay in his head. What was he supposed to do? He'd had a front seat to a live porno featuring the girl he was stupid in love with. Every image was burned into his brain.

Seeing what her face looked like when she came, *Jesus*. Watching her slurp cock like it was God's gift. He shook his head. Because at the same time it had killed him. Fucking *gutted* him to watch her take *three* other fucking men, right in front of him.

At least they were gone now. Well, mostly gone. That big bastard Mario was sleeping on a chair in the corner. A watchdog to make sure they didn't run off. Jagger wasn't a fucking idiot. He saw exactly how much Finn hated him.

That had been a mistake. Finn knew he ought to be playing it smarter. How would he get his chance to slice that fucker through the belly if he was always on his guard around Finn?

No, better to play buddy buddy, then, when the time was right, *strike*.

And how would Sophia feel about that?

She'd be pissed. No doubt. But something about this whole place was off. And no matter what she thought, these men were not the salvation she imagined they were. Jesus, most of them were half-starved and dehydrated. If Santa Fe were some Mecca out in the desert, they certainly weren't sharing the wealth with these sad fucks down here.

Sophia stirred in his arms.

"Shh," he murmured when she didn't settle right away like she had at earlier points in the night when he'd used the same tactic. This time, though, she blinked her eyes open and pulled away from his chest. Even though it was a relief to finally be able to flex his right arm and try to get feeling back in it, he hated to lose the contact with her.

She rubbed her eyes and looked around. Moonlight came in from the windows, enough to see a dim outline of the room and each other.

"Finn?" she asked in a whisper.

"Hey Soph," he said. Jesus but she was beautiful, all sleepy with her dark hair falling over her shoulder, so much cream-caramel skin on display.

She must have realized the same thing because she drew the sheet up around her even though she'd fixed her bra so that it covered her breasts.

She looked around the room. "Where is everyone?"

"Jagger went out, I don't know where. Leo's sleeping on the couch. And Mario's over there," Finn nodded to the corner of the room where the big man sat on a chair in the corner, his head tilted against the wall, snoring. "Jagger told him to 'keep an eye on us.'" Finn fairly growled the last part but Sophia just nodded, taking it in stride like it was no big deal.

"Right." Finn hopped out of bed. "Leo showed me where the bathroom is earlier. I'll take you."

Mario just snored on, not even stirring at their movements. So much for a guard dog.

Sophia dragged the sheet with her, wrapping it around her as Finn led her down the hall to a bathroom and stood outside while she did her business. He heard the sink turn on. Running water probably wasn't as much a shocking luxury to her like it was to Finn because she had it in her house when they turned on the water pump.

She came out five minutes later, the hair around her face damp. She must have taken the opportunity to wash up better.

"Okay," she whispered. "We can go back to bed now."

Finn nodded but then stopped, looking up and down the dark hallway. "Soph, we can get out of here. Steal a car or a bike and be halfway to Texas before sunrise."

She jerked back from him. "Why would you say that?"

"You don't have to do this. It's not too late—"

"Not too— I'm *married*," she hissed. "I had my wedding night and these men are my *husbands*." She brushed past him on her way back to the bedroom, knocking his shoulder with hers.

Finn sighed and dragged his hands through his hair. "*Fuck.*"

He followed after her. Why wouldn't she ever listen to reason? These men were dangerous. He had a bad feeling. A very bad feeling.

He stomped after her and pushed through the bedroom door.

But when he saw her curled up on the bed in a tiny ball, all the fight went out of him.

He went over and sat down, putting a hand on her arm. She jerked it away.

"Shit, Soph, I'm sorry."

She just grabbed the pillow and turned her back toward him, burying her face in it. At first he thought she was just being her normal obstinate self. But then he saw how her back was shaking.

Shit, was she *crying*? Had he made her cry?

"Soph. Sophia."

He rolled her towards him by her shoulders and she covered her face with her hands.

"Talk to me. Please. I'm sorry I'm such an ass. But you can talk to me."

She hiccupped and kept her face covered. "It's stupid," she said in a small voice.

She was killing him, didn't she know that? He'd walk through fucking fire for her, anything to keep her safe, to make her happy.

"Nothing you say is stupid. Come on, you can tell me. Did one of them hurt you?" He'd fucking kill them. He swore, if they'd—

But she just shook her head again. "You'll laugh."

"I swear I won't."

It took another few minutes of coaxing before she finally told him through hiccupping tears. "I didn't get to wear my mother's wedding dress. I got married in dirty jeans and an old t-shirt."

A surprised laugh burst out of Finn.

She finally dropped her hands from her tear-stained face, but only so she could glare up at him. "You swore you wouldn't laugh."

"Oh Soph," he shook his head, still chuckling. Her life had been on the line, she'd been all but kidnapped by strange men, paraded through a town of savage strangers, and she was upset about a *dress*? Only Sophia.

She smacked him in the chest and even that was fucking cute.

On an impulse, he cupped her face and dragged her forward, kissing her on the forehead. The way her breath hitched at the action had his own breath stuttering, though.

He moved back slowly, and for some reason, he wasn't pulling his hands away from her face. Jesus she was soft. So soft and breakable and perfect.

"It's not just the dress, okay?" she finally whispered. "I am scared. I have been for... well, ever since we left the cave, really. And yes, this place freaks me out. We don't know these men or exactly what they want. But we're here and I still think it's worth trying to accomplish the mission since we're already in this deep. But Finn, you have to know, I couldn't do any of it without— I need your help. I need... *you*."

And when she blinked up at him with those luminous green eyes of hers, Finn was caught. Completely ensnared, just like he'd been the very first day he walked into Jacob's Well and set eyes on her.

Except so much worse because now he knew her. He knew how the bright spots appeared on her cheeks when her temper flared and he knew how passionate she was, a passion that led her to throw caution to the wind she was so damn determined to make her life *matter*. She was beautiful and reckless and perfect, so fucking perfect and—

"Finn?" she whispered, her eyes searching his.

And then, without waiting for an answer, she lurched forward. Her kiss was clumsy but it was all Finn had ever been waiting for.

Still cupping her face, he devoured the lips he'd stared at so many times from afar, pressing her back into the bed.

She gasped and Finn slipped his tongue into her mouth. He didn't force it though. He just teased his tongue inside, savoring every inch, every single centimeter that was Sophia.

Jesus Christ, kissing her was better than every fantasy he'd ever had.

He groaned into her mouth and his hand slid around to the back of her neck.

And Sophia, oh Jesus, Sophia struggled with the sheet and then threw it to the side. And when it was gone, she slung her leg up and around his waist.

Her completely *naked* leg.

And she lifted her hips up against him, grinding into his hardness. Because there was no way, having her in his arms, having her lips on his, *finally*, that he wouldn't be hard as stone.

"Sophia," he groaned, pulling away from her lips and putting his forehead to hers. "That's not what this is about. We don't have to do that."

"You don't want to?" He'd never heard her sound so vulnerable or hurt.

"God, Soph, are you kidding me?" He shifted his hips into her. "Can't you feel how much I want you? Your body drives me fucking insane." After having her mouth, he couldn't go another second without it, so he kissed her again, long and deep. Jesus, he'd never let her ever think he didn't want her.

It took all his effort but he broke away from her mouth again. "But you've gone through a lot today. I'm not just going to be one more bastard who takes from you."

She was already shaking her head, though.

"Finn..." She reached up tentatively and pushed some of his shaggy hair back from his face. She swallowed before continuing. "You're my... my *husband*, too. And I want that. With you. Tonight. I want it to be real."

Aw fuck, she was seriously killing him. She knew that, right?

Just to make the torture complete, she rolled her hips against him again.

He was going to hell. That was all there was to it.

Because he reached down and ripped at the button of his jeans to free himself.

Sophia reached behind her and undid her bra, sliding it down her arms. Finn about passed out.

"Jesus, Soph," he breathed out, taking her in. He'd tried not to look while the other men were having sex with her earlier. He really had, but he was only human. Still, he'd only had glances of her in the few peeks he'd stolen.

But to have her here, underneath him, exposing herself just for *him*.

He dropped down to suckle on one of her dark pink nipples as he shoved his jeans and boxers down his ass.

Oh fuck. The tip of his cock nudged at her folds and she was hot.

And wet.

She was wet for him.

It drove him fucking crazy.

He suckled harder at her nipple but only for a moment because he missed the connection of her lips too much.

He shifted back up and took her mouth again.

Her legs had wrapped back around him and she rolled her hips against him, rubbing her folds up and down his length before he was even inside her.

"Jesus, Soph," he swore between kisses. "You're killing me. You feel so fucking good."

She smiled and when he pulled back a moment to look into her eyes, they were sparkling and excited.

She wanted this. She wasn't doing it out of some sense of obligation or because she thought she ought to as a new bride.

Finn reached down and grabbed his cock, dragging his tip up and down her slit and rolling it around where he thought her clit was.

Based on the way she arched her back, he thought he'd found the right spot.

He couldn't wait another second.

Still, he forced himself to ask. "You ready, Soph? You ready for me?"

She nodded. "Yes, Finn. *Please*."

Please. God. Killing him.

He felt around with his cock and finally lined up with the place where her body gave. Then he pressed in.

And she welcomed him in like she was made for him.

Because she *was* fucking made for him.

When she was born, Sophia Wolford was marked. Marked as meant for him, and him for her. He knew it with every cell in his whole goddamned body.

Especially his fucking cock.

Nothing had ever felt more right in his life than his cock coming home as he entered Sophia's body. Home. Pressing in further. Her body so fucking tight around him. So goddamned right.

Her mouth went taut and her face strained.

"Oh shit, Soph. Are you okay? Am I hurting you?"

His worry cut like a knife through the insane pleasure he was feeling but she just shook her head.

"No, it's good. Keep going. God, Finn, keep going."

Pleasure spiked at hearing her say his name. While he was fucking *inside her*.

"Say it again." He kissed her deep while he pushed in another inch. Fucking heaven. This was eternity. Being inside Sophia Wolford.

She squirmed, her hips rolling up restlessly against him. "What?"

"My name," he growled, sliding in the last inch.

"Finn," she cried as he swiveled his hips, trying to give her friction on that all-important bud. Seemed like it worked.

"That's right," he said, pulling out slowly, tortuously. Jesus, was pulling out even better? No, it was pushing in, he decided on his next thrust. Definitely pushing in. That feeling of breaching, of taking what the girl of his dreams was finally willing to give.

"Finn," she gasped again as he bottomed out and ground his groin into hers.

"Yes, Soph, I'm right here with you, honey. Tell me how good it feels."

"Finn, it's so good." A tear slid out of her eye. "I never knew..."

He pressed back in again and kissed her all over her face. "I know, baby." Emotion clogged his own throat. "Shh, I know."

They continued silently for awhile longer. The most precious minutes of Finn's whole stupid life.

This. This made it all worth it. The shit and the misery and the death and the blood. This moment with the most perfect woman on earth. Her clutching his back so hard her nails dug into his flesh. Her little breathy gasps between kisses as he learned her body. The feel of her nipples brushing against the hair on his chest.

"Finn, it's coming." She'd had her eyes closed, lost in the pleasure, but she opened them again.

Finn saw the whole fucking world in her eyes.

He couldn't hold back anymore. His hips jerked and he came as he looked into her eyes, and watched the surprised wonder as her own climax hit.

Afterwards, he clutched her to him and rolled so that she was on top of him. She weighed so little, he could still breathe just fine, and he didn't want to lose the connection with her yet. Every so often, he'd thrust a few times to give just enough friction so his cock would stay stiff. Even though he'd already come, he could stay hard for a good while after.

If he had his way, he'd stay just like this, his cock in the woman he loved, for the rest of his fucking life.

CHAPTER NINE

SOPHIA

"Rise and shine, lovely wife."

Sophia blinked her eyes open.

Where was—?

Then her eyes popped open wide. Holy shit! She was sleeping on someone. Like, *on* them. She put her hands on either side of him and pushed back.

Finn.

Right. Memories of last night flooded back in.

Him cupping her face so sweetly and her attacking him and kissing him... and then everything that followed.

She shifted to climb off him.

—which was when she felt him *inside* her.

Holy shit! His cock was still *in her*!!!!

How was that even possible? As she shifted, she felt him start to harden again. And she felt her body start to respond.

Her face flamed as she eased her body off of him. He slid out of her at last and his eyes opened. He didn't smile or even look her way, though.

He looked behind her and his eyes went hard.

Which was when she remembered that, *right*, it was another man's voice that had woken her.

She looked over her shoulder and saw Jagger standing there, Leo and Mario flanking him. Was spontaneous combustion an actual thing? Because she was pretty sure she was about three seconds away from it.

She jerked the sheet to cover herself, but Finn was laying on it, and she couldn't seem to yank it out from under him.

"Good morning, everyone," she said. "I hope you all slept well." Oh God, what if they'd asked how *she'd* slept? Oh fine, you know, I've just been screwing Finn for about five hours if you want to get technical about it. Because it still counted as screwing if his cock was inside her, right? Even if neither of them were conscious or, ya know, moving?

"So what's on the agenda for today?" She swung her head around to Jagger. Anything to get out of her own head. "Are we going to take a tour of the town? That's what we usually do in Jacob's Well whenever we get any newcomers. But I suppose every township has different customs. I'm happy to learn whatever yours are."

Sophia finally got the sheet out from under Finn and wrapped it around herself. "Or will we be starting off for Santa Fe first thing? Well, right after breakfast I mean. I really am very hungry. And thirsty. Though I imagine everyone around here is. I don't mean to sound ungrateful. The running water here is amazing. Does it come from an aquifer like ours does in Central Texas? It really is amazing that underneath all this desert are these underground rivers—"

She was rambling, she knew she was. Her friend Gail always got annoyed when she rambled but no matter how much she told herself to stop, words just kept erupting like some godawful fountain.

Thankfully, Jagger cut in.

"Actually we're heading back to Texas, not on to Santa Fe."

Wait, what? Sophia could only stare up at Jagger in confusion after his pronouncement.

"But..." It was really saying something that he'd rendered her speechless. It didn't last long though. She climbed off the bed, holding the sheet tight. "But the men! That's where all the soldiers are, right? We have to go get them so they can start marching toward—"

"We bring the women here first. The brides, I mean. Then you'll get your men."

Sophia's mouth dropped open.

"That's not what you said yesterday," Finn said, scrambling off the bed to stand beside Sophia.

Sophia nodded. Yeah. What he said.

"Actually," Jagger said, "We didn't really discuss it. We were busy with the..." his eyes scoured Sophia's body until she felt naked even though she had the sheet clutched as tightly as possible around her "...festivities."

"But that was the understanding," Sophia said. "I came here as an ambassador, to show you the process. Then the men from New Mexico come and fight, and they'll get to come back with brides."

"The ones who make it back alive," Jagger said, squaring his jaw and settling his calculating eyes down on Sophia.

His height advantage wasn't fair. She couldn't help that she was five foot five. But the fact that he was so much taller suddenly made her feel like she was a child arguing with her father.

"It's hard to convince a man to fight for any reason, but for the promise of a far-off bride who may or may not exist?"

"They *do* exist!" Sophia protested. "I'm proof!"

"It's not me you have to convince," Jagger said, eyebrows narrowing in apparent sympathy. Sophia got the cold feeling that he was just humoring her, though, like her father sometimes did. Like he was already bound and determined to get his way and *nothing* she said would ever matter one way or the other.

Which made her absolutely furious.

"You've already decided, haven't you? This isn't a discussion. You're just informing me."

She tucked the sheet tighter around her body. What a pompous, arrogant— And this was the man she'd let into her body last night, who she'd so wantonly begged to—

"I'm sorry, love." Jagger's voice softened. "I can't change the way the world works. But the only way you'll get your men is if you bring the women here first and hold lotteries or raffles or whatever you call them. Then the men will go, knowing they have something worth fighting for waiting back at home."

Sophia spun away from him.

Did this mean she'd been right yesterday to be distrustful of him? But what did he have to gain by taking her back to Texas first?

If Jagger thought to trick her, surely he wouldn't want to go directly into foreign territory and go bargain with powers stronger than him. He had to know he'd be dealing with her father if they went back to San Antonio and that such a man would be more difficult to fool than one naïve girl.

Maybe that meant Jagger was legitimate after all? If he thought he had a strong enough case to convince even the Commander of an entire territory?

But if she didn't go to Santa Fe, then how could she report back about the stability of the new government and the city first hand?

She bit her lip and looked around the big room, all but glowing as sunlight poured in the windows that lined two walls.

"What if we compro—" she started to say but Finn cut her off before she could finish the word *compromise*.

"Going back to Texas sounds good to us," Finn said.

"Finn!" Sophia swung around to look at him.

He didn't meet her eyes. He kept looking around the room at the other men. "We're already neck deep in this, Sophia. If they won't take us to Santa Fe, what are we gonna do? We don't exactly have any bargaining chips here. We'll get back to San Antonio and talk to your father. If he thinks bringing the women back is a good idea, then that's what we'll do."

Finn finally looked at her right as she stepped back from him. *They'd talk to her father?* After everything, that was still what it came down to, didn't it?

She'd always be the naïve, foolish daughter of the brave and fearless Commander. He'd rescue her from this like it was just another foolhardy misadventure. Sure she'd gotten herself in more trouble this time than when she and some friends stole extra rations of sugar to bake a cake for Davina's thirteenth birthday party, or when she stayed up past curfew and snuck out to go swimming in the pool at Jacob's Well by moonlight with her friends and some boys.

But the principle was the same. This was probably what Finn had been planning all along—to get her to a point where she realized her own stupidity and uselessness and finally turned back. So what was last night? He was just playing along until he could find any opportunity to get her back to Texas? Oh God, and when she'd attacked him and kissed him like that, he, what? Was just keeping her pacified and having sex with her was the path of least resistance to keep up the ruse?

"Congratulations," she turned on Finn and spat in his face. "I guess you'll be rid of me sooner rather than later."

"Soph, what? No, I—"

"I'll be in the kitchen preparing rations."

And then she swept from the room before any of them could see the hot tears burning in her eyes actually escape down her cheeks. God, she didn't know what to think. She wasn't sure if what she'd just accused Finn of even made sense, but everything was so mixed up. Why couldn't he have talked to her first and backed her play? Or at least figured things out together before just declaring what they wanted to do?

Her escape was short lived, though.

She ran down the hall almost blindly in the direction of the kitchen.

And ran right into the solid wall of a man's chest.

She yelped as she looked up.

It was Toby. Her fifth husband, who'd passed out after his fourth cup of homebrewed whiskey last night.

"Oh, sorry—" she started to say, but he cut her off with a nasty grin and by reaching around and mauling her ass with his big hands.

"Hey!"

She tried to swat his hands away but he only gripped her ass cheeks tighter, swiveling her and pressing her up against the wall. He followed with his body, crushing her to the cream-colored wall.

"Leo said you and me had lots of fun last night." His breath was foul and she turned her face away from him. "Shame I can't remember any of it. Guess you'll have to give me a repeat performance."

He ground himself against her and she shoved against him uselessly. God, this couldn't be happening. This man was her *husband*. He was supposed to worship her, not—not *assault her*. If this happened in Jacob's Well, her father would have his ass banned in three seconds flat.

But you aren't in Jacob's Well anymore.

"Get *off* me!" she screeched. After last night and this morning, there was only so much she could handle. And if this bastard thought for one second that she was going to let him—

"Toby." Jagger's sharp voice came from behind them and for a second, Toby tensed at the sound.

"You know we need to get going," Jagger continued. "If we're going to make it even halfway to Jal before sundown. You got the two men you're bringing along ready?"

Toby shrugged, finally stepping away from Sophia. The breath she hadn't even realized she was holding shuddered out of her chest.

"They will be," Toby said, picking something out of his teeth.

"Go check or I'm leaving without them," Jagger said. "I'll take Ramirez and Johnson instead."

Toby scowled and stalked toward the door that led to the stairwell.

Leo had come in right before Toby left and he looked toward Jagger. "You sure that's the best idea, boss?"

"Not now," Jagger snapped, his eyes shooting Sophia's direction.

Leo followed his gaze and nodded, leaving as silently as he'd come.

"There's breakfast in the kitchen," was all Jagger said to Sophia. "Eat up. We leave in fifteen."

Sophia lifted a shaky hand to push her hair back from her face.

Dear God, just what had she gotten herself into by marrying this group of strange and violent men?

———

Sophia didn't feel so good.

Four and a half hours into their journey and Sophia was so saddle sore, she couldn't imagine another hour riding the beast beneath her, much less a whole day.

Horses.

They were riding *horses* back to Texas.

She'd looked at Jagger like he was nuts when he'd led them out to the stables down the street from the courthouse.

Leo, Mario, and a couple of men that Sophia didn't recognize were carrying plastic bladders of water over their shoulders, so maybe that should've given it away but still. Sophia's mouth had dropped open and in spite of her determination to ignore Finn, she couldn't help her eyes shooting to Finn and mouthing, *he's kidding, right?*

But no, Jagger was most decidedly *not* kidding.

Nor did he take into consideration the fact that she'd lost her maidenhood last night and she was already sore *down there*.

No, he just hoisted her up on his horse and then swung up right behind her.

It had only given her the briefest satisfaction of seeing Finn's eyes flare when Jagger had taken her to ride on *his* horse. But then Sophia laughed at herself for her foolishness. Finn wasn't jealous. The anger she'd seen there had probably just been some sort of misplaced righteous fury on her father's behalf. Daddy's little innocent princess, getting even more sullied by the big bad wolf.

She'd sat up taller in the saddle at that thought and tried to look unaffected by the whole thing.

But her stoicism could only last so long because, dear God, it *hurt*.

Jagger and the others took a relentless and punishing pace and every time they jolted with the horse's cantering, Sophia's sex cried out in soreness. Her womb had taken a battering last night and this was just torture on top of it.

Still, she was determined to be just as strong as Drea would be in this situation. Drea, who was everything Sophia wasn't. No way Drea'd let a little thing like a broken hymen slow her down when the world still needed saving.

Though Sophia was growing less and less assured that any of this was going to be able to help anyone—not even herself, in the end.

That man, Toby, terrified her, if she was honest.

But he was her husband. He had as much right to her body as any of them. So that meant she had to submit to him, right?

It was the way she'd been raised.

But she'd also been raised to believe that a man should love and cherish his wife. That he should want to give all material wealth to her and sacrifice anything, even his own life, if it meant he could save her pain or injury.

But then, that hadn't been part of their vows, had it?

There had been no vow to love each other in sickness and health, in good times and bad, for richer or for poorer.

There had been no vows at all.

These men had promised her nothing.

And you promised them nothing in return.

So what about last night?

Because in reality, hadn't she offered them everything?

And they'd taken it, the four of them, each snatching a little piece of her heart. Because she didn't know how to divorce her mind and body. And she'd never wanted to. She'd looked forward to her marriage for so long because all she'd ever wanted was a family of her own, and to be loved.

And now?

The horse landed especially hard after taking a little leap and Sophia couldn't help grunting in pain as her thighs tensed around the large gelding.

"What's wrong?" Jagger asked.

He'd sat Sophia in front of him this time and she looked over her shoulder at him incredulously. "Are you kidding?"

He met her frown with one of his own.

"Um," she started but then trailed off. For all intents and purposes, Jagger seemed like a very intelligent man. But he was sure slow on the uptake with this one.

Her face went so hot she was sure she practically glowed pink in the midafternoon sun despite the long-sleeved linen shirt and hat Finn had tossed her way before they left the house this morning. She looked forward again when she saw Jagger's face soften some. She couldn't figure him out. Today he was taciturn and barely said a word to her.

How did she reconcile that with the man who'd been so commanding and in charge of her body last night?

Riding for hours through monotonous terrain only gave her time to replay everything that had happened the night before in *excruciating* detail.

And the fact that Jagger had been the first to breach her sacred place, and then how he'd gone on to... She'd had him in her *mouth*... and what was more, she'd *liked it*.

The whole first hour of the ride, all she could think about was that that part of his body was nestled right up against her rump as they rode the horse.

But then the saddle-soreness quickly set in and the bloom was quickly off that rose.

"Ever consider I might be sore because yesterday I was a *virgin* and three men mounted me?" she finally finished, her face averted. Jagger must have tightened his thighs sharply on the horse or something because the gelding, usually a placid ride, suddenly reared backwards and Jagger grabbed the reins from Sophia just in time to keep from being tossed off the horse.

"Jesus Christ," Finn swore, bringing his horse over to theirs in spite of threats from Jagger's two other guards, aka Toby's men, to stay put.

But Finn didn't stop. "Soph, are you okay?"

She winced, because though she and Jagger had managed to stay on the horse, landing had been another harsh reminder that she wasn't nearly as used to horseback riding as she ought to be. When she was younger, she'd loved riding horses but after The Fall, checking out a horse from the stables was a lengthy affair and besides, her father wouldn't let her go anywhere beyond the township's city limit, so what was the point?

Jagger slowed the horse down but trotting made it even worse and Sophia couldn't hold back the cry this time.

"Stop," Finn demanded. "Can't you see she's in pain?"

Jagger sighed, obviously frustrated, and Sophia wanted to both apologize profusely and to smack the man. It wasn't her fault she wasn't prepared to be hauled all over a foreign country on a smelly animal right after— Right after they'd—

Finn got down off his horse and then held out his arms for Sophia.

And in spite of how frustrated she was with him, nothing in the universe sounded better than getting off the horse. She was less than graceful as she slid off the horse and all but collapsed into his arms.

Hearing Jagger curse from behind her wasn't helping matters, especially when she could barely stand up once she was beside Finn. Almost immediately she collapsed to the ground.

"Shit, Soph!" Finn caught her right before she hit the dirt. "Water! Somebody get her some water!"

"We ain't got time for this." Sophia barely registered Toby's voice. Her whole body felt wrong. Floppy, like she was made out of jelly.

"Come on, let's get her out of the sun." Leo's voice. Another pair of hands helped Finn lift her and then she was being carried.

"Where? There's nothing, fucking anywhere. It's just flat, for miles." Sophia had never heard Finn sound so frustrated. Okay, that wasn't true—but apart from when he was arguing with *her*, she'd never heard him sound so upset. And there was an edge of panic she'd never heard in his voice before, ever.

"The trailer's coming up, right, boss?" Leo asked.

"About a half mile up."

"You think we can get her there?"

"Not sure. Don't think she's getting back on a horse today."

"We ain't got fuckin' *time* for this bullshit," Toby whined.

"I'll carry her," Finn said.

"Just sling her over a fuckin' horse an' be done with it. We got miles to make. You said so this morning, Jag."

"You think her father will appreciate us showing up with his daughter half dead of sunstroke and dehydration?" Jagger snapped. "She grew up pampered. I should have calculated for that." A pause, then, "You'll carry her?"

Finn hefted Sophia in his arms. "I got her."

Sophia blinked dazedly as Leo held up a water bottle to her lips. She drank several mouthfuls but then Leo pulled back. Rationing. Always rationing. And then they were moving again. Finn held her to his chest, arms underneath her back and her knees, bridal style.

Not exactly the way she'd imagined it.

Sophia buried her face against his chest and made an attempt to hurl her noodle arms around his neck.

The bounce of his footsteps was so much less jarring than the horse, though, and not on the place where she was sorest, she could have wept from gratitude if she had any extra water in her body to spare. But from the way Finn's breaths soon became labored, she could tell even through her fuzzy brain that this wasn't a workable long-term solution.

He wasn't going to be able to carry her a half mile, no matter his bravado or his stubborn pride.

This trip was showing both of them their limits.

It was humiliating.

It was humbling.

It might just be the death of her.

When Finn stumbled, Sophia thought for sure she was about to get a face full of dirt, or worse, cactus.

Instead, though, another pair of arms smoothly caught her up, transferring her from Finn's chest to another, much larger one.

Not a word was exchanged and Sophia had to squint up into the sunlight to see who her rescuer was.

Mario. Huge and silent as always. He didn't look down at her. He simply stared straight ahead as he held her cradled to his chest.

Unlike Finn, he didn't hunch with the weight of her in his arms or seem slowed in the slightest.

Finally, blessedly, Sophia let her eyes fall shut.

She was asleep before Mario's next footfall.

CHAPTER TEN

LEO

Leo stared in astonishment as his brother carried the woman up the stairs of the trailer twenty minutes later. Finn hurried up the stairs, slipping past him to push the door open.

Mario didn't get involved.

In anything.

Ever.

Well, he did when Leo asked him to. Jagger barked orders to Leo, Leo relayed them to Mario—even if they were all in the same room—and Mario did them.

It wasn't that Mario was mentally slow or anything. And he *did* talk. Just not that often, and never to anyone other than Leo.

Sometimes when Leo was busy doing something else, he'd come into a room and find Mario just sitting there, staring at... *nothing*.

It was like Mario didn't exist apart from Leo and that was a bit terrifying.

It was too much responsibility.

But it had always been that way. At least ever since Mom and Dad died.

Mario had only been eleven at the time and he'd witnessed their murders.

Leo had been out. The death riots had only just begun and he was sixteen and tired of being stuck inside. So he'd snuck out to his friends house and played video games all day.

And come home to find his parents dead, his house ransacked, and Mario— Mario was sitting there by Mom, covered in her blood, absolutely silent. Leo didn't know how many hours they'd all been there like that, but a lot of the blood on Mario was dried and crusty, so it had to have been a good long time.

Leo had been raising him ever since. If he had to devote the rest of his life to his brother to try to make up for the day he failed them all, so be it.

Mario was grown up now, just turned twenty last month. He was built like a brick shithouse. His neck was as thick as most guy's *thighs*. But he'd always be Leo's little brother.

And the last two days were the first time in eight and a half years that Leo had seen the spark of anything resembling life flicker in his brother's eyes.

Because of *her*.

Their wife.

When Jagger told him he wanted Leo as one of the husbands, Leo had immediately demanded Mario be another.

Jagger had seemed surprised. *I didn't think he—*

He does, Leo answered. He'd treated Mario to a trip to a brothel for his eighteenth birthday.

Mario had spoken one word. *Condom.*

A condom cost more than the whore herself but Leo was going all out and already had it on hand.

Mario disappeared upstairs with the first girl who approached him. He came back down forty-five minutes later.

Did you—

Yep.

How was it?

Never again.

The next time Leo visited a brothel, Mario stayed outside.

The truth was, Leo'd had no clue how Mario was going to respond last night when they'd all gone upstairs with Sophia.

But when she'd gone down on Mario, Leo had snuck peeks at his brother's face and been so shocked at what he saw there, he'd been distracted for minutes from the beautiful pussy in front of him.

Mario had looked *alive*. He'd looked like a man. Like a normal guy getting sucked off. Well, normal-ish. Mario'd looked like he was half in love with his wife already. And all she'd done was give him a blowy.

And then today, carrying her for what was more like a mile.

Leo hadn't told him to do it.

He'd just walked over and grabbed him out of the other sop's arms. Cause that guy was gone in love with her, too.

And then Mario had carried her here without a single look in Leo's direction.

Leo couldn't decide if he was upset by that or fucking elated.

Because on his worst days, if Leo was dead honest with himself, there were times he resented the responsibility of Mario.

Day in, day out, all day, every day, knowing that if he wasn't in the picture, his brother would just sit there and stare at the fucking wall? He'd forget to eat, and drink. Jesus Christ, there were days he had to remind Mario to take piss breaks. It was too fucking much. It was hard enough after the Fall to take care of yourself, much less yourself and another person.

Sometimes he wanted to scream at Mario—everybody's lost somebody. Get the fuck over it and man the fuck up!!!

And then he wanted to pound his own head against the wall. Because what kind of monster wished his own brother gone? Especially after what happened. Sure, everyone had lost someone, but Mario had only been *eleven*. And it had happened right in front of his eyes.

It wasn't something a person *ever* got over.

Leo had certainly met plenty of insane, violent fuckers since those days. Lots of other people had gone just as nuts after all that happened back then. At least Mario had just gone quiet and a little… unmotivated.

But what if it didn't have to be that way forever?

What if Mario found something else to live for?

Jagger and Toby and the others pushed past Leo after tying up the horses.

Leo hurried up the stairs behind them.

The trailer was abandoned who knew how long ago but was in good shape. Roof was still intact and it was so dry out here, the carpet hadn't molded or anything. It just smelled... unlived in. Musty, like an attic or a closet no one ever opened.

It was fully furnished still, too. Rioters must have missed it back in the day because everything was still in good condition.

Mario had laid Sophia on a dusty couch inside the trailer and he was crouched down beside her, pushing her hair out of her face.

And the look in his eyes was so... so fucking tender, Leo took a step backwards.

Who the hell had body snatched his brother?

"Here, I've got some more water for her." Finn came hurrying over with a plastic cup full of water, no doubt from the saddlebag Leo had seen him carrying inside earlier. The cup was a nice touch, though. Maybe he'd found it in the cabinets.

Leo had been to this trailer before. He'd slept here once on a trade run to Odessa. Jagger had been running trade through to Texas for a few years now. It was fucking dangerous because of that crazy bitch up in Colorado. She liked to think she had New Mexico on lockdown. No news in, no news out.

Jagger played it smart, though. He and his crew kept their mouths shut, hugged the southern border, kept quiet about the war and what was really going on in Colorado, and consequently, they lived like desert kings. Well, all right, Mario and Leo were more like servants to the king, but considering their access to water and food, it was more or less the same thing.

"Sophia." Finn held the cup to her lips. "Soph, here. Drink this."

He tipped the cup up too steeply and water dribbled down her chin and onto her shirt. She blinked up at him tiredly and to Leo's utter shock, Mario snatched the cup from Finn.

Mario cupped the back of Sophia's head and helped her sit up a little. Then he held the cup back to her lips, oh so carefully.

Mario treated her like she was porcelain, and slowly, she sipped water from the cup.

"Good," Mario murmured and Leo took another stuttering step backwards, hitting the door he'd just come through.

"Can I fuckin' talk to you?" Toby's ugly voice cut through the quiet room. "*Boss?*" The last word was tacked on snidely.

Jagger glared his direction, apparently not in the mood. Still, he jerked his head toward the hallway and Leo looked on as Jagger, Toby, and Toby's two thugs all headed to the furthest room and shut the door.

Leo barely waited a second before following them.

He spared one last glance his brother's way, only to see Mario completely absorbed in helping Sophia take another sip of water, Finn watching on anxiously.

Leo walked as quietly as he could down the hallway, wincing as his foot landed on an especially creaky patch of flooring right as he got to the door of the last bedroom.

He needn't have worried though, not with how loud Toby was being. Leo put his ear to the cheap door but he could almost make out the words even before he settled in.

"What the fuck? We just gonna sit here and pamper the bitch? I wanna get fucking paid, and I want to get paid *now*."

"You think her father's going to pay if we show up with her dead at his doorstep?" Leo recoiled at Jagger's impassive words but he didn't move his ear away from the door.

Toby scoffed. "Bitch won't be dead. But she don't have to be all plump an' shiny either. Who gives a fuck if she's a little road worn? In fact, I plan to wear that pussy o' hers out plenty before we get her back to daddy."

"You remain as ever the epitome of cultivation and gentlemanly pursuit."

"What the fuck does that—"

"We'll stay here until she's feeling better. And at no point will you rape her."

Leo breathed a little easier at that. Until Jagger went on.

"And as soon as we find a Satellite phone that actually works, we'll call her father and demand a king's ransom for her return. If he declines our offer, then you can do whatever you want to her."

Leo jerked back from the door, staring at it in horror.

He heard footsteps coming toward him and hurried back to the living room, only making it there right as the door opened behind him.

Sophia looked more awake now, and she was smiling sweetly up at Leo's brother. She reached out and squeezed Mario's hand, and the look on his face—Leo's heart flipped at seeing it. It was like when his brother looked at his tiny wife, he was seeing the sun rise for the first time in eight and a half years.

And right then, Leo knew that whatever happened, now there were two people on this earth he would lay down his life to protect.

CHAPTER ELEVEN

JAGGER

"How are you feeling?" Jagger sat on the edge of the mattress in one of the bedrooms. Because of the dry climate, the mattress had survived the years more or less intact and after they'd spread two semi-moth-eaten blankets over it, it was the most comfort they could offer Sophia.

"I'm fine," she said, two high pink spots of color rising in her cheeks as she tried to push herself up into a sitting position.

Finn was right there to push her shoulders back down and even Mario took a step forward from where he stood like a foreboding sentry against the wall, where he'd been a permanent fixture since they'd moved her in here yesterday.

The sun was going down now and after a day of Toby's bitching, Jagger had finally set him loose on the whiskey early before the dumb fuck made a scene of some kind.

This morning they'd sent Toby's two lackeys back to Carlsbad to pick up a trailer and bring it here. It would slow them down—already it was a day's wait to send them and another for them to get back with the trailer. But that was how long Jagger should have waited in the first place for his new bride to heal from their wedding night.

But he'd never expected for her to *actually* be a virgin! How the hell was any woman left on this earth still a virgin?

She shoved Finn away, eyes flashing. "I said, I'm fine. Stop treating me like I'm made of glass. So I should've drunk some more water and worn a hat with a wider brim yesterday. But I'm far less sore and I'm sure when your men get back tomorrow, I'll be fine to get back on the trail and—"

"Sure will," Jagger said. "Cause you'll be riding in the trailer."

Her mouth dropped open. She'd been sleeping when Jagger told Leo and Toby's guys to go back for the trailer.

Toby's men had looked less than pleased at the prospect, their eyes immediately moving to Toby. Disloyal sons of bitches. Jagger was their Governor.

Not for much longer if Toby had his way, no doubt.

It was why he'd insisted Toby's right hand men come along. Just how bold would they be? Would they try to kill Jagger outright on this little trip?

Well he was staying a step ahead of them.

Because that whiskey Toby was downing so eagerly in the other room?

It *might* be laced with arsenic.

Not enough to kill the bastard. But it would keep him weak and he'd have the hangover from the seventh level of hell come tomorrow morning.

It was also a handy excuse for the stomach upset and all the vomiting that would be coming in a few hours. Not that that would deter Toby from drinking if the past were any indication.

But it would keep the man from coming anywhere near Sophia during their little respite.

"I don't need a *trailer*," she said, aghast. "I'll get used to the saddle. I was just especially sore because of—" her eyes dropped and she fiddled with the edges of the blanket. "Well, you know."

But then she sat up, smiled cheerily, and threw off the blankets.

"I'm fine. Much better now. I'll go get dinner prepared, even. I've just been lazing around all day and—"

Jagger moved in front of her to block her, then urged her back down on the bed and sat beside her.

"Don't be stubborn, little dove." He pushed a lock of hair back out of her face. Her hair was so soft and when bright green eyes flashed his way in surprise at the gentle touch, he almost pulled back.

"I'm sorry," she whispered, and the vulnerability in her eyes sliced him in the guts in a way that took him off guard. "This isn't how I envisioned the first few days of my marriage."

"Nothing to be sorry for," he said, unable to look away from her. He forced himself to, though.

It was one thing for the big oaf Mario to be bewitched by her. But Jagger? He'd hardened himself to everything soft left in the world a long, long time ago.

Not even Sophia Wolford could touch him.

He'd enjoy her while time allowed and then fetch the best ransom he could get for her from her bigwig father.

That was all.

"But if you are feeling better…" Jagger put his hand on her knee and slid it up her thigh. "I can think of another way we could pass the time."

"Jesus Christ, she's been ill," Finn jumped in but Sophia just glared at Finn and put her hand on top of Jagger's to stop him from pulling away.

Her bright eyes came back to Jagger's. "Don't stop. I'm fine now. And I— I've been wanting to. To try it again."

Her cheeks were pink again as she looked from man to man. There were only the three of them in the room, Jagger, Finn, and Mario. Leo had gone with Toby's men so they could bring back extra water. At least that was the excuse Jagger had given. Really he'd wanted eyes on them at all times.

Leo never liked to be separated from Mario but Jagger had overheard Mario telling his brother it was fine, one of the few times Jagger had ever actually heard the giant speak.

Leo had promised to come back as quickly as possible. Another reason to send him along.

Jagger watched Sophia's tongue slip out to lick her lips as he slid his thumb up her silky inner thigh even higher.

She was wearing the tiniest pair of sleep shorts he'd ever seen since it was hot, and a barely there tank top that did little to hide her peaked nipples.

He reached up to pinch one and she let out a little breathy moan.

Finn, who was seated on the other side of the bed, stood up and dragged his hands through his hair, pacing away from the bed.

"Finn," she called and he spun to look back at her. Poor kid's face was agonized.

Jagger couldn't read the look on Sophia's face. Things had been tense between her and the boy, he'd noticed, but it looked like Sophia was offering some sort of olive branch.

And because the guy wasn't a dumb fuck, he took it, swallowing hard and walking back toward her. Right when he clasped hands with her, she reached out her other hand to Mario.

Mario was far quicker than Finn in hurrying to her side.

He didn't stop there, though. He came to the foot of the bed and climbed up between her legs. The big man clearly had an agenda.

Jagger lifted an eyebrow as Mario's big fingers coasted up the outside of her thighs and then slid in the top of her shorts.

Sophia got the message and lifted her hips. Mario pulled her cotton shorts and underwear down in one swift motion, all the way down off her legs, exposing her pretty, pretty pussy. She kicked them to the side and then Mario slid reverent hands back up her inner thighs.

Jagger climbed off the bed and shoved his pants down, then took himself in hand.

He'd step in later, but here at the beginning, it was hot as fuck just to watch.

CHAPTER TWELVE

MARIO

Mario was touching her. She was letting him touch her. So soft. And hot. And when she looked down at him, she smiled.

She didn't look at him like he was a freak. She didn't pull away from his touch.

The opposite, in fact. She seemed to relax against his hand as he caressed up and down her thigh.

He wanted to put his cock inside her.

He wanted it very badly.

But she'd hurt afterwards the last time and he would not do anything that might hurt her.

Touching her would be enough. It would be so much more than enough. More than he'd ever known.

He opened her legs and she spread herself there before him like a flower blossoming to the sun.

Mario leaned in and inhaled her sweet scent.

And almost passed out from how aroused he was.

He thrust his hips against the bed for friction because he thought he might die without it.

And then he extended his tongue and licked the edge of her soft, wet petals.

A shudder shook through her legs. He knew instinctively it was one of pleasure and not revulsion or fear. She wanted his touch. His touch affected her the same way hers did him. Her wetness was proof.

She wanted *him*.

Him, who was barely half a man.

He flattened his tongue and licked her from bottom to top.

Once, and then again.

She squirmed against his face like she was seeking something but he didn't know what. He knew almost nothing of women. What if he couldn't please her? He hadn't forgotten the way she'd screamed around his cock the last time. He knew women could come.

Leo knew how to make women come.

But Mario had only slept with that whore the one time and it had been cold and sterile feeling. The woman had seemed bored the whole time.

Nothing like Sophia.

Mario turned to Jagger, who was standing to the side, stroking his cock and watching. "How?" Mario asked.

Jagger nodded and came closer. If there was one thing Jagger loved, it was giving orders. Mario picked and chose the ones he wanted to obey but this was one time he'd be grateful for the instruction.

"Here," Jagger said. He reached between her legs and began to massage a spot at the top of her slit. "This is her clitoris. If your rub and suckle it just right, it will bring her pleasure beyond belief."

Mario stared intensely as Jagger pulled the folds of her sweet little pussy back to expose an engorged nub.

"See that?" Jagger teased his middle finger in a circle around it and Sophia's whole body jerked. "That's what you want."

"How hard?"

"Listen to her body. Sometimes she'll want it soft. Other times she'll want it merciless. Sometimes she'll want you to tease your teeth along it."

Sophia shuddered again, like just them talking about it brought her intense pleasure.

Jagger must have noticed the same because he smiled. "You like hearing me tell him how to eat you out best?"

Jagger slid his fingers down her juicy pussy and thrust one finger inside her hole.

Mario was tired of just watching, though, so he lowered his mouth back down, ignoring Jagger's hand in the way, and started to lick just the very tip of his tongue all around her clitoris.

She immediately started to respond, whining out the sexiest little noises Mario had ever heard in his life.

Mario should have died eight and a half years ago. There wasn't a day that went by that he didn't wish he had.

Except for today.

Today he was glad he was alive.

As he sucked on his wife's sweet little pleasure bud and felt her respond beneath him, he was so, so fucking happy to be alive.

CHAPTER THIRTEEN

SOPHIA

Oh God, what were they doing to her down there? It was so intense and foreign feeling and pleasurable. She hadn't let go of Finn's hand but she could feel how stiff he was beside her.

She hated that. As good as it all felt, knowing Finn was still upset kept her from truly letting go.

She didn't understand.

Fine, he wanted to keep her safe for her father's sake.

But he'd seemed to enjoy what they'd done together the other night, even if it had meant more to her than it had to him. He'd been hard and his seed had spurted.

Did he not want her like that anymore?

He was turned away from her, so she couldn't tell if he was affected by what the other men were doing to her. She frowned. He was so stubborn, even in this.

But he was her husband, goddammit.

And if he wanted to pawn her off on her dad as soon as they hit San Antonio, he had another thing coming.

She'd heard the wives talk about seducing their husbands. Vanessa had confided in her about how her husbands weren't enthusiastic about the marriage at first. But Vanessa had slowly brought them around.

Well Sophia refused for this marriage to be anything other than an absolute success.

So Finnigan Knight better get his act in shape, and if he thought *he* was stubborn, well then he clearly didn't know her as well as he thought he did.

Sophia let go of Finn's hand only long enough to tug her tank top over her head. It had a built-in bra, so she was completely exposed now.

Finn moved like he was going to get up again but she grabbed his hand before he could.

"Finn," she said, not able to help the breathy quality of her voice. What they were doing to her down there did feel *so good*.

"Kiss me, Finnigan."

Finn turned back to her and looked so torn, Sophia was startled.

And then his eyes dropped to her naked breasts.

Fire blazed up from her core and she couldn't help arching her breasts toward Finn.

"Touch me," she whispered.

Finn reached down a shaky hand like he was half in a trance.

But then he paused, his eyes flicking down to Jagger and Mario. When he seemed like he might pull back, Sophia grabbed his wrist and tugged him down on to the bed with her.

He lost his balance and landed sideways, but on top of her.

Worked for her.

She grabbed his face and kissed him, pouring all of the passion she was feeling and her rising pleasure into the kiss.

Finn held back for about two whole seconds.

And then he devoured her back. The hand that had been so tentatively outstretched now solidly grasped her breast.

"*Ohhhhh*," she cried into Finn's mouth, wrapping her arms around his neck.

"Oh God, Soph," he said, his voice deeper than he'd ever heard it before he dived in even deeper for another kiss.

Mario was quickly catching on to whatever it was that Jagger had been showing him because his tongue was absolutely merciless as he drove her closer and closer to her orgasm.

She clutched desperately to Finn's shirt, glad he hadn't taken it off in spite of the fact that she wished she could touch his skin. She was afraid she'd leave scratch marks if he didn't have the shirt on, though.

He rolled his thumb back and forth across her nipple.

That was all it took.

It was like a blast wave of light lit in her core and exploded outward, up to the top of her head and out to the tips of her fingers.

It was sharp and quick this time, though, and as soon as it passed, she wanted more.

Finn had pulled back and was looking at her like... like... well, like he'd never looked at her before.

Not like she was a chore or an obligation.

But like she was a woman.

A woman he desired.

"I want you, Finn," she whispered. "I want to taste you. *Please.*" She didn't care if she was begging. She wanted more of him. She wanted him to look at her like that always. She wanted to look up at him as she pleasured him and watched him lose his damn mind over her.

"Sophia," he gasped.

"I want— I want—" She swallowed, feeling so mortified but driven by the insanity of her desire to connect with him for longer. For more. "I want to suck you. So hard until you spill your seed in my mouth. Down my throat."

"Jesus Christ," he swore, his eyes darker than she'd ever seen them, and full of indecision.

No. She wouldn't let his stubborn pride ruin this moment. She reached down between them and felt for his shaft through his jeans.

He was hard. He was hard for her. The knowledge was so intoxicating she didn't waste any more time.

She unbuttoned his jeans and then grinned when he shoved them down his legs. She tugged him forward but he was the one who climbed on the bed and straddled her chest, his long, hard penis right in front of her face.

Her breath hitched and she looked up his chest to his face.

His eyes were wide, like he couldn't believe what he'd just done. He shifted as if to climb right back off again but Sophia wrapped her arms around his thighs, thrilled when her hands came in contact with his ass, settled right above her breasts.

She squeezed his flesh and jerked him forward. Closer to her mouth.

And then she lifted up and took the tip of him into her mouth, all the while watching his face.

His stomach caved in as he sucked in a breath through his teeth, but he didn't throw back his head or close his eyes.

He stared directly down at her.

Their gazes locked and Sophia had never felt more naked.

Two men were licking and fingering her pussy but it was this, Finn watching her while she took his most intimate body part into her *mouth* that felt as if she was being cracked open like a nut and exposed as her most intimate self.

She pulled one hand from his thigh and tentatively touched the sack underneath his large member. She'd always been curious about what *balls* were and now to feel them up close and personal.

To be touching *Finn's balls*. Another hot *zing* of pleasure shot down her spine and she groaned around Finn's cock.

His mouth dropped open and his eyebrows scrunched together like he found that especially pleasurable.

So Sophia did it again. Groaning long and low as she pulled her other hand around to grab the base of him while she continued rolling his balls with her other.

"Jesus Christ," he hissed, sounding like he'd just run a marathon. "Jesus Christ, Soph."

Soph.

It was the name he'd called her ever since they were just teenagers back in school. But now they were so much more. Now she knew what he looked like as his pleasure ramped up. She knew what his cock looked like. What he *tasted* like. A little bit of his seed had already erupted and she eagerly licked it from his slit and then started bobbing up and down on him.

"Oh *fuck*." He braced his hands on the wall above her head and always, always his eyes were on her. His words and noises became more incoherent the longer she was at it. She loved the way his hips jerked almost involuntarily.

He was close. She didn't know how she knew, but she did. She prepared herself for his seed. Last time, Jagger's had been unexpected and she'd choked a little on it.

But this time she prepared. Plus, Finn reached down and touched her cheek.

"Soph. Soph. Christ, I'm— You should pull off."

Did he think she couldn't handle it?

Besides, she wanted *all* of him. So she only suctioned harder and swallowed him as far down her throat as she could manage.

And when he erupted, the shock and the pained pleasure on his face was the most beautiful, powerful thing she'd ever seen, his gaze never moving from hers.

Mario suckled her clit just right and her back arched as another orgasm hit her. Finn dropped a hand to cup the back of her head as his hips jerked slightly and even more of his seed spilled into her mouth.

She swallowed it down as best as she could amid her own pleasure.

Finn climbed off her as soon as he was finished, collapsing to her right. And then he grabbed her and kissed her deep, heedless of the fact that she'd only barely finished swallowing his seed.

"Jesus, Soph," he choked out, pressing his forehead to hers for a moment before devouring her lips again.

His eyes searched hers and it looked like he was about to say something else. But just then, Jagger climbed up on the bed.

She turned to look at Jagger and he dropped down to kiss her.

She blinked in shock and then immediately looked over at Finn. Would he be mad?

Finn's eyebrows were furrowed like he was conflicted, but not mad especially.

Jagger cupped the back of her head and urged her back toward Finn. "It's all right. Keep kissing him. I just wanted a taste."

Finn looked as surprised by the action as Sophia felt but she eagerly grabbed at the opportunity and reached for Finn again.

His lips were only a little less eager but at the slightest coaxing from Sophia, he was kissing her just as hungrily as ever, maybe even more so.

Jagger began kissing down her chest, focusing his attention on her breasts.

And then he began to rub his cock up and down her slit. Her breath hitched and he came back up to whisper in her ear even while Finn continued kissing her.

"I won't put it in, little dove. I know you're still sore. But feeling how wet and soft you are drives me fucking insane. Now kiss Mario. Thank him for what a good job he did learning how to suck your delicious little clit."

Sophia kept clinging to the back of Finn's head even as she turned to the left where indeed, Mario was waiting, his big warm body spread out on the other side of her.

She dug her fingers in the long, raggedly cut hair at the back of Mario's head and pulled his face toward hers.

Mario's lips were clumsy against hers but eager.

All the while Jagger took his cock in hand and rubbed himself up and down her drenched sex, using his hardness to rub and circle her clitoris.

Sophia bit and sucked on Mario's bottom lip while Jagger continued using his cock to pleasure her. The low, guttural groan Mario rewarded her with was so freaking sexy.

It was unreal.

It was all unreal.

Being surrounded by these three gorgeous men, all intent on her pleasure?

She couldn't wrap her head around it.

She broke off from Mario and turned back to Finn.

Sharing her seemed the most difficult on him, so she wanted to make sure he felt included.

His lips were right there to meet hers and after several long minutes when she turned back to Mario, Finn didn't simply lie passive.

He lifted her hair and suckled the back of her neck, teased and bit at her earlobe, and best or worst of all, she wasn't sure which, he whispered in her ear. "You're beautiful. So goddamn beautiful, Soph, it about slices me in half."

Jagger kept playing with her down there, even teasing the tip of his cock into her opening. She could feel the huge width of him. But he kept his word. He didn't push inside. But after the endless teasing and the multiple orgasms, she was about ready to beg him to.

He notched his head at her entrance, pressing in the barest bit, and then he'd slide it up again through her folds to her clit where he'd continue his tortuous game of cat and mouse, pulling back right before she was ready to fall over the edge.

Mario had become especially enchanted with her breasts, licking and flicking her nipples with his fingers and tongue, and Finn took the opportunity to monopolize her mouth again.

And then Jagger dropped his hips and began grinding on her in earnest, applying so much delicious pressure, sliding his fat cock up and down, the tip of his head catching on her nub with every thrust.

"Oh," she gasped against Finn's mouth. "*Oh!*"

And then her gasps became a wail as she came harder than she had all night.

Finn drank up every cry, cupping her face as tears poured down her cheeks at the pleasure, his frantic whispers about how beautiful she was, how fucking beautiful she was, ringing in her ears.

CHAPTER FOURTEEN

JAGGER

They were back on the road two days later. The men had come back with a lightweight open trailer hitched to the horses. It had good tires on it and fared well enough on the terrain without being too much of a strain on the animals. They tied a large piece of old nylon over the open top to protect Sophia from the sun.

Sophia continued to argue that she didn't need such preferential treatment but Jagger didn't miss the look of relief on her face when they all saddled up on the morning of the fourth day and he ushered her in to lay on the pallet he'd put down in the trailer beside several plastic 5-gallon jugs of water.

Toby looked like shit as he swung himself up on his horse. At least he managed to keep his seat.

Jagger didn't feel bad about it. He'd warned him not to drink so much. Granted the bastard hadn't known the whiskey was tinged with arsenic, but still. At least it had kept him away from Sophia the two days they were all holed up together. He'd been either drunk or sick the whole time.

Toby's men kicked their horses so they rode on either side of Toby, no doubt to catch him if he fell off as they went.

This was obviously not the first time they'd dealt with him hungover.

Jagger smirked and shook his head.

"Ride out!" he called and urged his horse forward.

They rode hard that day to make up for lost time. Leo and his brother led the horses that pulled Sophia's trailer. They stopped at Lindsey Lake to water the horses but that was the last natural water source for sixty miles.

By sundown, Jagger felt confident they'd made it at least twenty-five of that sixty. They watered the horses and made camp.

Everyone was exhausted from the day's ride and too tired to make trouble if they'd had a mind to.

Sophia cooked a couple of hares Jagger'd found this morning in the traps he'd set out the night before.

Finn slept on one side of her and Mario, who'd apparently designated himself her bodyguard, took the other.

Jagger didn't know what to make of that and he was too tired to consider it much before he dropped off to sleep with the rest of their makeshift camp.

The next day was more of the same.

Long empty stretches of knee-high scrub brush and horizon in all directions as far as the eye could see.

Jagger imagined it was like being at sea. He'd liked books about the sea when he was a kid. Old historical ones about the British and pirates and long endless days of doldrums where a crew might be trapped in the middle of nowhere with nothing but the nonexistent wind and their prayers to save them.

In the books, salvation always came one way or another but now Jagger imagined the reality of the many crews that slowly dehydrated and starved to death.

Reality was always so much less pleasant than the fictions men told themselves so they could sleep at night.

But Jagger was a man and no longer a boy.

So as nice as it might be to lay with Sophia, as pleasant as her kisses might feel and her mouth on his cock, by the time they got where they were going, it all had to come to an end.

On *his* terms, not the goddamned fickle wind's.

Because fuck knew there was no God.

CHAPTER FIFTEEN

TOBY

That uppity bitch got to ride like the queen of fucking Sheba no matter that Toby was the one *really* suffering.

Toby glared at the trailer and the orange nylon that reflected the late afternoon sun so bright he winced and looked back ahead as his horse continued plodding along.

Toby was her fucking husband and he had fucking *rights*. Literally. He had the right to fuck her. Any time he wanted. Any way he pleased.

Not that he'd got to assert them since the wedding night, and he couldn't even fuckin' remember that.

Well fuck that shit.

Tonight he was gonna take that little cunt. She was gonna ride in that fuckin' carriage? Fine. He'd give her somethin' to be sore about. He'd ride *her* good and hard tonight.

Maybe even give Joey and Tom a spin.

Then Toby glared at Jagger. If that moody motherfucker wasn't in his way every fuckin' time he turned around.

Toby would have been Governor of Carlsbad ten times over by now if it wasn't for Jagger fuckin' Kincaid.

Though if Toby had his way, him and his boys would take care of that smug motherfucker before this trip was done.

They'd get the money and then put a bullet straight between his eyes.

Toby's hands gripped the reins tighter just at the thought. Jag thought he was so slick, always a step ahead of everybody else.

Toby'd show him who was *really* in charge.

Three hours later, they came upon Jal just as the sun was setting. Jagger held up his hand. "Hold up. Let me go ahead alone. Don't any of you move till I come back with the go ahead."

Toby rolled his eyes. "Why the fuck not? Place's a ghost town." He gestured at the empty streets in the distance, pistol in hand.

"Put the gun away," Jagger hissed. "They're watching us right now."

Toby wanted so bad to lift his piece and land that bullet in Jagger's forehead this very second. But fuck, he'd waited this long. *Wait till the payment's in hand*—that'd been his motto for years now and there was a reason he'd lasted this long and had it as good as he did.

Jagger rode out in front of them about twenty feet, then raised both his hands high overhead. "The moon rises high over the desert in the winter," he shouted. "Jagger Kincaid here, at your service, with a small party, humbly begging passage."

Toby sneered. Dumb fuck was plain out of his damn mind. Desert heat had finally got to him, that was clear as day.

Toby was about to pull his gun again and ride forward toward town when all of the sudden a whistle came—first one, then another, then another and another.

And with the sound, men popped up out of nowhere, right out of the ground like they were gophers. Except for the fact that they all held machine guns pointed at Toby and everyone else.

Motherfuckers! Where the fuck did they come from?

Toby looked a little closer at the one nearest him and saw that shit, there was a little human sized hidey hole that had been dug into the otherwise flat landscape.

And the bastards had them surrounded.

CHAPTER SIXTEEN

SOPHIA

Sophia peeked her head over the edge of the trailer at Jagger's shouting, lifting the nylon up so she could see. Her eyes shot wide open when she saw the men appear out of nowhere with guns pointed at them

At first she ducked back down again, her heart thumping a mile a minute.

But then after another long moment of quiet, she lifted up and peeked out again. Jagger had ridden out to one of the men with a machine gun and was talking calmly to him.

The man hadn't dropped his gun but he nodded at something Jagger said and gestured him forward.

"I'll be back in five," Jagger called. "Don't make a move. Any of you."

Sophia dropped back to the bed of the trailer. Don't make a move. Not a problem. She was on it.

She thought she might have held her breath the whole time he was gone. But far sooner than she was prepared for, the nylon on the trailer was whipped back.

She shrieked at being exposed.

But it was Jagger.

Beside him were Finn and Mario, and a man Sophia had never seen before. He was young, maybe her and Finn's age, and he looked just as surprised to see her as she was to see him.

"You didn't say you had a—"

"This is our wife," Jagger said, reaching out a hand for Sophia. She took it and sat up, letting him pull her to the edge of the trailer. She quickly pulled on her socks and the soft leather boots Jagger had given her back in Carlsbad. Her blisters had mostly healed up since she'd barely worn shoes since the wedding, so it didn't hurt to pull the boots on.

Jagger helped her down from the trailer once she got them on. It felt good to be on solid ground, especially since Finn and Mario immediately flanked her. "She's under our protection," Finn made sure to say.

The man nodded. "Fair enough." Then he looked to Jagger. "If you're friends with Grandpa Bill then you know his ways. You don't fuck with us, we won't fuck with you."

"Words to live by," Jagger quipped. "Come on, let's get out of the open."

The man nodded and they all started forward.

Jagger took Sophia up on the back of his horse for the last of the ride into town. She clung to his waist. She wasn't sore anymore. After two days being stuck in the trailer, it felt a little surreal to be up on horseback and well, for things to be *happening* again.

Now that they were, though, she wasn't sure she shouldn't have been happy with the boredom of the trailer.

They were obviously walking into a settlement of some kind.

But as they got closer to town, it looked just as dead and abandoned as it had from the outskirts. The landscape was as flat as ever and Sophia couldn't see any signs of life. Anywhere.

"Where are—" she started to ask but Jagger cut her off.

"Jal is the last stop before you hit Texas and it was hit hard in the war," Jagger spoke quietly so only she could hear. "All the border towns were. The Queen of the Colorado territories was determined to end her war at our borders."

Queen?!

But Sophia didn't have a chance to think more on his shocking words because he was hurrying on, obviously intent on passing along the basics before they got where they were going.

"She didn't want word of her resources ever reaching the Texans because she didn't want another war on her hands. So her solution was to absolutely decimate the populations of the border towns even after she'd won the war and taken all the women. Her armies slaughtered every man living in Jal."

Sophia looked around her at the empty streets and swallowed hard, suddenly imagining the streets filled with bloody fighting.

Now that she looked closer, she could see bullet holes in buildings. Everywhere. She shuddered and held on tighter to Jagger.

"So who are these men? They came in afterwards and occupied what was left?"

"No," Jagger said, his voice still hushed. "Bill and his family were here the whole time. They hid. Bill was a wealthy man and one of the few men in towns with a basement. He stuffed all the men of his family—and he had a large one, sons and grandsons and cousins and cousins' cousins—all into the basement of one of his businesses and they rode out the storm. Legend goes that they stayed down there for three days and three nights. And when they came out, every single person they'd ever known was dead and left to bloat in the heat where they'd fallen."

Sophia gasped in horror.

"It took them weeks to bury everybody."

There was no time to say more because apparently, they'd arrived. Sophia looked around as Jagger brought the horse to a standstill outside a huge warehouse. Just like the rest of the town, there was nothing around. No people. No sign of life. Nothing.

The men with machine guns had walked with them, escorting them through town. One knocked on the door of the warehouse, with a unique knocking pattern of several quick raps followed by silences of varying lengths and more rapping.

Jagger swung down from the horse and then helped Sophia down. Mario was by her side in an instant, Finn quickly following. They were her shadows. Not that she minded, especially on a day like today, heading into the unknown. She reached out a hand to both of them and gave them a quick squeeze to show her appreciation.

The warehouse door opened to a man in his late forties or early fifties. He looked them all over and then motioned them in. As every person entered, they were patted down.

Finn stepped in front of Sophia. "Don't you even think about laying your hands on her."

Jagger put a hand on his arm. "Finnigan. It's fine. Let him, or she can't come in."

"It's fine, Finn," Sophia echoed but Finn just jerked his arm out of Jagger's grasp.

Finn only marched up to the man patting them down and put his finger in his face. "You touch her inappropriately and he—" Finn pointed back behind him to Mario, "—will rip your head off."

The guy's eyes followed Finn's gesture and Mario slammed his fist into his other hand menacingly.

"Hey man, if you're a friend of Bill's, we won't disrespect your woman."

The way he'd worded that didn't exactly inspire the most confidence in Sophia, but when she got to the man, he patted her down the same way he had everyone else and didn't try to cop a feel even though she was just wearing a sundress. She thought she got off easier than everyone else, actually, because when Mario growled from behind her as the guy skimmed the back of his hands up her legs, he backed off.

"Okay, you're fine," he said quickly, gesturing her inside.

She blinked in surprise as she stepped through the door. She hadn't seen any windows from outside so she'd expected it to be dark—but there were *lights*. *Electric* lights.

Not a ton of them, but they hung from the ceiling in regular enough intervals to be able to see. The large space wasn't all open, parts of it were portioned off by hanging sheets to make smaller rooms, others by stronger wooden partitions that had been set up, even a few made of metal, but there was a large open space where people gathered in the center of the warehouse. Several large couches were set up around the space, along with a few loungers.

Sophia started to do a quick headcount when she froze in place.

"There are women!" she whispered in shock, hurrying forward even ahead of Jagger.

"Sophia, wait," Finn said but Sophia was already off. These people were friendly with Jagger and they had women among them, so they couldn't be that bad.

Frankly, after not setting eyes on another woman in almost two weeks, the sight of not just one, but *four* was so welcome, Sophia's grin was bursting on her face as she hurried up to the group of about fifteen people.

"Hello," Sophia said, holding her hand out to the first woman she came to. She had stringy blonde hair and a pale face, and looked maybe five years older than Sophia. It was hot in the warehouse and all the women wore skirts and tank tops, no doubt to stay cool. "I'm Sophia. You have no idea how good it is to see another feminine face."

The woman jerked back from Sophia, not just like she was startled, but like she was scared. She had large, fearful blue eyes.

"Oh, I'm sorry," Sophia dropped her hand, feeling terrible for scaring the girl. "I shouldn't have just come barging in like that. I'm with Jagger. He's a friend of Bill's." That seemed to be the magic phrase around here but the girl only backed away more.

"Don't go running off like that, dear," Jagger said, coming up beside Sophia right as a big man with a white beard and a red face pushed through the crowd and held out his arms wide. He wore a soiled tank top that might have once been white but was now an indeterminate grayish brown.

"Jagger, my boy!"

"Bill," Jagger said, walking forward and embracing the man.

This was Bill? He looked like a homeless, half-deranged desert Santa.

He pulled Jagger into a tight embrace, clapping him hard on the back several times before letting him go.

"And who is this vision at your side?"

"Of course, sir. Where are my manners? This is Sophia Kincaid, my wife."

Sophia's head shot to Jagger. It was the first time he'd called her by his name.

Kincaid.

It was stupid to get caught up about something so inconsequential when she was face to face with so many strangers.

Especially when desert Santa smiled her way. Sophia was about to smile back but then he looked her up and down appraisingly, stopping and staring at her chest.

Was he seriously just ogling her right in front of Jagger, even though he'd just said she was his wife?

She was wearing one of her sundresses because she hadn't wanted to put back on her dirty jeans, and it got hot in the trailer under the tarp, but now she was regretting it. She crossed her arms over her chest in an effort to cover the scooped neck of the dress.

"You sure about that?" Bill looked back to Jagger. "We could use another good earner. Gorgeous girl like her, she'd earn us a pretty penny every night. You know I'd give you a fair price for her."

What?!

Sophia about choked on her own tongue. Her eyes shot to the other girls in the group and sure enough, one of the men from outside had sat down on the wide couch and pulled her down into his lap. At least Sophia *thought* he was pulling her onto his lap.

Really he was just midway to pushing her onto the floor. Then he unbuckled himself and pulled her by the hair until she was up on her knees and sucking his—

The sight was blocked by Finn stepping up beside her.

A growl came from her left and Sophia looked over to see Mario beside Jagger. Jagger, though, just laughed and slung his arm across Sophia's shoulders.

"Alas, it's true love. And, as you can see, my men are partial to her, too. We couldn't bear to lose her."

Bill eyed Mario and Finn for a tense moment, and then let out a hearty laugh. "Well I had to ask. I'm a businessman after all."

"That you are," Jagger agreed with an easy smile.

"Come, there's stew on," Bill said. "Get off your feet. Food before business anyway."

"You're too kind."

How could Jagger smile at the man? Sophia fumed, her hands fisted as he led her across the concrete floor of the warehouse to the furthest wall where several picnic tables had been set up end to end. And as much as he'd detailed about the settlement on the way over, how could he have forgotten to mention this little detail?

She wasn't an idiot. She knew in theory this kind of thing happened in the world. And much worse. Did these men use these women like those monsters who'd brutalized her mother? How could Jagger treat this man like a friend when he— when he—

Sophia's attention was distracted by another of the women, older, maybe in her late thirties but also wearing a mini-skirt and tank top, who moved between a make-shift kitchen and the tables.

They'd broken up the concrete in the corner—Sophia couldn't imagine how long it had taken, and had a recessed fire with what looked like a tunnel that had been dug to carry the smoke out underneath the warehouse walls.

But Sophia was far more focused on the woman herself. She didn't have the blank, scared expression of the first woman. She introduced herself as Meredith, but didn't say anything beyond that. She had a pleasant but aloof smile, and if she was surprised to see Sophia among their company, she didn't show it.

"So that man," Sophia said to Jagger as they sat down. "He owns these women? And he— He prostitutes them to his men here?"

Please, *please* tell her she'd misunderstood.

Toby must have been standing closer than she'd realized because though she'd been whispering, he sneered behind her.

"Not these men. They get it for free cause they're family. Bill takes the girls round to settlements nearby. Why didn't you just say this was Bill's place, Jag? Shit, if I knew Bill and his girls lived this close, I'd be out here every other week spendin' my scratch on these bitches. You only have 'em out to Carlsbad a few times a year."

Sophia jerked back from Jagger. He had them out to... As in Jagger arranged for these poor girls to be used as prostitutes in the township he governed?

"That's exactly why no one knows about this place," Jagger said with a tight jaw. "They aren't regular brothel girls. Bill just takes them out every so often to get enough money for supplies. Two months a year at most."

Sophia gasped. Did he think that made it better?

Sophia got up from the table and took several steps away from Jagger.

He stared at her darkly. "Sophia, get back here."

She just shook her head, though. This place, these men, God, even *Toby*, who she was officially *married to*, if you could call that sham affair on the steps of the courtyard a wedding—it was suddenly too much.

"Sophia," Jagger said again, his voice heavy with warning.

But that only made it worse. Did he think she was one of his girls like these girls were Bill's? Would he decide to sell her if he ever got down on his luck and needed a few bucks?

Her mother's screams echoed in her ears.

She turned and fled.

"Whoa there, filly, where you think you're going?"

Toby caught her, jeering. "Having all these girls around have got me thinking it's time for me to remind you of your wifely duties."

She screeched, fighting to get away from him.

"Sophia!" Finn's voice sounded very far away.

But the next second, Toby was yanked off her and thrown to the ground.

Mario stood in front of her, his chest heaving. He didn't say anything, but his big hands came to her face, eyes searching hers.

She nodded shakily. "Thank you, thank you."

She realized their error the next second, though, when something solid smacked into the side of Mario's head and the huge man crumpled to the ground.

Sophia screamed and jumped, backing away even more when she saw Toby wielding a long steel pipe.

"You bastard, what did you do to my brother?"

Leo had been talking to a group back in the center of the warehouse but he came running when he saw his brother go down.

Suddenly the lights overhead in the warehouse started flashing and everyone who'd been merely observing before jumped up and started running.

"Stations!" Bill roared.

Sophia looked around in utter confusion. What the *hell* was happening?

Jagger had jumped up from the table and ran to intercept Leo who'd still been headed for Toby. "It's not the time for this."

Sophia could barely hear him above the rest of the mayhem but Finn was soon at her side, too. Toby's men had finally stopped restraining him and she grabbed Finn's hand.

Leo fought against Jagger's hold at first but Jagger shoved him in the chest. "Look around! Do you know what this means?" He waved at the lights and the general chaos around us. "It means people have been sighted coming into town." He looked up at the flashing lights, apparently making out some pattern because the next thing he said was, "From the *Texas* side of the border."

Leo finally paused, looking up. "Shit." He ran a hand through his hair, then looked down at his brother. He pointed a finger at Toby. "I'm watching you, you little shit."

Then he jerked out of Jagger's hold, hands up. "I'm cool, I'm cool. So what the fuck do we do?"

"Nothing, unless Bill asks," Jagger said. "They have a protocol. They haven't stayed hidden out here for eight years because they're stupid."

But just then, they heard swearing come over a crackling walkie talkie. "Shit, Dad, they've seen the horses outside. They're headed your way."

"Fuck!" Bill slammed the table and looked Jagger's way. "Knew I shoulda brought those beasts in right off." Then he shook his head and pressed the button on the walkie. "How many?"

"Twenty-five. Trucks and motorcycles."

Bill swore again. "You boys don't do anything. Stay hidden until they get here. Then we'll attack from both sides. They know we're here. We can't let a single man leave."

"Understood. No survivors."

"Over and out."

No survivors? They intended to kill every single one of the men coming to attack? Or maybe those men out there weren't even thinking in terms of 'attack'? Maybe they'd just seen what appeared to be a ghost town and had approached thinking that maybe they'd find a water source.

And now they were walking into an ambush.

Sophia didn't have long to stand on the moral high ground, though. Everything was happening too quickly.

Bill suddenly looked Jagger's way. "We could use every able-bodied man who knows how to fire a weapon. If they get through that warehouse door, it isn't just me and mine who'll be at risk."

Jagger nodded and started snapping orders of his own. "Finn, Leo," then he looked at Toby's two guys. "And you two and Toby. Go with Bill's son, Clive. He'll get you weapons."

Finn looked unsure, probably about leaving her, but Sophia let go of his hand. "Go. There's no point to any of it if we don't survive the day."

He pressed his forehead to hers for a long moment and then he ran in the direction Jagger had pointed.

Leo ignored Jagger and dropped to his haunches to see to his brother.

Jagger sighed and looked to Sophia. "Sophia, go with the women." He pointed to where one of Bill's men was herding them in the center of the warehouse behind the metallic partitions. "Stay safe."

Sophia was about to argue. After all, Dad had taught her to shoot as well as any other boy in all of Jacob's Well but when Jagger's eyebrows furrowed and he asked it again, this time with a plaintive, "*Please,* Sophia. I need to know you're safe or I won't be able to concentrate. Neither will Finn," she relented and nodded.

Sophia scurried towards the center of the warehouse right as gunfire broke out. She screamed and dropped to the ground before realizing it was outside the warehouse, not inside yet. Still, she crawled the last little bit around the partitions to join the other four women. They were all huddled against an inner wall, clutching one another.

The eldest woman, Meredith, who'd been serving dinner looked over at Sophia and hissed, "Keep your mouth shut, no matter what happens. If they manage to get in and find out there are women here, they'll come for us first thing." She shuddered, then glared Sophia down. "We've got a good thing here, so don't make a goddamned peep."

So Sophia clapped her hand over her mouth to keep her shriek silent when, the next moment, all the lights of the warehouse went out and suddenly everything went pitch black.

It was likely just a tactical move. If the warehouse dwellers were familiar with the layout of their home, or maybe even had some night vision goggles, then they'd have the advantage if intruders did get in.

As soon as she'd thought it, brief spurts of gunfire broke out. *Inside* the warehouse this time. Every noise was magnified by the echo chamber of the concrete flooring and steel walls. Instead of her mouth, Sophia was soon covering her ears as she hunched into a ball and tried to make herself as small as possible.

It was official.

She *hated* the outside world. This was the second time in as many weeks as she'd been shot at by people who didn't even *know* her. People in this world just went around indiscriminately killing one another. She'd thought, she didn't know, that things had gotten *better* in the last eight and a half years? There were laws and mobs didn't go around raping and killing anymore. But God, she hadn't realized—it was just as savage as ever out here, even if the savagery took different forms than it used to.

Everything had seemed so black and white only days ago—about who she should marry and what she should do—but now Sophia had no clue what to think. All she knew was that she'd never longed for her girlish Pepto-Bismol pink bedroom back in Jacob's Well so hard as she did right this minute.

But you can't go back there.

Jacob's Well was occupied by Travis's troops.

There was no going home.

No running back to Daddy and hiding her head in the sand any more. She thought she'd wanted freedom but she was starting to realize she hadn't known how good she'd had it.

When a stray bullet pinged against the steel of their partition barrier, one girl began to weep. Her heaving and hiccupping gave her away, no matter how many times Meredith whispered a hushed, "Shhh. Quiet now."

Men shouted and cried out along with the gunfire, though, so Sophia doubted anyone heard the girl.

It didn't mean Sophia felt any safer. What if the initial count had been wrong and there were more than twenty-five men? Or they had more powerful weapons?

And Finn. God, *Finn*. She should never have let him leave her side. She should have *demanded* he stay with her, that he—

"There you are."

Sophia barely stopped herself from screeching when a light flashed in the darkness, revealing Toby's face.

He was holding a lighter.

"You fool," the woman hissed, but he'd extinguished the light before she'd even finished chastising him.

What was he doing here? Had Jagger ordered him to come and keep watch over them? At least he hadn't turned on the light until he was around the corner of the partition. No one else should have been able to see it.

"Hey," Sophia hissed when she felt Toby's hand feeling around blindly in the darkness. "That's my leg."

Instead of pulling his hand back, though, he just reached higher, grabbing her thigh in a crushing grip.

"I know. If this is what it takes for me to be able to assert my husbandly rights without your fuckin' bodyguards around, so be it."

Sophia felt her eyes fly wide open. Uselessly. It was pitch black. But she reared up her leg that was still free of him and kicked downwards as hard as she could, scrambling backwards when she heard Toby's *oof* of pain.

The next second, though, he was back and more furious than ever. He landed on top of her.

"No!" she screeched. "Get off of m—"

But her words were cut off by a hand over her mouth.

A small, feminine hand.

"Are you insane?" Meredith hissed. "Quiet or you'll get us all killed."

Toby laughed and ripped the bodice of Sophia's sundress down the middle. Sophia's scream was muffled by Meredith's hand and Toby's weight kept her immobile no matter how hard she fought to get him off.

No! This couldn't be happening. She tried using the self-defense moves she'd practiced so often in her room, but she couldn't get her elbows up or buck him off. In all those scenarios, she'd been *standing*, not already on the ground.

Finn! she tried to call. *Mario!*

But they couldn't hear her. Even if Meredith hadn't been covering her mouth, the gunfire was only getting louder and more rapid every second.

And Toby was trying to rape her right in the middle of it all.

He shoved her legs open and thrust himself against her. Oh God, no. She felt him hard through his slacks.

Why the hell had she worn this fucking sundress? If she'd been in jeans he would have at least had a little bit more of a fight but with the stupid sundress all he had to do was flip it up and unzip himself. Her underwear were no barrier at all.

Oh God, oh God, oh God. Sophia felt herself start to hyperventilate. Because this wasn't a nightmare, she couldn't even pretend. The sweaty man on top of her was real and she couldn't twist out from underneath him and now he was unbuckling his belt and any second he'd— he'd—

Oh God, he was pulling it out. *He was pulling it out*.

She felt it against her leg.

No, he would not put that fucking thing inside her. He wouldn't.

She bucked more furiously than ever, putting her feet against the concrete and using every ounce of leverage she could manage.

Toby punched her.

Once in the face and again in the gut.

She coughed, dazed by the pain, all the while her mind was screaming at her, *no, don't stop fighting, don't stop*—

Because he was reaching down again. Shoving aside her underwear and positioning himself. About to—

"Sophia!"

Sophia looked dazedly in the direction of the shout. She still couldn't see anything and her mind felt fuzzy. But she still had the brainpower to bite Meredith's fingers and then shout, "Help!" when the woman jerked her hand back.

"Sophia!" came the shout again, closer now.

There was the briefest flash of light, and then Toby was hauled off of her.

"Jagger, wait. She's nothing. You know we're just going to—" Toby started to say but his words were cut off by a sickly gurgle.

Sophia's hand flew to her mouth as she scrambled backwards even as she felt a mist of wetness coat her face.

Oh God, did he just—?

"Sophia. Are you okay?"

Sophia blinked and wiped at her face. Had Jagger really just— Had he *killed* Toby?

Light flashed again, the spark of a flint, just enough to see Jagger crouched above Toby's lifeless body, his throat slit. Sophia turned away and hugged the wall.

The next moment, though, strong arms surrounded her. She fought at first but Jagger just kept holding her tight.

"Shhh, you're okay now," he whispered into her ear, holding her head tight to his chest. "He'll never touch you."

When he only held her and didn't try to touch her in any other way, Sophia finally melted, burying her face against him.

In that moment, she just wanted him to make it all go away. Go away, go away, go away, just like daddy always used to.

But it wasn't just Toby she saw now when she closed her eyes.

No matter what you do, you do not come out of the closet. Promise. Promise mommy you won't move!

And she hadn't moved.

Not even when her mother began screaming downstairs as rioters broke into their house.

When man after man violated her mother, Sophia did nothing. She didn't move out of the upstairs closet.

She did *nothing*.

She'd been as bad as Meredith. She let them do as they would to her mother just so that she could save herself.

Fat tears slid out of her eyes, soaking Jagger's shirt.

Her entire life was one long story of selfishness after selfishness. Time and time again, she'd let others sacrifice themselves for her.

Her mother. Her father. How many times had she heard that her father had created Jacob's Well just for her?

And when Dad had come and rescued her that day after the men finally left and she'd continued to hide in the closet—too scared to even go down and check on her mother, she was such a coward—all she'd been able to feel was happiness that she herself was still alive. Her mother was dead but the relief at being saved was so overwhelming, Sophia hadn't been able to stop crying. She'd never known if they were tears of joy or grief.

And what kind of person did that make her? She'd been so ashamed. So horribly ashamed. So she'd focused on being the best daughter anyone could ask for. She'd give back to the community and do enough good to outweigh the bad.

But it was never enough, was it?

Even trying to finally do something selfless, to come out here and help raise an army was back-firing horrifically. What would Dad say when he found out what happened to her if she died here today? That she'd been lost in a gunfight in New Mexico?

Although, as she frowned and hiccupped, the noise of gunfire was quieting. She pulled back from Jagger's chest and swiped at her face with her forearm.

One last volley of gunfire made her jerk back against Jagger and his arms tightened around her again.

Afterwards, though, it was silent. Eerily silent for long moments that turned into minutes. Finally a sharp whistle broke the quiet. Several other whistles of varying lengths and tones responded.

And then the warehouse was flooded once again with light.

Sophia winced and covered her eyes.

"It's safe," one of the other girls breathed out in relief.

"How do you know?" Sophia asked, voice wobbling. She still hid her face in Jagger's chest, like if she just stayed there long enough, she could pretend Toby wasn't there, dead, on the other side of him.

Because that was what she was best at, right? Pretending the bad things weren't there.

"The whistles. They're signals. They said it's all clear."

"All the same," Jagger said. "I think we'll stay right where we are for a while until it's confirmed."

Meredith and the others nodded.

But after a while, two sandy-haired men came around the barricade looking for the women and confirming it was safe to come out. They stared down at Toby's corpse in surprise.

"He got caught in the crossfire," Jagger said.

The men nodded even though anyone with a pair of eyes could follow the trail of blood from Toby's body over to where Sophia and Jagger were huddled in the corner against the metal partition.

At least Jagger had resheathed his knife at his belt, but still, it was obvious what had happened.

The men just nodded, though, apparently uninterested in any affairs beyond their own. "It's all clear." They gestured for the other women to come out, which they did, obediently.

"Have you seen our friends?" Sophia asked, hiding behind Jagger, but she had to know. God, were Finn and the others okay? Please let Finn be okay. Finn had to be okay. And Leo and Mario. "The ones who came with us?"

"Not sure. They're just starting to clean up and bring guys into the infirmary."

Jagger got to his feet and helped Sophia up. She held the tatters of her dress together. She felt the shame thick. Everyone would see. Everyone would know. But she had to find out if Finn was okay, if—

The next second, though, Jagger had pulled his T-shirt off and draped it over her head.

She looked up at him, surprised and grateful and— and she didn't even know what else. So much was happening so fast. His eyes caught hers though, and silently, he helped her put her arms through the sleeves of the shirt.

"We caught one of the sons of bitches," the taller of the two men said to Jagger conversationally, ignorant of whatever moment they were having. "He's telling quite a story. Says he was promised a bunch of land if he joined up with Travis's fighters near San Antonio. But then the army switched sides when some badass bitch came in and took the city over and the Army's loyalty with it."

Sophia's head snapped in the man's direction. Badass bitch? Did he mean Drea?

"So he and a bunch of his friends deserted when they realized they weren't going to get nothing they'd been promised and ran west."

"Where'd he last see the army?" Sophia asked.

"Ask him yourselves."

As they came around the last of the steel barriers, the man gestured toward the end of the warehouse opposite of the kitchens. In the distance, Sophia could see a crowd of men circled and hear shouting.

"But you'll have to hurry, before they tear him apart."

Sophia looked to Jagger, horrified, but he just steeled his jaw and took her arm, urging her quicker down the makeshift hallway created from the rooms of hanging sheets on either side of them.

"And who else knew you were coming this way?" she heard Bill ask as they got closer. "Eh? Who else did you tell?"

"No one. No one, I swear!"

Jagger pushed through the crowd until they got to the front. A man who looked like a younger version of Bill raised his fist but the skinny man on the floor whose face was already bloody held up pleading hands.

"I swear I'm telling the truth! Why would I lie? Everyone I know is dead." He started to weep. "They're all dead. There's no one left."

Bill stepped back, his face pinched like he smelled something distasteful. "This sniveling idiot isn't lying. There's no one else coming. Go ahead and take him out back and—"

"Wait!" Sophia said, jumping forward.

The man on the floor looked up at her and begged, "Please. Angel, save me! Don't let them kill me!"

Sophia swallowed hard. He was already beaten so badly he could barely open his left eye. "All right," she forced herself to whisper. "I might be able to save you. But only if you tell me the truth."

She crouched down so she was at his level, but still far enough away so he couldn't jump forward to touch her.

"Anything," he said. "I'll tell you anything you want to know."

"Tell me more about the war," Sophia said. "Is the army you left marching on Fort Worth? What do you know of their numbers versus Colonel Travis's numbers?"

The man looked down and Sophia's stomach sank. What didn't he want to tell her?

"Look at me," she ordered with steel in her voice. "I can save you. But only if you tell me the truth. The whole truth."

Someone behind her moved like they might protest her words but she lifted a hand to silence them. She knew the men of this settlement would do whatever they wanted to do to this man regardless of her promises—but *he* didn't need to know that.

"Well, Miss," the man finally looked up at her, and it was only then that she realized how young he was. Maybe only sixteen or seventeen. "That's part of why we bugged out. We knew that army's doomed."

Sophia felt the air whoosh out of her chest but she strove to keep her facial expression pleasant and calm. "Oh? Why's that?"

"Cause Colonel Travis has twice as many troops and before all the sat phones went down, he'd just got another whole army of mercenaries to fight for him from the old Southern States Alliance. I'm good at sneakin' and I was huntin' for some extra bread when I overheard it with my own ears. Travis was talkin' to Army command. So that lady's army is walking right into a trap."

Sophia stood back up again, her back snapping straight.

She had to get this information to her father and Drea. They had no idea what they'd be facing when they got to Fort Worth.

They'd be outnumbered three to one.

Hired mercenaries against rebels plucked from the countryside. Yeah, there were some trained forces on their side in the Army that

Drea apparently led now. If she'd taken San Antonio, then she had more professional fighters. But a large part of the Army was still men like those from Jacob's Well—farmers and Scrappers and construction workers—men who hadn't picked up a weapon since the War for Independence eight years ago, if then.

"And the woman's Army—when were they planning to march north for Fort Worth?"

"They're already headed there, Miss. We bugged out the third night but they're probably nearabouts Austin by now."

"Thank you for your honesty," Sophia said to the man. To the *boy*.

"So you'll spare me?" He looked at her so earnestly.

Sophia bit her lip as the men holding his arms behind his back hauled him to his feet and then began to drag him to the warehouse door.

"No," he shouted. "No, she promised! I told the truth. You promised!"

Sophia shrank back as the warehouse door slammed behind them, hands going to her face. They were going to kill him. Oh God, they were going to kill him. Maybe if she ran after them and tried to argue for his life, that he *had* been helpful, that maybe his words could help them win the war—

Bang.

The dull sound of a gunshot stopped her in her tracks.

Yet another person to add to the tally marks against her soul.

"There was nothing you could have done," Jagger said, taking her arm.

Sophia wrenched her arm away from him. And then she looked around, remembering. "Where's Finn? And Mario and Leo?"

Her stomach sank to the floor. "Oh God," she whispered, shaking her head.

"They were fine last I saw," Jagger said quickly. "Leo was with his brother where we left them and Finn's probably just helping clean up."

But Sophia knew in her guts that the first thing Finn would do once the fighting stopped was to come looking for her.

"Where was Finn when you saw him?"

"Other side of the warehouse."

"Show me."

Jagger nodded and when he didn't move fast enough, Sophia started running.

She didn't make it to the end of the warehouse though. In the center where the couches were, a makeshift triage center had been set up.

"I'm fine," Finn argued. "Just put a bandage on it and I'll be—"

Finn. He was safe. Oh thank God.

"Sit still," said one of the women, a brunette who looked only a little younger than Meredith, as she urged Finn to lay back on a long couch. He was shirtless and his shoulder was bleeding copiously down his chest. "We've only just got the bullet out. We still have to stitch it up."

"Finn!" Sophia yelled and ran over to where he sat, his face pale and features pinched with pain. "Oh my God."

She crouched at his feet and looked up at him.

His face relaxed as soon as he saw her. "Thank Christ you're okay."

He grimaced in pain right after though, as the brunette started to sew his shoulder up. She looked like she knew what she was doing at least. She even used one of those circular doctor's sewing needles and she made quick, tight stitches.

Sophia looked around. "Have you seen Leo or Mari—" But even as she asked it, she saw Leo leading Mario toward them, Mario holding a hand to the side of his head where Toby had clocked him.

Toby.

Even thinking his name sent a sick shiver through her stomach.

He's gone now. And Finn and Leo and Mario and Jagger are here. That's all that matters.

Except that wasn't true.

Her Dad. And Drea and everyone she'd ever loved were all in danger. She thought she could be such a hero, coming out and getting them the extra troops they'd need.

But even if Jagger *was* telling the truth about men from New Mexico coming to fight if they got their brides, which she beginning to doubt, they'd never get there in time. Even feeding and providing enough water for the seven of them plus their horses had been tricky and Jagger was one of the wealthiest New Mexico had to offer.

But hundreds of troops—much less *thousands*?

The logistics alone involved in moving that many men across a desert landscape were mind-boggling. Sophia hadn't really understood it until she'd gotten here.

She shook her head. It had been a fool's dream, all of it.

She looked over to Jagger, who watched the whole scene coolly.

Jagger wasn't a fool.

So what was his agenda? His *real* agenda?

Because she was done being the helpless maiden who got everyone around her injured or killed.

CHAPTER SEVENTEEN

JAGGER

"Why did you marry me?"

Jagger turned around in surprise at Sophia's voice.

It was nighttime after the battle and he'd slipped outside for some fresh air and, frankly, to get away from the stifling *humanity* in that fucking warehouse. So many fucking people, every time you turned around.

Privacy was one of his most prized privileges. He'd fought hard for it. To have plenty but also to be able to close the door and be alone whenever he wanted? That was the definition of living like a king to him.

He'd had his priorities in life. He knew exactly what he wanted and where he was going.

Until he'd picked up the sat phone off that bastard, called that stupid fucking number, and her breathy, angel-sweet voice came over the line. Promising heaven and dooming him to hell.

"So?" Sophia pressed. "Why'd you do it? Because you and I both know it's not to help me raise some stupid army."

Ah. He knew it was only a matter of time before she saw the truth of things. She was too smart not to, not once she saw how life was out here.

But by that time, he'd thought it wouldn't matter. They'd be well on their way and whether she was willing or not wouldn't have mattered. Like he'd told Toby, willing was easier to deal with but only marginally. They already had the trailer. Tying her up and tossing her inside it wouldn't make much difference either way.

Except for the fact that his priorities had suddenly shifted underneath him like quicksand and he didn't know what the fuck he wanted anymore.

No, that wasn't true.

In the second he saw Toby lying over her struggling body, he knew very clearly what he wanted.

He wanted to kill Toby, firstly, and then, no matter the cost, he wanted to protect her.

Protect her?

What the *fuck*?

Jagger didn't protect people. He took advantage of them. He used them and then threw them away like wadded up tissue, without another thought.

But this girl. This fucking girl. She'd gotten underneath his skin from the very moment he'd met her, walking the desert in those ridiculous socks and house slippers. That was the perfect word for her—ridiculous. She was a china doll running around recklessly in a world full of hammers.

Jagger knew better than to care about anything so fragile. He'd already had his heart shredded by another china doll.

"Say something!" Sophia shoved him in the chest and it barely even rocked his center of gravity.

He grabbed her by her forearms. They were covered in goosebumps and he didn't think it was just from the chill of the night air. "What do you want me to say?" he hissed. "You've already guessed it."

Sophia blinked like she didn't want to believe it even as she gasped, "You were going to trick me?"

Going to? Didn't she see how deep in she already was?

Apparently understanding was dawning because the next thing she said was, "You *did* trick me."

She tried to pull away from him but he didn't let her. "Sophia," he warned, "I'm going to let you go, but we're going to talk about this."

"Fine," she said through gritted teeth.

He released her arms and she took several steps back from him. There was a three-quarters moon out, so he could make out most of the features of her face. And she looked pissed.

"I still don't understand. What were you trying to trick me into doing?"

Jagger threw his hands up. "Coming to New Mexico? Marrying me so I'd have a woman to warm my bed? Maybe getting us a few more women for our community? Take your pick."

Sophia sucked in a sharp breath. He watched something crumble in her. The last of her innocence maybe—between what had happened to her earlier in the warehouse and now this revelation.

It made him glad he hadn't told her the entire truth about what he and Toby had planned. Because he hated to see that look on her face. As much as he'd given up on hope or goodness himself, the fact that there was someone out there like Sophia who'd still been able to believe for so long, to embody so much beauty, so much goodness, who'd managed to remain so unspoiled...

He stepped forward and grabbed her face, pulling her into a bruising kiss.

She smacked at his chest and he was about to pull back when, for one sweet, perfect moment, her lips gave against his and she was kissing him back.

He pushed her back against the warehouse and lifted both her arms above her head, then fit a knee between her legs.

But just as he reached down to lift up her skirt, she yanked her arms back down and shoved him away from her.

"Get the fuck *off* me," she spat, stomping the heel of her shoe on his toe for good measure.

Jagger stepped back both in surprise and pain but Sophia took the opportunity to shove him again, and he was already a little off balance so he ended up stumbling several more steps backwards.

"How dare you, you bastard?"

She followed right on his heels. "You tell me you lied to me, that you brought me and Finn all the way out here for *nothing*, married me under false pretenses, and then have the gall to think you can *maul* me and I'll just let you?"

Jagger smirked. "I don't know, seemed like you were enjoying yourself, little dove."

She made a noise of outrage and then went to slam him in the chest again but he caught her arms before she could.

"Let *go* of me, you fucking bastard."

"Look, I get this might not be the fairytale you thought you were signing up for, but this is real life." He shook her by her arms. "This is what happens in the real world."

"That is such an excuse!"

"Fine!" He said, his every last nerve raw where his skin contacted hers. "I'm a bad man. You've caught me out. I'm a bad man who's done bad things. I planned to do bad things to you. But then I met you… and things changed."

"Oh bull *shit*." She swung her forearms around from underneath, breaking his hold on her and stepping back, feet shoulder-width apart, features furious as she faced him down.

"Will you stop fucking cursing? It only makes me want to take you over my goddamned knee."

She looked about three seconds away from steam pouring out her ears. "I won't be going over your knee or anyone else's. I'm my own woman and I make my destiny from here on out. I don't need any fucking *man* telling me what I can and cannot do. I'm perfectly capable of—"

"Capable? Yeah, coming out completely unprepared into the desert and almost getting yourself killed really showed how capable you are."

Her eyes lit like she wanted to murder him. Fuck but it made him hard. He hadn't been kidding about wanting to spank her. He didn't know what it was about this girl but she drove him fucking insane. She made him forget all the other bullshit. She made him *care*.

"So what now?" She threw her hands out. "Why even tell me the truth? Why kill Toby if your plan was just to abduct me and keep me as your sex slave?"

He raised a finger sharply. "Don't lump me in with that bastard."

"You think you're so different? You thought I'd still welcome you in my bed once I learned the truth? Then you would've been the same as him. A rapist pig."

"I've never taken a woman by force in my life." Every word made the vein in his temple pulse more furiously.

"And what about the women you were hoping to dupe into coming back with us? You were hoping to turn them into slaves, too?"

"Actually I was just hoping to come home with a sack full of gold after ransoming you back to your father."

Fuck knew he hadn't meant to confess it, but there it was.

The truth.

Sophia's mouth dropped open in shock, and out of everything that had been revealed in the last fifteen minutes, it was this that made her look the most appalled and betrayed.

Fucking *women*.

"And I'm telling you all this because I'm a fucking idiot." He threw his hands out. "You've made a fucking idiot out of me. Normally Leo and his brother would be on my side no matter what but you've got them both wrapped around your little finger, and then I went and killed the only other man on my crew who would have backed my play." Toby's men were gone too. One killed in the skirmish earlier, and the other seriously wounded.

"And now I'm telling you everything like even more of a fucking idiot but it doesn't matter because I wouldn't have been able to go through with the plan because again," he thumped his chest, "you've made me a fucking idiot."

"What does that *mean*?" Sophia cried, only sounding half as exasperated as Jagger felt.

"It means I *care* about you." He shook his head. "And I don't care about anybody."

"Great. Don't I feel special."

Why did she have to twist everything he said? He was trying to tell her something important but she just threw everything back in his face. He was *trying* here, didn't that count for anything?

"Hey, what's going on out here?" Leo's voice split the quiet night as he pushed open the warehouse door and a rectangle of light spilled onto the dark ground. "Sophia?"

Mario was right behind Leo, pushing the door out, his head swinging around until his eyes landed on Sophia.

Once he zeroed in on her, he barreled toward her, glaring at Jagger. "Sophia?" he asked, his giant's voice rough and rumbling. It was the second time in as many days that Jagger heard it after years of only silence from the big man.

"I'm fine," Sophia said, a bitter edge to her voice as she spun away from Jagger and stomped toward the door.

Mario glared at Jagger and Jagger glared back. He almost hoped the big man would pick a fight. He felt like punching something. And maybe like he deserved to get his own ass kicked.

As soon as Sophia disappeared inside the warehouse he turned away from Leo and Mario and walked away into the night, hands on his head.

Shit, take a breather, Kincaid.

It was better that she knew. She'd be done with him. They'd end this farce of a marriage. Maybe he'd see her back to her dad safely and then he could forget any of this bullshit had ever happened.

He ran a hand roughly down his face and then squeezed his eyes shut. He was too old for this shit anyway.

The warehouse door slammed as Leo and Mario followed Sophia back inside. Ten minutes later, Jagger fortified himself with a deep breath and followed them.

Everyone was settling in for the night so he grabbed a sleeping pallet that had been set out for the visitors and took it to the outer edges of the circle near the fire. It cooled down dramatically at night but the air was still plenty stifling to Jagger. He was good with being on the outskirts. Lone wolf suited him just fucking fine.

And if his conscience was so bothered, how come he could fall asleep so quickly, huh? Because within one breath and the next after laying down and closing his eyes, he was out.

Jaggy, Jaggy, come see! Pretty kitty! Pretty kitty!

Jagger groaned. Not now, Marilee.

Jaggy, pretty kitty! Come see!

But once Marilee got something in her head, there was no getting it out and she just kept jerking at his arm sleeve. "*Jaggy. Jaggy, Come!*

He blinked his eyes open. But instead of his little sister with her big, sunny smile and bright blue eyes, it was a corpse. Maggots wriggled out of her eye sockets and her mouth was opened on a lipless scream.

Jagger shot up to a sitting position, almost banging heads with Sophia. "What the—?"

But Sophia clamped her hand over his mouth before he could say anything else. He glared at her and yanked away from her hand, looking around them. It was the middle of the night, at least he assumed so since there were no windows in the warehouse. But everyone else was still sleeping and the fire had died down.

There was just barely enough light to see by. Sophia was frowning down at him, like she was about to ask if he was okay. But then she notched her chin higher.

"You wanted to sell me? Fine. Then take me to Fort Worth and sell me to Arnold Travis."

CHAPTER EIGHTEEN

SOPHIA

3 Hours Earlier

Sophia stomped back inside after Leo and Mario came and interrupted her infuriating conversation with Jagger.

It had all been a *lie*!

He'd tricked her, been planning to use her, and of course she'd fallen hook line and sinker for it. She was everything Finn had ever accused her of being—innocent and naïve to the point of it being a disability.

She'd almost gotten them *killed*! And for what? So she could walk into her own kidnapping? Jagger had been planning to extort her father for money while they were in the middle of a *war*.

She couldn't even handle thinking about how humiliating that would've been. What if they'd actually made it to her father and one of Jagger's men, like Toby, had gone to Dad and asked them to waste precious resources retrieving his foolhardy daughter? God, especially at a time when they needed every bit of gold and other valuables they might have to spend on supplies so they'd even have a chance to fight back against Travis.

Not that they *did* have a chance.

Sophia dropped her face to the floor.

A touch at her back had her pulling away and jerking around to look behind her. Mario withdrew his hand, his eyebrows knit in concern. He was hurt by her rejection.

But couldn't they see? She was a disaster. She always fucked everything up.

She just wanted to fight for what she believed in, too. She wanted to be able to sacrifice everything for her country.

She wanted to prove that if it ever came to it again, she wouldn't hide in the fucking closet.

Instead she'd dragged Finn away from where he could be useful and had gotten him shot by deserters in fucking *New Mexico* of all places.

So when Leo tried to come close she held up a hand. "Don't. I'm fine."

And then she stalked off, feeling like a child throwing a tantrum and hating herself even more.

If only someone would just go and *kill* stupid Arnold Travis she thought after excusing herself to the 'bathroom'—one of two small curtained off rooms with a port-a-potty. Sophia pinched her nose and paced the small room.

Instead of these huge armies fighting against each other, if only someone could just get close enough to Travis and stab him in the neck with a dinner knife or something, when he was least expecting it.

Like when Drea walked right into that room full of badass bikers. Sophia remembered being shocked, appalled, and impressed beyond words when she heard the girls Drea had rescued recounting what happened. Drea walked straight up to the head of the gang and pretended to give him a lap dance.

Then she cut his *dick off*!!!

No one ever expected women to do things like that. Women had been beaten down and subjugated ever since The Fall. But now apparently Drea was leading an *army*.

But it wouldn't be an army that would be able to get to Travis. He probably wouldn't even get near the battlefield. No, he'd send his mercenaries, all the while staying nice and safe back in Fort Worth.

But this war wouldn't be over until that man was dead. Without him, though, the entire coup would fall to pieces.

Sophia had listened to her dad talk enough times about how paranoid Travis was. He never let any one of his lieutenants become too powerful because he never wanted any of them challenging him.

If he was killed, there'd be a power vacuum yes, but there wouldn't be anyone else on hand to readily fill it. And without anyone to pay the mercenaries, that contingent would disappear and the rest of Travis's forces would soon follow, even if Travis's lackey's started battling amongst themselves for the mantle of President. Sophia doubted they'd be able to get it together quickly enough, not if Drea's army was as far advanced as that man had said.

Five minutes later, by the time Sophia had actually used the restroom, washed her hands as best she could with the sliver of soap and bucket of water, she knew exactly what she needed to do.

She'd go to Fort Worth and kill Travis herself.

Of course, Finn, Mario, and therefore Leo, would never agree to her plan. They'd only get in her way and try to stop her.

She knew her chances were slim.

Very slim.

The mission was most likely doomed, in fact.

But so was Drea's Army. Even if Sophia managed to get word to them in time warning them of what was waiting for them in Fort Worth and they pulled back, Travis's Army would only come hunting them down in short order.

Terrible times called for drastic measures.

If Sophia died, she died.

But she had to try.

So Jagger was her only real option. He'd planned to extort her father while he was on the losing side of a war for God's sake. He wouldn't cry too many tears over her.

But first.

She had to say goodbye.

Finn was still recuperating in the recovery area they'd set up in one of the curtained off rooms. The lights had dimmed after dinner and everyone in the warehouse was quieter as they readied for bed.

Sophia pushed aside the curtain and saw Finn was sleeping on what looked like a futon mattress laid out on the concrete. There were three other men in the room on similar pallets, all asleep.

Finn had passed out soon after the woman finished with the stitches earlier, which she'd said was good, just part of the body's defense system to repair itself after such a shock.

Sophia didn't know about that, but Finn's coloring did look better. She didn't want to wake him but she couldn't help crouching down and then bending over to press the gentlest of kisses to his forehead, barely a whisper of her lips across his skin.

His eyes jerked open as he startled awake.

"Shit," Sophia whispered, pulling back. "I'm sorry. Shh, it's just me. Go back to sleep."

But Finn only braced himself on his elbows and tried to raise up on the mattress to look around, immediately wincing in pain when he did.

"Finn!" Sophia hissed. "What are you doing? Lay down."

She pressed him back down to the bed by his good shoulder.

His hand immediately reached up and took hers. "How long have I been out?" And then he grimaced.

Sophia winced in sympathy. She couldn't imagine how much a *gunshot* must hurt without pain medication. They'd only had a couple of ibuprofen to spare for him since it was a relatively 'minor' wound.

"Finn, I'm so sorry." Sophia sat down on the bed at his good side. "I'm so sorry I ever got you into any of this. You were right. We never should have come."

Finn's eyebrows furrowed. "Don't say that."

Sophia scoffed. "Wha—?"

"Okay, so all the getting shot at and almost dying hasn't been optimal." He grimaced again but then his face went earnest and he squeezed her hand. "But Soph, I wouldn't take back one second of the past couple weeks because…" he trailed off, then swallowed hard. "It took me thinking I was about to die to realize I'm a giant fucking idiot for not just telling you this sooner."

His eyes searched hers. "I love you, Sophia. I've loved you for years. Almost since the first moment I saw you when I walked into town that day."

Goosebumps rose all over Sophia's skin. Was he being serious? There was no way he—

She turned her back to him, her hands trembling as she gathered her knees to her chest. "That's not funny, Finn."

His hand came to the small of her back. "I'm not joking, Sophia. This is me. Loving you more every day since I first walked into town and caught my first glimpse of you. Everything I've done since that day was to improve my odds in the pools so I had a better chance of being chosen in the lottery as your husband."

Sophia gasped and turned back to him. "What are you— But you—" She broke off again, closing her eyes and seeing him walking into Ana Martinez's house. Ana was one of the unmarried older women in town who was past her childbearing years who chose to give her favors freely to men of her choosing. It was little wonder she'd accepted the strapping eighteen-year-old Finn into her bed when he'd come calling.

"I know you used to go see Ana Martinez. I saw you once."

She didn't miss Finn's flinch at the name.

"You saw that?" His voice was quiet, and that was all the admission she needed to know she hadn't mis-seen that day.

Still, she was a woman now, not a naïve girl. Men had… *needs*. Finn might have liked her, but it didn't mean he was going to wait all those years for her to grow up and be eligible for a raffle to— well, to—

"It's not what you think, Soph."

Sophia scoffed again. "I'm not a little girl, Finn. And it's fine. Whatever. The past is the—"

But Finn just kept shaking his head, so vigorously that soon he was wincing and grabbing at his wounded shoulder.

"Finn! Stop it, lay back."

She put her hands on his chest again and he grabbed both of them in his.

"Sophia, I was a virgin on our wedding night."

"You were—" She blinked in confusion. "But you—"

"I did go to Ana's. So she could teach me about sex. And how to, you know," his face flushed slightly, "to please a woman. But Soph, it was always with you in mind. I've never been with anyone except you. It's always been *you*."

He's injured, she reminded herself as she all but threw herself at him, trying to keep free of his hurt shoulder as she grabbed his face and kissed him with all her might.

"I love you, too," she murmured between breaths, kissing up his chin to his ear—God she loved the way he always had this scruff on his face, she loved the way the rough bristles felt against her lips—and then back to his mouth.

"I had the biggest crush on you forever," she said, running her hands through his hair, "and then when we got older and spent more time together, it was more. But I thought you didn't feel—"

"I did," he rumbled before devouring her lips again. "I do."

"*Ohhhhh*," she groaned into his mouth.

"Soph, I need you. I need to be inside you. Right now."

"Finn," she shook her head, "You're hurt. We can't—"

"Pull my jeans down and straddle that sweet ass over me right this goddamned second, Soph, or I swear, bullet wound or not—"

This might be the last time you see him.

Because no matter how sweet this revelation was to hear, could she really let it change her plans? Right when she'd finally decided to be brave? No. No, this didn't change anything. Even if it felt like it changed everything.

So even though she second guessed herself the whole time, she took one glance around at the other men who were still asleep, then undid Finn's jeans and yanked them down far enough to pull him out.

Her sex clenched the second she did. He was so aroused, hard and thick and warm in her hand. She felt her slickness in her panties and suddenly couldn't shove them down quick enough.

She climbed on top of Finn before she could think better of it and positioned him at her entrance.

Sex was still so new that she wasn't sure she had him in the right place, but as his hips gently nudged upwards, he began to slip inside like it was the most natural thing in the entire world.

"Oh God, *Finn*," she gasped, pulling her hair over one shoulder so that it fell like a curtain between them and the rest of the room.

Finn's eyes glittered in the dim glow of the overhead warehouse lights.

"I love you, Soph," he said as she sank down inch by inch on top of him until he was fully seated inside her.

As she looked down into his eyes and finally saw everything he wasn't trying to hide any longer, it was so intense, so much, so perfect, so *full*, she couldn't help the tears that started leaking down her cheeks.

"Hey, don't cry."

But she just shook her head and dipped down, holding herself up by her hand beside his head so she didn't put pressure on his hurt shoulder.

First she brushed her nose back and forth against his as she squeezed all of her pelvic muscles around his length inside her.

"Jesus, Soph," he choked out and she smiled, finally kissing him and starting to shift her hips forward and backwards.

God, it felt so insanely good to slide up and down on his shaft like that, grinding down against his groin on every downstroke and getting friction exactly where she needed.

It came swiftly. Being with Finn, being with him like *this*, knowing he *loved* her, and knowing this might be their last time, oh God—

"Finn," she gasped, clutching the bedclothes beside his head even as he said, "Jesus Soph, I don't know how long I can—"

And then together, they both tensed and spasmed like one single trigger had been pulled.

Finn grabbed the back of her head and dragged her down for a kiss as he thrust deep and she felt him spill inside her.

She writhed against his hard shaft, the heat exploding outwards from her core and lighting every nerve ending on fire.

She disappeared into him.

The future disappeared, and the past, and everything that wasn't *them*, and this moment.

She held onto it for as long as she possibly could, clutching onto it, onto *him*—

But eventually, the heat dissipated and the dark of the dim room returned. There was Finn's labored breathing and her own and she realized she was lying more on him than she'd intended and she might be hurting him.

"Your shoulder," she said in alarm, trying to shift off to the side, but he just wrapped an arm around her waist, holding her still.

"Shh," he whispered. "Just a little longer."

Looked like she wasn't the only one wanting to hold on.

She bowed her forehead to his chest. *Oh, Finn.* Why couldn't they have found this back in Jacob's Well? During a normal Raffle, with the world not insane and ready to tear itself apart?

But that world was gone. And if she ever wanted anyone to ever have it again, she had to try. She had to or she'd never be able to stand herself.

"I love you," she whispered as Finn blinked heavily and his arm around her waist went slack. "Always remember that."

He just squeezed her tighter for a moment before his arm went loose again. "Love you. Always," he sighed, sounding contented.

And it was with those words ringing in her ears that she pulled away from him and took what might be the last look she'd ever get of him, before turning to go and look for Jagger.

CHAPTER NINETEEN

JAGGER

This was for the best. Jagger knew it was. He wasn't the good guy.

And hey, if Sophia wanted to go on some suicide mission, who was he to stop her? Plus, he'd get paid out of the whole deal. All this pesky emotional bullshit would be finally over and done with. Pussy wasn't worth this BS, that was for *damn* sure.

"Here's the coin your dad and I agreed on." Jagger handed over a bag of gold to Bill's son—melted down, purified, and stamped into coins in Odessa. "With more coming your way when I return with the vehicle."

Bill's son, Jagger had forgotten his name, nodded and looked Sophia up and down.

Jagger wanted to step in front of Sophia to block her from the ugly bastard's gaze, and then was immediately annoyed at himself for the impulse.

She's nothing to you.

And he was about to offload her, thank fuck.

The man held out his hand for the bag of gold but before he could snatch it, Jagger pulled it back. "She's gassed up? I don't want to be running out of gas and be stranded ten miles out."

The man's eyes narrowed. "Dad told you she'd have half a tank. You calling Dad a liar?"

Shit. Hillbillies and their fucking pride. The smallest misstep could get your head blown off.

"Of course not," Jagger said magnanimously. "Just wanted to double check and make sure there was no miscommunication."

He held the bag of gold back out. After all, if Bill really wanted to, he could order them all killed so he could just *take* the gold, but Bill was usually a longer-term thinker. If he killed Jagger now, that meant one less stop he'd be able to take his pussy-posse to for business.

Well, no doubt whoever took over in Carlsbad if Jagger were dead would still welcome them, but Bill knew with Jagger he'd have no trouble coming with his girls, but more importantly, *leaving* with them. And fuck knew it was far safer bringing his girls to Carlsbad than it was venturing into Texas.

And sure enough, Bill Jr. or whatever the fuck his name was, handed the keys right over. And when Jagger and a dour-faced Sophia climbed in the Jeep a few warehouses down, she fired right up.

Sophia had changed clothes and was back in her jeans that the other women had washed and dried by the fire, with a small backpack over her shoulder and the boots he'd given her on. Her jaw was rigid, like she was working hard to look strong and determined.

Jagger didn't know which of them she was trying to fool.

Not your problem.

He shook his head, put the Jeep in drive, and sped out of the warehouse as soon as Bill Jr. pulled the door open wide.

Jagger drove for hours, roads he knew were clear—both of debris and trouble. He didn't head straight east. Whenever he and his crew ventured into Texas, they always made straight for Hell's Hollow. Taking the same path now took them a little out of their way, but knowing the roads were more important.

Sophia fell asleep almost immediately.

Well, she pretended to at first. Her eyes were shut but her body was tense and strung tight. It took a good forty-five minutes before she finally relaxed and her breathing evened out.

Not that he gave a fuck.

He had one mission. Get her to Fort Worth and offload himself of the gigantic headache that was Sophia Wolford.

He'd get his money for her and be on his way.

His jaw tensed and he glanced her way again as the sun rose, bathing the baby-soft skin of her cheeks in light.

Fuck but she was beautiful. Why'd she have to be so goddamned beautiful? And sweet, too. Well she could be a damned firecracker when she wanted to be, but underneath was a core of caramel. Soft and gooey and just sweet as hell. She wanted to pretend she was so hard but he didn't know who she thought she was kidding.

They'll eat her alive in Fort Worth.

Jagger jerked his eyes back to the road, grinding his teeth.

Not his problem.

She wasn't his problem anymore.

He'd made his peace with who he was and the life he lived. She wasn't the first girl who'd had a harsh wakeup call to the brutal realities of life.

It happened every day. Well, it would, if there were any innocents left. The fact that girls like her were rare only meant that her fate was all that much more inevitable.

So what if he facilitated bringing that reality check on sooner rather than later? He was only giving her what she wanted. What she asked for. She was walking in with eyes wide open.

No, she's not. She has no idea, not really. She can't even comprehend what they'll—

The Jeep hit a pothole that was especially deep because he hadn't been paying fucking attention to the road like he should.

Sophia jerked awake, letting out a little surprised yelp and grabbing for the door and dashboard.

Jagger managed to keep the Jeep going though the shocks got

another workout as the back wheels hit the same pothole, jostling them just as hard a second time and rattling his teeth.

"Wanna watch where you're going?" Sophia said, looking behind them at the road. "God." She put a hand to her forehead and then scrubbed it down her face.

Jagger just glared at her. "Do I look like I need a backseat driver?"

Sophia crossed her arms over her chest and turned firmly toward the passenger seat window, giving him her back.

Fine with him. The less said between them, the better as far as he was concerned.

"Where are we?" she asked after several long moments of silence. "How long have we been driving?"

"About seven hours. We're passing just north of Hell's Hollow."

Sophia drew her knees up to her chest at hearing that. "We're not going there, are we?"

Jagger sliced a glance over at her. "Might be able to get more for you if I sold you there," he muttered. "And without half as much bother."

Her mouth dropped open and he rolled his eyes.

"I said we were *passing* north of the city. That's what I meant. We're just passing by, all right?"

"Have you done that before? Sold women in Hell's Hollow?"

He hadn't. But he just shrugged. "Gotta make coin one way or another."

Sophia withdrew as far from him as she could get without pushing the door open and jumping out of the Jeep.

"You aren't even capable of human feeling, are you? God," she shook her head, "you've never loved anyone or anything in your whole life, have you?"

"Shut up about shit you don't know anything about," he said, a warning in his voice.

But of course she had to just keep pecking at him. Pecking and pecking and pecking.

"Oh please. Whores you fuck don't count. Come on. Can you tell me you've ever cared about anything? Mr. Nothing Matters There's No

Meaning in the World." She scoffed. "I bet you would have sold your own family if it could have turned you a profit."

Jagger stomped the brakes, stopping the Jeep in the middle of the desolate backroad. Then he turned and got right in Sophia's face.

"I said to shut the fuck up about shit you don't know the first thing about."

Her eyebrows shot to her hairline. "Wha— I don't understand."

Jagger yanked back from her, slamming his head back on the headrest. "Fuck!" he shouted. He banged the steering wheel with the palms of his hands. "Fuck, fuck, *fuck!*"

Sophia jumped every time he swore and he wished he was beyond caring. He so fucking wished.

"I had a sister, okay?" he finally said, staring out the front windshield. "A twin fucking sister. We were triplets, actually, but we were born premature. Our brother died the day we were born and my sister, she was—" He broke off and sucked in a long breath.

Jagger had been small as a kid but he'd eventually caught up with the other kids. But Marilee, she always stayed small. His little dolly, he used to call her.

And it felt like from day one it had been his responsibility to take care of her. He was the strong one. He could learn things quick but she always had trouble. She had to be kept back, put in special classes.

Jagger had to be the best he could be because everything he achieved, he was doing for both of them. He got top grades and a full ride scholarship to UT and went on to law school. It all had to mean something, right? He had to accomplish something great, to be extraordinary. He couldn't waste a single day of his life.

Because otherwise, what was it all for? They'd been in the same womb—why had it been him who got to thrive and not her? If anyone deserved the best in life, it was his sister Marilee.

"She had developmental disabilities and only got to about a third-grade learning level. She was the best person I ever knew."

He swallowed and closed his eyes, remembering. Marilee had her days, of course. She could throw tantrums to end all tantrums and they were harder to manage the older she got. Her own limitations frustrated her. She always wanted to do the things Jagger was doing. She wanted to go to dances and out on dates and she loved the fantasy of going to college and living on her own even though it wasn't a real possibility. She was so curious, too. She had an infinite curiosity about the world.

"She got sick when Xterminate hit Texas."

"Oh Jagger," Sophia murmured but he ignored her. She didn't understand. Everyone knew someone who'd gotten sick, he knew that. It was different with Marilee. At least it had felt like it was, like it should be. It was *Marilee*. His twin. He'd been with her from the moment of his conception. She couldn't *die*.

"As soon as she started showing symptoms, I packed her up in my SUV and started driving to Georgia. To the CDC. They'd have the cure first, I figured, and I was going to make sure my sister was first in line."

Jagger shook his head at how stupid he'd been. How fucking naïve. It had just literally been incomprehensible that he'd lose her. She was too *good*. So much better than him. So much more deserving.

It all had to mean something. Her life couldn't have been for *nothing*.

Except of course it could be.

"We got there and the doors were locked, of course. No one was getting in. Tons of other poor fucks had the same idea as me and there were sick women as far as the eye could see. Marilee suffered for weeks, all of us out there hoping a cure would come any day. Right in time before the end."

"But it didn't," Sophia said.

Jagger smiled thinly and finally looked her way. "Marilee died in my arms, terrified and confused about what was happening to her and begging for me to make it better."

Sophia's eyes closed. "Oh God, Jagger, I'm so sorry."

He turned away from her, looking back out the front window. He didn't want her sympathy. He just wanted her to understand.

"So I started driving back to Texas. I thought, at least I can give her a good burial. I was going to bury her under the weeping willow in our back yard that she always loved playing under. Maybe give her some peace in death at least."

He blew out a sharp breath. "I even made it all the way back to Texas. I was thirty minutes away from my house when rioters blocked the road. They broke the windows of the SUV. And when they saw her body in the back, they set it on fire."

Sophia gasped but Jagger just kept going. "I jumped out of the car. I got clear of it before the whole thing blew."

"So you see," he said, still staring out the front windshield, "there's no fucking point to anything. I kept wanting there to be meaning—in her life. In her death. But I finally saw the truth. Life is just fucking chaos. Random and cruel. The only way to survive is not to let any of it touch you."

"No," Sophia cried. "No, you're wrong. You're so wrong. Do you think this is what your sister would have wanted?"

"Oh fuck you." He couldn't stand being in the car with her another second. He shoved his door open and jumped out of the Jeep, stomping down the empty road. At least she'd decided to throw her little shit fit while they were in the middle of nowhere.

But of course she couldn't leave well enough alone and let him blow off steam by himself. Her door slammed shut and then she was right beside him.

Fine. She wanted to press the fucking point? Well he wasn't going to hold back.

He spun on her and pointed his finger in her face. "Don't pretend to know what my sister would have wanted. She wouldn't have understood this world. Her world was small and nice and safe. When she got sick and everything became so chaotic, she was only confused and constantly upset and begging me to make it better and I couldn't. I fucking couldn't, don't you fucking get it?"

"At least she had an excuse for us sheltering her. She *couldn't* understand. She literally couldn't comprehend what was happening on an intellectual level. But you—" He shook his head.

Sophia looked down at the ground but he could also see she was hardening her jaw. "So it's my fault my dad wanted to keep me safe? That he loved me the way you loved her? If she hadn't been disabled you wouldn't have taken her to the CDC or wanted to honor her after she died?"

"Don't fucking twist my words," he spat.

But she shook her head. "I'm not the one twisting shit. You've come up with this nice clean justification for the way you live your life. The world's fucked and shitty things happened to you, so nothing you do is really your fault. That's handy."

"You're such a fucking princess. Looking down on everyone from your ivory fucking tower and pretending you understand an iota of what it means to suffer—"

Her scoff was full of so much bitterness for a second she looked and sounded nothing like herself. "You ever think there's a reason I don't talk about my mother?"

Jagger frowned. He'd never thought about that. He'd just assumed there was a Mrs. Wolford, tucked away fat and happy somewhere while her husband went to war and her wayward daughter snuck out of the safe little nest.

"Maybe because I hid upstairs in the closet while she got raped to death. But you know, it's not usually one of those topics you bring up at a get-to-know-my-new-fiancé dinner. Not that we had one of those. No, you made sure to seal the deal before I could really take stock and think through my options. Then again, if I had, I guess you might have just killed me and Finn. Or Finn at least. I suppose I was still too valuable. You can't ransom back a dead girl."

Jagger bit the inside of his cheek. "Every time I start to feel a little bit of sympathy for you, you just go and keep talking and then you piss me off again."

"Oh no, am I making the big, bad gangster mad? I'm shaking in my boots."

Jagger stepped into her space, making her back up all the way to the Jeep until she was pressed against the passenger side door. "You just never know when to stop, do you?"

"You don't scare me," she said furiously.

"Like I said, you're a little fool."

She spit in his face.

The little—

His hand flew to grip her around her neck and her breath caught. He didn't squeeze but Christ, he could feel her fluttering pulse against his thumb. "Somebody needs to teach you a lesson before it's too late." He held her life in his hands.

"Oh yeah?" She hiked her chin up defiantly but Jagger didn't miss her nervous swallow. Or the spark in her eyes as her gaze locked on his. "And who's gonna teach me? You, I suppose?"

"You bet your tight little ass," he growled before crushing her lips with his own, never letting up his grip on her throat.

This goddamned woman. He never knew which way was up around her. He didn't feel like himself. She made him feel— She made him want—

But her hot body against his felt too good and the next thing he knew, he was pulling her around the Jeep, yanking open the back door, shoving the bags of supplies to the ground and dragging the back seat down flat.

Then he hoisted her up and came down on top of her.

He had to be inside her.

Right the fuck now.

Apparently she was on the same page because in the same short space of time, she'd kicked her boots off and shoved her jeans down. He helped pull them off one leg, dragging her panties off with them.

He had to be inside her. He had to get in-fucking-side her.

He jerked the button of his fly undone, yanked his jeans down, and then finally, Jesus, finally, he gave one hard *thrust*.

"Fuck," he yelled as he went hilt deep inside her, her wetness giving smooth passage. Smooth, but not easy. Because fuck, she was so tight. Always so goddamned tight. Her sweet, fresh, all but virginal little pussy.

She felt so good, so fucking perfect, and it pissed him off.

"Why the fuck," he pulled back and then slammed back into her, "do you have to piss me off," he did it again, rotating his hips and grinding down against her in a way that made her mouth drop open with pleasure, "so fuckin' bad?"

She reached up and grabbed the front of his shirt, all but ripping it as she dragged him down to her mouth. She stopped just short of kissing him.

"Maybe because it's the only way you'll let yourself feel anything," she said, sounding no less pissed.

She wrapped her legs around his waist and tried to control his pace from below, shifting her hips up and down to fuck herself on his shaft.

"Oh I don't think so," he growled, shifting her so that he held her ankles up near her head. "You take what I give you. When I give it to you."

She started to protest but then he started to fuck her again. Long, slow strokes he made sure she'd feel, right where she needed it.

And finally, fucking finally, she stopped fighting him. He wasn't sure what flipped the switch. If him repeatedly hitting that spot inside her finally pushed her over the edge of pleasure or what, but her eyes went all soft.

She looked at him the way he caught her looking at Finn sometimes.

"Oh Jagger," she sighed, reaching up like she was going to touch his face.

He shook his head and grabbed her wrist, pinning it to the bed of the Jeep. But she just kept... *looking* at him. Like she— Like she—

"Don't," he snapped.

"You can't stop me," she whispered. "It's too late. I see you. I see you, Jagger."

Wisps of her dark hair fanned around her face and he wanted more than anything in the world to let go of her wrist and her ankles, to push them back, to cover her face with kisses—

No. No. He wanted to fuck her. That was all. She'd pissed him off and she was still his wife, his property for the next 24 hours so he'd fuck her if he—

"Maybe I'm young and we both know I'm naïve. But it *does* mean something," she said. "It means something, the two of us being here. In this moment. You being inside me and me loving you."

Why the fuck did she have to go and say that? If he had another hand available, he'd have slapped it over her mouth before she'd ever gotten the words out. But he didn't and she'd said it.

Why? *Why?*

All he'd wanted was a little distraction. Life was miserable and then you died. So he tried to make it a little less miserable along the way. A little coin. What pleasures he could scratch up here and there.

But then he'd made that stupid fucking phone call and she'd picked up.

Sophia squeezed around him and he lost himself in her for a long moment. In and out, pleasure lighting up his spine but no, fuck no, he wasn't letting go of this any time soon.

She arched up into him, her breasts like everything else about her, so perfect. He couldn't see all of them but in her tiny little tank top, enough were on display for him to imagine. He wanted a year to explore her, to worship every inch and—

But tomorrow she was going to go sacrifice herself on some doomed fucking mission.

No.

He wouldn't let her.

He'd tie her down right here. Or back in his room in Carlsbad.

He'd keep her as his sex slave, just like she'd accused him of.

He kissed her, insane now that the damn was breaking. Fuck. Fuck, he needed her. He— He— He lov— He *needed* her. He couldn't let her go. Not now.

He kissed her deep. So deep she couldn't breathe except for when he gave her air. She couldn't move except for when he pulled out and then it was only so he could thrust back in.

She'd forget all her foolish ideas. He'd make her. He'd make her forget everything except him. Except what he felt like inside her.

But she's so stubborn.

Her father had tried to keep her safe and look how far that'd gotten the man. Finn, too.

They weren't Jagger, though.

He let go of her wrists and her ankles and slid his hand back to her throat.

"Now, you're going to give me what I'm about to take. You're going to give it to me because for once in your goddamned life, you're going to do what you're told, do you understand me?"

Her eyes were wide, but she didn't say anything. No nod, no nothing.

He squeezed slightly around her delicate throat. "Do you understand me?" he asked, allowing a growl into his voice. He'd make sure she understood him before he was through, that was fucking sure.

"Suck." He shoved two fingers in her mouth and, eyes still wide, she did. "Harder," he demanded.

She sucked harder.

Fuck, she was perfect.

"Squeeze on me, little dove. I want to feel how much you want it."

Her breath hitched and she did as he said. He could feel her inner muscles contracting around his cock.

He thrust his fingers in and out of her mouth in an imitation of what he was doing to her sex. Her saliva coated his fingers as she slurped and sucked.

Good.

She'd need the lubrication for what he had planned.

He pulled his forefinger out of her mouth and dropped it down to her anus.

If he thought her eyes were wide before, it was nothing to how they popped open when he slipped his finger into her ass.

Her entire chest bowed up off the flattened seat, in shock or pain or pleasure, or all three maybe by the look on her face.

Jagger just kept pushing in, pausing to stretch as he went.

"That's right, little dove," he said, licking his lips in anticipation. "Let me in."

Before she was probably ready he started probing with his second finger, stretching her around the entrance first and then pushing inexorably inside.

She squeezed on his cock harder every centimeter he intruded. He rolled his hips to grind against her clit as he continued.

And he'd make her fucking dance and sing for him tonight. Considering the way she was already squirming on the bench seat and breathing so heavily, it wouldn't take as much work to get her on board with his idea as he'd initially thought.

Jesus, her eyes were bright, so bright and he could tell she was in it—that place he'd only gotten to maybe once or twice in his life before The Fall, when you were having sex with a person and you got to that place where you were removed from it all. The rest of the world dropped away, who you *were* even dropped away, you didn't even know you were in it until you came out of it. It was a separate plane of being where if you were lucky, if you were very fucking lucky, you got to connect on a deep fucking level with another human being.

And Sophia was there. He could see it in her eyes. Maybe because she especially needed the rest of the world to drop away right now. Maybe because she needed a commanding touch. Maybe because she was just really fucking horny and he was in the right place at the right time.

He didn't fucking care.

But he was going to worship her and keep her there for as long as possible. He dropped down to one elbow beside her head and kissed her deep.

Instead of fast strokes in and out with his cock, he moved slower. Jesus, her body gave so beautifully. Her legs dropped open to receive him even deeper and *fuck*, sinking into her was the most amazing feeling in the world. He pushed in, savoring the feel of her.

"Squeeze babe. Squeeze on me."

She did and he teased her, thrusting in and out with just his tip and making sure to rub against her clit each time he did. All the while teasing her ass with two of his fingers.

Her chest arched and she let out the most delicious little noises. Her eyes were closed as she lost herself in pleasure but no, he wanted her to know exactly who was bringing her all these feelings.

He pulled out of her sweet little cunt and positioned his cock at her back hole. Her eyes flew open even wider. He propped himself up with the hand he'd been fingering her ass with and ran his other hand up through the valley of her breasts and then back to her throat. Her nostrils flared the instant he gave a slight squeeze.

"You're strong, little dove. Strong enough to take what I'm asking you to give. The strongest person I've ever known."

Her breath hitched as he pressed the head of his cock to her little puckered anus.

"Let me in. Give into me." He ran his thumb over the thrumming pulse point on her neck. She was either terrified or excited or both.

"Trust me," he demanded, knowing at the same time that trust was the one thing that couldn't be commanded. It had to be given freely.

Would she?

His own chest went tight with tension as he waited for her reaction.

But he should have known—his little dove had never met a challenge she backed down from. Her little chin notched higher and she relaxed her legs that had clenched up tight.

"I trust you," she whispered.

He took the opportunity and pressed in, his cock still wet from her cunt. Her body stayed relaxed and he knew the control that took—or rather, paradoxically, the giving up of control it required.

But when Sophia gave, she gave completely. She always had.

So Jagger was able to not only push the bulbous head of his cock in her tight as fuck little anus, but he was able to keep pushing, continue invading, more and more and more.

Her breath came in little pants and her eyes had never been so dark as her gaze locked with his.

Jagger reached for her hand, interlocking his fingers with hers and then pinning it above her head.

He pushed the last bit until his balls were flush with her ass and she cried out. It had to hurt. He wasn't ignorant about that. He was well-endowed. But she'd still let him into her deepest, most secret place. She'd done it without a blink of the eye.

I trust you.

He bowed low and kissed her.

She kissed him back hungrily, almost like she needed his lips to help ground her in this moment.

He'd give it to her. She who gave so selflessly, how could he do anything but give it all back to her? Everything. He wanted to give her fucking everything. Christ, she was making him crazy. He didn't know who he was anymore. He couldn't think. Not while he was buried inside her. Not while her sweet lips were working so eagerly against his and her little tongue curiously sought out his.

He couldn't do anything except bury the hand not holding hers in her hair and then, because he couldn't stand it another moment, he began to pull slowly out of her tight, hot hole.

She groaned but he didn't think it was in pain now.

He rolled his hips forward and down so that his groin gave her friction where she needed. But that wasn't enough, he decided, so he disengaged his hand from her hair and lifted up so he could reach between them.

Her hips shifted eagerly into his hand, which meant her ass was twitching and squeezing around his cock.

"Jesus Christ," he swore.

He was supposed to be the one in command here, but every second he felt less and less in control.

And when she started to roll her hips, really fucking him back, restless little cries escaping her throat as she chased her pleasure, holy fuck, he was gone. He was just fucking gone.

He slipped two fingers in her cunt and teased her clit with his thumb as he upped his pace thrusting in and out of her ass.

That seemed to be what did her in. The gentle whisper of his thumb on her clit plus the hard pounding pressure in her ass.

"Jag—" she screamed, hips lifted to press more firmly against his hand.

He dropped down and kissed her voraciously as the orgasm slammed through him. Fucking blinding. Fucking amazing.

He was a fucking *god*.

He pumped into her. Once. And then one more thrust. And one final—

And then he collapsed against her, rolling slightly to the side so he didn't crush her.

He rested his head on her breast and she caressed her fingers through his hair and for a brief moment, his life was complete. It was a contentment a man like him rarely felt. Okay, *never* felt. He never felt like this.

He lifted his head to look at Sophia, only remembering now he'd started all this to make a point. To show her she was his. To show her that doing what she was told would make her the most satisfied and happy she'd ever been.

But then he saw it. She wasn't dozing in contentment. She might have been his completely while they were making love—and there could be no other term for what they'd just done—but already, barely a minute afterwards, and he could see he was already losing her.

"Why are your eyes still saying goodbye?" he whispered.

CHAPTER TWENTY

SOPHIA

Jagger pulled away from Sophia. She didn't try to cover herself as she sat up. She had nothing to hide from him anymore.

Moments before as she'd stared down at him, she could see all his walls were down and he looked content. Even *happy*. Maybe for the first time since she'd met him. Because of her. Because of what they'd just shared together. Because of the life they could have had together.

And her chest had squeezed in pain because she knew it wouldn't last.

Jagger shook his head like he couldn't believe her. "You're still planning to leave me." It came out as a choked whisper.

Oh God, why did this have to be so hard? She reached out for him but he jerked back. "Jagger, please. This doesn't change anything. I still have to go."

"No. You don't. Don't go. Don't do this."

He grabbed the hand she'd just held out to him, going up on his knees. "Run away with me. Back to New Mexico. There's no war there.

Live with me in Carlsbad. You'll have everything you ever need. We'll pick up the others. We can be a family. A real family."

Hadn't he heard anything she'd ever said about her home? She couldn't forget Dad and everyone else she loved. She couldn't run away and pretend they didn't exist.

"I can't." Tears pricked her eyes, knowing she was hurting him. Maybe it would have been better if she'd never pressed it earlier, never made both of them own up to the love between them. But it was too late for that. And yet it still didn't change things. "I have to do this. I have to go."

Jagger pulled back again, yanking his jeans up and getting down from the back of the Jeep. He only made it two feet before spinning back to her.

"Why?" He threw his hands up. "Your pride? To prove something to yourself? To your father?"

"No!"

Then she stopped. Was he right? Was this ultimately just another immature stunt on her part?

Maybe an assassin was the best way to deal with Travis... but did it have to be *her*?

It should be someone more experienced. Someone who'd actually killed before. Someone like Drea.

But Drea was too important. And sometimes Sophia's other friend, Shay, talked about what it was like living with Travis before she'd escaped him. She'd been his woman for years, borne him two children and knew him better than anyone. Shay had talked about the girls he liked to collect and Sophia knew that someone like her—young, pretty, and inexperienced—would be valuable to him. She'd actually have a chance at getting close to him.

And they were all out of time. The confrontation was coming and it was coming *soon*.

She'd already told Jagger all that and knew those sorts of facts weren't what he was looking for, though.

"I don't know how to explain it." Sophia pulled on her underwear and hopped down from the Jeep. "But I just feel like it has to be me. Travis and my dad were friends once."

Jagger had his back to her so she walked up to him but stopped short of touching him.

"This started with my family. I need to be the one to end it. Or at least I need to try."

He turned around and she could see he was about to argue again so she held up a hand. "And my dad *did* teach me how to fight. Hand to hand and with a gun."

His jaw went rigid. "You couldn't fight Toby off."

Her whole body went clammy even at the mention of his name and she turned away from him. "You really know how to build up a girl's self-confidence."

"Jesus, Sophia, stop." He reached out and grabbed her arm to stop her. "I just don't want to do something that neither of us can take back." His eyes searched hers. "I don't want to live the rest of my life full of regret over what we do today."

All she'd ever wanted was to crack Jagger open to get to the real him, and here he was. The center of him was loving and gentle and loyal and, she also could see, so, so afraid of being hurt again like he'd hurt when he'd lost his sister.

She stepped forward and clasped his hands, lifting them to his chest between them. She kissed his knuckles and then looked back up into his eyes.

"But don't you see? Neither do I. And I'll regret it for the rest of my life if I don't do this."

And, though he probably wouldn't appreciate hearing it, it was him who'd shown her she was strong enough. She'd been so afraid thinking about the task that lie in front of her she'd barely been able to fall asleep once they got on the road earlier. Once she finally did, her dreams were full of terrifying monsters, all teeth and hands, but she couldn't escape, she was too weak to even run away.

But just now, Jagger had shown her her own strength. She was brave enough to submit and receive him.

Courage wasn't doing the brave thing *without* fear—it was doing it *in spite of* the fear.

He let out a long sigh, his eyes falling closed, his shoulders slumping. "Stubborn little dove." He dropped his forehead to hers.

They stayed like that for a long while, until finally, reluctantly, she broke the silence.

"It's time to go," she whispered.

He shook his head. "Don't ask me to do this." His voice broke, and when she looked up, there were tears in his eyes. "Please."

Quieter, a hand to his face, she whispered again, "It's time to go."

CHAPTER TWENTY-ONE

SOPHIA

For the first few hours of the second leg of the drive, Jagger was silent. But as the sun started heading for the horizon, he reached for Sophia's hand and interlocked his fingers with hers.

Sophia looked over at him in surprise. He didn't say anything, though, or even look her way. He just kept a tight hold of her hand for the next two hours until they were stopped by border guards at the edge of Fort Worth.

Sophia couldn't help squeezing Jagger's hand tighter as two guards approached the Jeep. They wore the black camo she'd heard Travis's men always did. But hearing about it and seeing it were two different things—somehow seeing the stupid camo made it feel real.

Shit. She was really here. Really *doing this*.

"Sophia, I can turn around right now—" Jagger whispered.

"No." She pulled her hand away from Jagger's before either of the guards noticed. She'd spent some precious water to wash and then changed into a sundress before they got back on the road but she huddled down into her seat. Playing her role of scared little captive. She wished it were more of a performance.

"No one's allowed in—" the first guard started to say, but Jagger cut him off.

"I got a girl to sell. She's a 4. Only been active two weeks."

The guard who'd come around Sophia's side scoffed. He reached through the open window and grabbed her by the chin, jerking her face up. He was a short man with yellow teeth. "A 4? Fuck, if you're gonna lie, at least make up a believable number. Face like this, I woulda gone with 400, even though you and me both know it's more like ten times that."

It was barbaric, the 'rating system' that determined the price of a female slave—the number of men she'd slept with, combined with how long she'd been sexually active.

"And two weeks my ass," said the guard on Jagger's side. "I can see from here she's more 'n thirteen, so that's a whopper if I ever heard one. Bet her cunt's more worn out than an old leather boot."

Sophia's chest went tight at their crude talk, but she steeled herself because she knew much worse was coming.

Jagger had told her in excruciating detail what the usual process of selling whores involved, in a last ditch effort to dissuade her before they'd gotten back in the Jeep. He'd never sold any but had been in the room and seen it firsthand in Hell's Hollow.

But while she might be naïve, Sophia wasn't an idiot. And she'd told herself she could handle it. No matter what. No matter *what*.

"You think I'd show up at this gate if I was lying? I know Colonel Travis takes only the best. Me and my men found her hiding out in a bunker with her brother, along with another sister. She was untouched. I know we coulda got even more if we'd left her that way," Jagger smirked, "but what can I say? My men hadn't seen pussy in an age. Boys will be boys. If Travis likes this one, I'll bring the other sister next week."

The supposed 'second sister' was a little bit of insurance, so they didn't just kill Jagger and take her without letting him go. Sophia knew it was cruel to ask Jagger to bring her here, especially after they'd discovered what they meant to each other. But she couldn't think of another way into the city. And at least she'd know Jagger would walk out of it alive.

The guard holding Sophia's face let go and shook his head. "I still say he's full of shit." He reached for the door handle and jerked it open. "But I ain't had me any sorta bitch in weeks so let's have at it."

Jagger growled and grabbed Sophia's arm, jerking her close. "Say the word, I jack these two up and we get the hell out of here."

She shook her head. "Make it look good," was all she whispered in the second before the guard got the door open. "They have to believe I'm struggling."

She saw in Jagger's eyes how what she was asking killed him. And she didn't look away as she started pretending to struggle in his hold and shouted, "No! Let me go!"

He clenched his teeth as he grabbed her other arm and swiveled her so she faced toward the door the guard now had open.

"Only an inspection," Jagger barked. "Travis wouldn't be fucking happy if his 4 became a 5 or 6 just because his guards couldn't keep it in their pants."

The guard glared at Jagger before grinning lecherously at Sophia. "She really is a looker. Course it hardly matters if her cunt's as used up as old chewing gum."

He whipped up the skirt of her sundress and yanked her legs open. She'd taken off her underwear and put on another of her sundresses—wanting to look as authentic as possible—a decision she wasn't sure if she regretted now or not. She'd certainly never felt more exposed in her life as the hot autumn wind slid across her nether bits.

But all of this had been so much simpler in theory than reality, hadn't it?

Because when she felt thick fingers on her, roughly pushing inside her when she wasn't even the littlest bit wet, her cry of pain wasn't just for show.

"Fuck me," the guard said, looking past Sophia to Jagger. "She's tighter than fuck."

"No fuckin' way. Lemme feel."

Sophia squeezed her eyes shut as the second guard came around and the entire thing was repeated.

I'm not here, she chanted to herself. *This is not my body. I am not here. I am not here. I am not here. I am not here. I am not—*

"Sophia." Jagger shook her and she looked up, only realizing then that the guards had stepped back to talk. No one but Jagger was touching her. She shoved her skirt down and yanked the car door shut.

"Soph—" Jagger started to say but she just shook her head violently back and forth. No. She couldn't handle him being sweet or worried or anything else right now.

Jagger swore under his breath and slammed the steering wheel. Sophia ducked her head. It was unfair to ask this of him. It was all unfair and maybe she *couldn't* do this and he was right, she should have told him to turn around and drive, *drive—*

"Okay," the first guard said, coming around to Jagger's side. "Both of you, out of the vehicle. I'll be driving you into town." He pointed to a van beside their makeshift guard tent.

The second guard opened Sophia's door. She closed her eyes and whispered a silent prayer as she let herself be dragged out of the Jeep and over to the van.

There were four more 'inspections' and an hour and a half wait locked in a room that Sophia was pretty sure had been a closet in a former life.

It was the longest hour and a half of her life since the last time she was locked in a closet, waiting, waiting, waiting to find out her fate while her mother was downstairs being tortured and murdered.

Oh, and she was gagged, so there was that, too.

Where was Jagger? Were they treating him alright? It was true that Jagger had been smart and mentioned that made-up other sister, as a protection against getting killed right on the spot. He, unlike her, was very familiar with this world.

Trust nobody. Finn told her that and it wasn't the first time she'd heard it. Henry had said it to her once, too. Henry, the older man she'd had a dumb, girlish crush on after she saw Finn go in to see Ana Martinez. Henry was a friend of her father's, a man who could do no wrong in Sophia's eyes. But then he'd betrayed his family, even his wife.

Sophia had been shocked when she learned the truth. She'd looked up to Henry and admired him from afar for so long. He was always well-dressed and well-mannered, so civilized.

But people weren't always what they seemed. Jagger, for instance. He was rough, gruff, and lived like an outlaw, but underneath—okay so it might be really really *far* underneath—he was good and kind.

And Sophia could be the opposite of what she seemed, too. So she looked like some sweet, naïve, scared little thing? Fine. She'd use it to her advantage.

Of course, it would help if she didn't actually *feel* quite so terrified.

The door to the closet opened and Sophia blinked against the sudden light, lifting a hand to shield her eyes.

Someone just grabbed the arm she'd raised, though, and dragged her to her feet out of the closet.

"Ow," she cried, stumbling along after the man. He wasn't anyone she'd seen before. She looked left and right, surprised to see she was in a... *hotel room?* They'd put a bag over her head at the last guard station before coming into the city proper.

But as the guard dragged her out of the hotel room and down the hall, she recognized where they were. All the lights were working, which meant the electricity was on.

This was the Omni Hotel. The same place where the former President used to live before Travis had him killed and took his place.

Of course he lived here, he probably considers it a status symbol that validates his Presidency.

There wasn't much more time for thinking, though, because the guard who had her was soon knocking on a door down the hall.

"No!" Sophia shrieked around the gag in her mouth. "Let me go!" Though it sounded more like. "*Eh ee o!*"

The guard just shook her roughly, rattling her brain, it felt like. "Don't give the President any lip now."

Then the door opened and there was Arnold Travis, sitting on a couch with a glass of bourbon, chatting and smiling with Jagger, who was doing the same.

"And here she is," Jagger said, standing when the guard dragged Sophia in the room.

Sophia remembered to struggle, but only barely.

Arnold Travis, in the flesh. She'd heard so much about this man he'd become mythic in her mind. She'd expected an eight-foot giant.

But he was just a man. Shorter than she expected. Shorter than her father. And his shoulders weren't even very broad.

She'd spent a lot of time looking at men, daydreaming about her would-be husband, cataloguing every man she came across as a potential.

And everything she saw in Arnold Travis was... lacking. How could this be the man who had an entire nation on its knees?

Jagger suddenly sprang to his feet, taking her attention. His gaze kept shuttling back and forth between her and Travis and she frowned before remembering to school her features into distress and hate.

"I lied to your guardsmen, your excellency," Jagger suddenly said. "While this woman is a 4, that was true, I concealed her identity until I was speaking to you face to face. The girl before you is Sophia Wolford, only daughter of your greatest enemy, Eric Wolford."

Sophia felt all the blood drain from her face.

No.

Why?

The confusion was followed quickly by fury, especially when Jagger continued. "I hope there might be some small compensation to be gotten for bringing her to you?"

Jagger had betrayed her. It had all been a lie. She'd loved him and he'd—

"You'll get your money," Travis growled as he shot to his feet and stalked toward her.

Tears squeezed from her eyes as she looked past him to Jagger, who wouldn't look at her. "How could you?" she shouted into the gag, but it was unintelligible.

She started to fight like a wildcat against the men holding her arms from behind and Arnold Travis smiled a cold, reptilian smile.

And then he punched her so hard the world went black.

CHAPTER TWENTY-TWO

ARNOLD TRAVIS

"Well that felt good," Travis chuckled as he stretched out his hand and looked at the bitch laid out on the floor at his feet.

Eric's little girl, huh? Looked like she'd grown up since Travis had last seen her. He wouldn't have recognized her if he hadn't had his spies watching everything Eric did for years. It was clear the little tart thought she could sneak in undetected and what—kill him?

He smirked down at her, then looked up at the man who was with her, the smile falling from his face. "Start talking. Quick, if you don't want one of my fine guards," he gestured around the room and his five men all stepped forward, "to put a bullet in your forehead."

"It's a long story," the man said, hands up. "We confiscated a sat phone of a man headed west into New Mexico. That's where I'm from. He was some sort of diplomat on the run after you'd taken over. There were all sorts of numbers programmed in the phone, so I started calling them."

The man, Jagger, pointed at Sophia, still passed out on the floor. "That one answered and we convinced her to come to New Mexico."

Travis scoffed but the man continued, telling a story about a naïve girl and a group of men only too happy to take advantage of her.

"She actually *married* you?"

Jagger smirked and nodded.

"We were going to ransom her back to her father, but then I realized she'd probably be worth much more to you, considering all she told us about you and her father."

"What did she say about me and him?" Travis's jaw locked even thinking about Eric. His one-time best friend turned longtime enemy.

Nine years ago, Travis had called Eric a brother. He was the only person Travis had ever let close. But Eric had stuck a knife in Travis's back the first chance he'd had, no matter all Travis had done for him. Poetic now that Eric's daughter got to experience the same thing.

Travis would never forget the day Eric betrayed him. They'd gone to that army base in San Antonio to get troops and supplies after D-Day. They were going to remake the nation together, as brothers.

Travis only did what needed doing that day—what anyone would have done—but Eric, always the Boy Scout, was too perfect and precious to get any blood on his hands. But if anyone else did, well Eric was only too happy to judge *them*.

Because he considered such things beneath him.

Travis knew Eric had always secretly felt that way about him. Eric with his happy family and their fancy fucking house. Travis had been an idiot to think Eric had ever given a fuck about him. No, Eric had never been able to see past the trailer park and the endless string of foster parents and the secondhand clothes.

Eric had everything handed to him on a silver fucking platter while Travis had to fight for every goddamned inch.

And then for Eric to have the fucking *gall* to stand there that day on that army base and look at Travis like he was a stranger...

"*For fuck's sake!*" Eric shouted. "*You're covered in blood. What the fuck happened?*"

Travis blinked and wiped his face, only then looking down and realizing he was covered in blood. "It's not mine," *he said, stupidly thinking that was why his best friend was upset.*

But Eric only took a step back at his words.

Still, Travis was riding the high of whooping ass in his first battle and he was eager to share it with Eric. "I ran into a little trouble over at the Commissary. Nothing me and my men couldn't handle. And look, we got a helicopter. Supplies too. And a bunch of guys wanna join up. They're tired of this bullshit. They see that if they want shit in this life, they gotta take *it*. It's gonna be true now more than ever. We just gotta make sure we take it first."

Eric stumbled back a step but Travis just kept nodding. "You should've seen me, man. I just started talking, and they were all totally with me from word one. The system's been rigged for years. But now's our chance. We can finally take what's rightfully ours. We can be kings."

It was the first time Travis had been able to really see it and believe it—all the potential of this brave new fucking world. For the first time, there would be an equal playing field, no more deck stacked against him, and he could have the life he'd always deserved.

"Jesus." *Eric shook his head, then ran his hands through his hair.* "Jesus."

Eric looked freaked out and he was pacing back and forth. Which pissed Travis the fuck off. Why wasn't he celebrating with him? But no, Eric always had to obsess about morality and doing the right thing.

Travis liked to believe Eric had invited him to live at his house during high school after he found him sleeping in the janitor's closet—his foster dad had kicked him out of the house again—because they were best friends.

But sometimes Travis wondered if Eric hadn't just done it because it was the right *thing to do. And fuck knew Eric Wolford couldn't live one day of his goddamned life without doing the* right *fucking thing.*

When they'd gotten to college and Eric had found Connie he'd certainly ditched Travis quick enough in exchange for the family life. Not that it had lasted long. Soon it was just Travis and Eric again, joining the army and getting deployed together for a tour. They went their separate ways in their next deployment but now they were back together again, like it was always supposed to be. If Eric would just—

"How many?" *Eric choked out.*

"What?" *Travis asked.*

"How many men? Did you kill just now?"

Travis looked at him like he was from a different planet. "Are you serious with this bullshit?" *He'd looked forward to this day his whole life, and now Eric was squabbling about—*

"Bullshit?" Eric exploded. "These are people's lives *we're talking about!*"

"Yeah and it was either them or me," Travis shouted right back, thumping his chest. "Would you rather it was me back there dead?"

"So it was self-defense?" Eric looked at him like he was pleading for him to say yes. Which pissed Travis off even more. "Did they start firing first?"

Travis just shook his head. Eric was really doing this. He was really fucking doing this. Over a decade of friendship and he was willing to sacrifice it over what? A couple of dead fucking kids guarding a commissary, after the goddamned apocalypse had happened?

"I cannot believe this fucking bullshit. After all the years we've known each other? After all I've fucking *done for you?*" Travis shoved Eric hard in the chest. "You'd be rotting in a fucking prison *right now if it wasn't for me!*"

Eric recovered from stumbling backwards right before he fell and stood back up again. His eyes were swollen from crying all week like a little bitch over his dead wife. "Just tell me who fired first," he begged.

"Your daughter would be dead *if it wasn't for me!*"

"Who shot fir—"

"I DID!" Travis screamed right in Eric's face, spittle flying. "I fucking did! I went into that commissary and saw some fuckers with guns guarding the supplies and I ordered all my men to fire. And I pulled out this gun right fucking here," Travis whipped out his gun from the back of his pants and pointed it right at Eric's forehead, "and when they were on the ground, begging for their fucking lives, I ended *them.* Just like I did to the fuckers who got in the way of my smuggling operations in Nigeria, Syria, and Lebanon."

"Why the fuck do you think I kept getting promoted so much quicker than you? Think." He banged the barrel of the gun against Eric's forehead. "I knew how to play the fucking game. Something Eric the Boy Scout always refused to fucking do."

Travis finally pulled the gun back, waving it around them, to the soldiers who'd lined up behind him, along with the ones who'd grouped behind Eric.

Travis could feel the tension mounting between his soldiers and those Eric had managed to recruit and he fucking reveled in it. This was what it was all about. Men being real men. Barely leashing the animal inside them that wanted to tear each other to fucking pieces.

"This is the real world, Eric. Wake the fuck up."

Eric just shook his head and took a step back from Travis's gun at his fore-

head. His voice was choked, "I loved you like a brother." He swallowed and stood up straighter. "Let me and my men pass. I'll go collect my daughter, and then we never have to see each other ever again."

Just like that, Eric thought he could write Travis off. Eric just got to say the word and poof, Travis no longer existed to him.

Privileged fucking bastard. Did he think he wouldn't have to pay for this? That there wouldn't be a reckoning?

Not that day, but someday.

Someday.

A day like today.

Travis had let two people close in his whole fucking life, and both of them had betrayed him. Eric Wolford, and Travis's own bitch, Shay, the mother of his kids.

He'd deal with Eric first, and then he'd go after Shay.

Eric's daughter groaned at Travis's feet, shifting and grabbing for her head as she came back to consciousness.

The rush of adrenaline at finally having the single thing Eric cared most for in the world—fuck, it felt good. It felt really, *really* good. More satisfying than even getting rid of that weakling of a President and installing himself as President instead.

Travis pulled his long, sharp knife from the sheath on his belt and bent down, pressing his blade to her throat. She was still gagged, so she couldn't say anything other than making horrified little squeaks.

"Just the smallest bit of pressure, and your life is over," Travis whispered with a grin. "Just give me an excuse. Please. I beg you."

He could see her pulse fluttering in her throat like a terrified rabbit's. He laughed. "Wow, I really would have thought Eric's daughter would have a little more fight in her. But that's okay." He bent down and whispered. "When I rape you, over and over until you have no tears left, it won't have mattered if you fought in the beginning or not."

Her eyes flashed furiously up to him. She had her mother's eyes.

Travis had hated that bitch. She'd been the first one to steal Eric away from him. So even though he hadn't intended to mark the girl yet, the tip of the knife pierced her neck, drawing a small prick of blood that began to spill like a tiny waterfall of red down her neck.

Travis had always been fascinated by blood. It was so bright and chaotic. When you cut into a person, the blood tended to spray so messily.

And the screams, Travis liked those too. He liked to draw it out for as long as he could. How many cuts, how much blood could drip and spray and congeal and then drip and spray the next day, and the next, and the next, before a person's eyes finally went distant, their soul finally separating from their suit of meat?

Travis lifted the flat of the blade to his tongue and licked the bead of her blood caught there.

Her eyes widened in horror and Travis smiled because that was part of the fun, too. Slowly breaking down the mind along with the body until they admitted you were their god, the only determiner of their life and death.

"We're going to have a lot of fun together, honey," he whispered, grinning down at Eric's terrified daughter.

But just as he was about to order one of his guards to start dragging her behind him as they left for his villa, movement out of his periphery had his head jerking up.

Right in time to see the man, Jagger, running straight toward him.

Travis laughed as the man tackled him to the ground, several feet away from Eric's daughter, immediately grappling with him for the knife.

He was strong, Travis would give him that. When he slammed Travis's wrist to the floor, it almost even hurt.

But there was no fucking way that, this close to what he wanted, Travis would be cheated out of it.

Travis held onto the knife with a death grip. And seconds later, his guards were pulling the man off of him.

Two other guards held Eric's daughter immobile, her mouth dropped open in a shocked O of surprise as she watched them pull Jagger off him.

"I'm sorry, Sophia," the poor bastard said, voice stricken. "I'm sorry. I knew he recognized you. As soon as he saw you, I knew he recognized you so I was trying to find the best way to—"

Enough of this sappy bullshit.

Travis flipped his knife around and sank it into Jagger's guts, hilt deep.

CHAPTER TWENTY-THREE

SOPHIA

"No!" Sophia screamed, fighting against the arms holding her and trying to get to Jagger. He stumbled several steps backwards, his hands dropping to his stomach as Travis ruthlessly yanked the knife out.

Travis's guards were immediately there, grabbing Jagger's arms so he couldn't lunge at Travis again.

Jagger hadn't betrayed her after all. He'd just seen what she hadn't. Travis had *recognized* her somehow. She didn't especially look like either of her parents. But he'd still known— Duh, he hated Dad. It would have been easy to run surveillance on him... and his family.

Stupid. She should have thought of that possibility. So Jagger had done the only thing he could think to—pretended he was selling him the daughter of his enemy so he could take a chance at killing Travis himself.

Except he'd failed.

He'd taken his chance when Travis had that knife out. It had been desperate but he had to know it might be his last time in a room with Travis. And Sophia hadn't realized what was happening until too late.

She hadn't believed in Jagger. She'd thought he was just another Henry and that there really was no one she could trust.

She could kick herself, though, for not trying to help once she *did* realize what Jagger was doing. She could have helped him hold Travis down, or tried to get the knife sooner, or caused some sort of distraction so he could—

But she hadn't and now Jagger had a bleeding abdominal wound, blood seeping down his shirt as he covered it clumsily with his hands.

The blood was so *bright*. Sophia could only stare on in shock. It was so bright. This couldn't be real. Blood wasn't really that bright red, was it?

Arnold Travis couldn't *really* have her captured, could he? She hadn't walked right into this horrible trap, had she? Dear God, what had she done?

"Tie him to a chair," Travis ordered sharply. "And get me a fucking camera. Now," he shouted when his guards didn't move fast enough.

The guards not holding her began scrambling to obey Travis's orders.

Sophia could only weep as orders were repeated over walkies and more guards appeared at the door with both a camera and rope, plenty of rope.

They tied Jagger to a chair without doing anything to address his wound. His head hung groggily but he was still conscious. Oh Jagger.

She'd done exactly what she'd sworn she wouldn't after all—she'd forced another person to sacrifice their life for her.

Travis could have ended Jagger's life easily with the knife. But it was clear he meant for Jagger to suffer. Sophia cried harder. What had she done? What had she *done?*

She fought when the guards came for her. But she was no match for three grown, trained men. They picked her up and carried her to where Travis pointed. To the bed.

She screamed into the gag as they tied her spread eagle to the four posters of the bed.

Travis took off his shirt. Then his jeans.

He came toward the bed in just his boxers. She knew he was only as old as her dad, but he looked far older. His hair was mostly silver with bits of brown whereas her dad's was the other way around. And Travis was muscular but lean and brutal looking, like a jackal.

Sophia tried to calm her breathing. She was fucking hyperventilating. She couldn't— She had to— He was about to—

Travis grinned down at her, then he looked up to one of his men. "Are we recording?"

Sophia spun her head to look at the man with the camera, right as he nodded.

"Eric, long time no see," Travis said, and Sophia's whole body went stiff at hearing him say her father's name. No. Oh God, no.

"I had a visitor today. You'll never guess who." Travis smiled into the camera and then gestured down.

Sophia squeezed her eyes shut, knowing the camera was panning down to her.

"Oh don't be shy. I'm sure Daddy wants to see all of you." Travis slapped her and her eyes popped open with the blow.

Then he pulled the gag out of her mouth. She wrenched her head away from him the second he got it off, turning her head away from the camera.

Travis just laughed some more, a noise she knew would haunt her until her dying day.

He skirted his hand up her thigh and Sophia struggled against the ropes tied at her ankles, no matter that doing so only made them chafe and burn.

"Get off her, you sick fuck!" Jagger yelled.

Travis just climbed on the bed, jerking her skirt up and exposing her to the camera. "That's her erstwhile defender you hear shouting. Go ahead, get a shot of him."

The cameraman swung toward Jagger who continued shouting epithets and fighting against the ropes the guards were still securing around his arms and legs in spite of his wound.

"Stop, Jagger," Sophia cried, her throat thick with tears. "Stop."

"Isn't that sweet?" Travis mocked. "She's so concerned about her man." He shook his head. "But gotta say, he's not in the best shape."

Then Travis looked back down at Sophia as he climbed in between her legs. "Your little girl here, now, that's another story. She looks very, very good. Mighty scrumptious, actually."

Travis bent down and ground himself against her and she turned her face away, shuddering in disgust at the feel of him on top of her.

You can do this, Sophia. It would be like earlier with the 'inspections. She'd close her eyes. Pretend she wasn't here. That this wasn't her body. She'd get through it. Stay alive for another day. Another opportunity to kill Travis.

Travis pinched her nipple until she couldn't help but cry out. Then he did the same to the other.

"You hear that, Eric?" Travis shouted over her. "That's the sound of your little girl screaming because you aren't here to help her."

"Come closer," he waved to the cameraman. "See your daughter's cunt, Eric? See how close I am to it? She's tied up. She can't go anywhere. I could fuck her all day long. You can see how hard I am for it."

Sophia had her eyes squeezed shut and she wished she could shut her ears to the disgusting, foul things he was saying.

She could feel Travis through his boxers. He was hard. And large. It would hurt.

It wouldn't be like earlier with the inspections, either. She wouldn't be able to pretend she wasn't here. Not while he was defiling her with that.

And he meant to send this to her *dad*. Oh God, *please*, she begged, though she didn't know what she was even asking for. Still, she couldn't stop begging. *Please, please.*

"Are you seeing this, Eric? See how easily it'll be for me to destroy your little girl's cunt? I won't be gentle about it, either. If I'm going to turn her into a brothel girl to sell to the highest bidder, I'll need to break her in good, won't I?"

Tears poured out Sophia's eyes, listening to her future detailed so horribly.

Any second, he'd push his boxers down and shove inside her.

Any moment now—

But to her shock, Travis backed away and climbed off the bed.

"Of course, friend, you could save her from that fate. I'll offer you a deal—for old times sake, let's say. If you walk through my door within 5 days, I'll let you exchange yourself for her. She'll go free, completely untouched."

"No!" Sophia shouted. Oh God, this was worse than anything Travis could do to her. No, she couldn't let Dad die for her just like Mom did. "No, Dad, don't!"

"Oh shut up, you dumb whore," Travis said, turning and slapping her again. Unlike his first slap after the camera had turned on, this one had all his weight behind it and she was quickly stunned, pain exploding all over the left side of her face.

She blinked in confusion, Travis's voice coming from far away. "Five days. Don't be late. I'll barely be able to stop myself from fucking this sweet, tight little cunt in the meantime, so if you don't show, then it's open season on your little girl."

CHAPTER TWENTY-FOUR

JAGGER

"I need to see Eric Wolford," Jagger gasped, shoving the truck door open at the rebel checkpoint outside Cleborne.

"Hey, stay back." Two soldiers in green fatigues raised weapons on him and several more came running toward the truck.

Jagger put his arms up. Or tried to, anyway. He stumbled and fell to his knees, a hand clutching his stomach where he'd been stabbed in the gut.

The world tipped sideways and then swam back into focus.

Hold it together. Fucking hold it *together*. Just a little longer.

She was back there. Sophia was back there with that monster and Jagger had to let them know. He had to get her help.

Travis's men had put him in a truck an hour and a half ago and sent him south with Travis's message and Jagger hadn't been sure he'd be able to make it ten miles, much less forty.

But he had. He was here. So close to finishing his mission.

He fought through another bout of faintness as he reached into his pocket.

"Hands where I can see them. Now or I'll fucking shoot!"

Jagger pulled out the tablet loaded with Travis's video message.

"Take this," Jagger heaved for breath. "Eric Wolford." Spots danced in his vision. "His daughter."

Sophia's face flashed before his eyes and then it was only blackness as he crumpled to the ground.

CHAPTER TWENTY-FIVE

ERIC WOLFORD

What do you mean, you thought she'd be here?" Eric yelled at Finnigan Knight. The boy who'd run off with his daughter two and a half weeks before had come back half an hour ago and Eric had only just been notified about it. He'd had the boy brought immediately to him.

The boy who had somehow lost his daughter several days ago.

"I mean," Finn said, pacing back and forth in the trailer they were currently using as Command Central, "that we got intel that Travis has an army of mercenary ex-Southern Alliance soldiers and you're even more outnumbered than you thought."

"What?" Drea snapped. "How many?"

Drea, Eric, plus several of her top commanders including David, Jonathan, and others were crowded in the living room of the trailer area discussing their planned assault on the capital. The trailer park in Cleburne was only forty miles outside Fort Worth. They had maps of the city, of the old tunnel systems underneath the city and the strategic points where they thought they had the best chances of breaking through scattered on tables set up throughout the room.

"You'll be outnumbered three to one." Finn looked back and forth from Drea to Eric.

Drea swore and looked to her commanders who immediately began talking heatedly amongst themselves.

"What does that have to do with my daughter?" Eric asked Finn impatiently. Ever since Eric made the decision to go help Drea instead of follow his daughter three weeks ago, he'd been haunted wondering if he'd done the right thing. Drea had needed his help *immediately*, he'd told himself. And she had. She would have died if he hadn't shown up in the eleventh hour. So he couldn't bring himself to regret his choice.

But when he'd gone looking for his daughter after the dust had settled and they'd taken San Antonio, she was nowhere to be found. Once he realized she and Finn had taken one of the Jacob's Well trucks, he knew going after her would be a fool's errand. They could have gone any one of a hundred different routes to get to Santa Fe.

And Sophia was of age, as much as he'd wanted to deny it. She was a grown woman who could make her own choices. Something Drea regularly reminded him of. Sophia wasn't helpless, and Eric had done as much as possible to teach her to defend herself. Plus, she had Finn. Eric hadn't known him well, but the little he did reassured him that Finn was a reasonable boy who knew something of the real world. Surely he'd keep Sophia from getting into too much trouble.

Except here was Finn. *Without* Eric's daughter.

"When we woke up and found Sophia gone, I was sure she'd come straight here to warn you." Finn dragged a hand through his hair. "I don't even know where the hell else she and Jagger would *go* if not here."

There was a brief knock at the door and then a soldier stepped in without waiting for a reply. "Sir, there's another one."

"I said not to disturb us," Eric snapped.

"I know, sir, but you were also mad when we didn't bring *him*," he pointed at Finn, "to you right away. And well, there's another one. Says he knows your daughter and has a message from her."

Eric and Finn looked at each other. "Where is he?" Eric demanded at the same time Finn asked, "What's he look like?"

"Never mind," Eric said. "Just take us to him."

"Eric." Drea reached a hand out to him, concern etched in her features.

"It's fine," he said over his shoulder as he hurried after the soldier. "Stay here. I know you need to deal with the new intel."

They were on the eve of their assault and what Finn had told them could change everything. But Eric couldn't care much about the war right now. He'd have to leave that to Drea.

Ever since he'd gotten back from Afghanistan eight and a half years ago to find his wife left for dead in the Death Riots and his little girl hiding in a closet upstairs, he'd sworn to devote his life to protecting Sophia. He'd built Jacob's Well township for her, so she could have a safe and happy childhood. And when the time was right, it was meant to be a place for her to marry good men and create a family apart from the ugliness and violence of the outside world.

Eric expected the soldier to lead him to the border defense line, but instead he took them toward the infirmary trailer.

"Why are we here?" Eric asked.

"The fella was in bad shape. Near passed out right after he got here and said his bit about finding you."

"What do you mean, bad shape?" Finn asked as they jogged up the stairs and pushed the trailer door open.

"You'll have to ask the doc. All I know is he was bleeding from his stomach, soaked his bandage through and—"

"Jagger?" Finn exclaimed as soon as he got through the door. He rushed forward to the man on the cot in the center of the room. "Where's Sophia?"

"Back," said a medic who tried to block Finn's way. "Hey, get back. This man's going to die if we don't operate. *Now*."

Eric stared down at the man in the cot. His shirt was off and he had an ugly, inflamed stomach wound. Not a bullet wound, but maybe a knife? And it looked like he'd lost a lot of blood.

And Finn had called him *Jagger*. This was the man who'd supposedly last been with Sophia. But Sophia wasn't with him and he had a life-threatening wound.

So where the *fuck* was Sophia and what the hell had happened to her?

Eric was about to shove the medic out of the way and grab the man to shake him until he told them where Sophia was, but he lifted a wobbly arm to Finn and spoke in a gasp, "Tablet. Sophia."

He was only able to get those two words out before he fainted dead away.

"What the fuck does that mean?" Eric yelled.

"Sir, he did have this on him when he arrived." Another soldier, not the one who'd come to get him, stepped forward with a small handheld tablet. They used to be a commonplace item but ever since D-Day when EMP attacks had fried most electronics, it was rare to find one that worked.

But this one not only worked, it was fully charged.

Eric swiped to turn it on and then almost dropped it when he saw his daughter tied to a bed on the screen.

Along with Arnold Travis.

Eric choked and fell to his knees, clutching the tablet to his chest as he did, though, careful not to drop it. Finn swore behind him as they both continued to watch and listen.

Eric wanted to smash the tablet to pieces when he saw his one-time best friend touch his daughter's thigh. And then he threatened the most vile—

Eric dropped the tablet to the floor, unable to trust himself not to throw it across the room.

"Five days," Travis said over the speakers. "Don't be late."

Eric roared in fury the second the message cut off. But he knew what he had to do. If it was a question of exchanging his life for his daughter's, well, there was really no question at all, was there?

CHAPTER TWENTY-SIX

SOPHIA

Arnold Travis was a monster. How had her father ever been friends with this man? She couldn't understand it.

His thugs had thrown another black bag over her head and taken her to a different location after Travis filmed the horrible video and sent Jagger off to deliver it.

At least it meant Jagger had a chance at safety, if he could get there in time before he lost too much blood. And if he didn't have any trouble on the road. And if Drea's soldiers didn't shoot him on sight when he came rolling up to the rebel encampment.

She had more immediate worries, though. She'd assumed Travis lived in the Omni Hotel like the previous President had, but it looked like that assumption was wrong. She'd been taken to an opulent mansion that was old, hundreds of years old. It was likely a museum before D-Day with how well all the woodwork had been preserved, but Travis had taken it over as his personal residence.

He didn't throw Sophia in another closet like she might have expected.

No, he gave her a spacious room upstairs with a view of the city. It was beautiful. She'd only been to Fort Worth once before but then, like now, it was astounding to see an entire city with electricity to spare. They'd managed to restore the electrical grid several years ago. It was powered using solar energy and the extensive wind farms mostly in the Panhandle.

A guard and 'lady's maid' stayed inside the room at all times so escaping wasn't exactly an option. Plus, though these weren't exactly the circumstances she'd imagined, she couldn't get closer to Travis than living in his *house*. She'd just wait for her opportunity. So far he wasn't even binding her hands.

He's that confident you're no threat.

Well, she'd prove him wrong. She'd prove everyone who'd ever underestimated her wrong.

She'd learned upon waking that Travis required her presence at breakfasts and dinners, no exceptions.

He'd also laid out lingerie and a skimpy dress for her to wear. She put on the underwear but refused to touch the rest of it.

"Please, Miss," the maid kept asking. "It'll put him in a terrible mood if you don't do what he says."

"I don't give a rat's ass if he's in a bad mood."

"No, you don't understand—"

"I'm not putting that on," Sophia said coldly. "If you want to try to wrestle me into it, you're welcome to try."

The woman just sighed then nervously bit her lips and looked downstairs.

Sophia did go downstairs for breakfast but only so she could get a sense of the mansion and look for anything she could use as a weapon.

To her dismay, there were only butter knives set out. The sharpest thing on the table were the forks.

Travis glowered at her as soon as she sat down. He, naturally, sat at the head of the ornately laid table. Flower arrangements in crystal vases lined the center of the table.

Servers came in with plates of steaming omelets and orange juice in fancy wine-glasses, big globes on small, delicate stems.

Travis threw his napkin in his lap impatiently. "Why haven't you showered or changed into the clothes I sent up for you?"

Sophia glared right back at him, lifting her chin. "I'm not your fucking puppet to dress and dance at your say so."

"Oh but you are," he snapped. "At dinner you'll wear exactly what I have my girls lay out for you. And you'll eat every single morsel set in front of you."

"Fuck you," Sophia spat. She could only remember saying the curse word a handful of times in her life but it made her feel the tiniest bit of power now, when she felt otherwise terrifyingly powerless.

The cold smile that touched Travis's lips was not reassuring, though. It sent a chill down Sophia's spine.

"No," he said, standing and walking around the table. "I think I'll fuck..." He looked around the room. "Which of you was it that was supposed to dress her this morning?"

There were four women standing at different points along the wall and they looked back and forth amongst themselves before the girl who'd attended Sophia that morning stepped forward. "Me, s- sir," she said shakily.

"Did I or did I not instruct you to dress her for breakfast in the clothes I sent up?"

"You did, sir, but she wouldn't—"

"Did I stutter?" he roared.

"N-no sir."

"Over the table. Right in front of Miss Wolford. If she's too good to wear my clothes and eat my food, maybe she'll appreciate a show instead."

"No," Sophia tried to say, suddenly terrified of where this was all going.

"Too late now. Actions have consequences. Maybe your daddy shielded you from that basic fact of life, locked away in your ivory tower in that township of his, but this is the real world. So wake the fuck up."

Then he looked to the terrified girl still huddled at the wall and shouted, "Now!" He pointed to the table and she ran to Sophia's side.

The woman started to bend over, face down, but apparently she wasn't fast enough. Travis took two strides and slammed her into the table by the back of her neck. He did it so violently, without any care for the table setting that Sophia's glass of orange juice went flying, shattering the globe and leaving only the stem behind.

The woman didn't fight his force, though. Not even when blood dripped down her face from the glass cuts, staining the white tablecloth below.

Travis grabbed her thin dress and ripped it down the middle, exposing her back.

Sophia gasped at the barely healed over marks she saw there, up and down the woman's back. And she was even more horrified to see Travis pulling his belt off.

"Stop it," Sophia screamed when he began to beat the woman with it. Fresh red welts appeared everywhere the belt struck.

She had to stop him. Her eyes darted around the table, and not really thinking it through, she grabbed the broken stem of the orange juice goblet and swung it toward Travis's exposed neck after he landed an especially brutal hit.

Surprised flickered in his eyes only a moment before his arm came up to deflect Sophia's swing.

Sophia cried out in frustration and she grabbed the only thing left to her—a fork. She pretended like she was going to go for his neck again. When he went to block her, she jabbed downwards with all her might, stabbing the fork into his thigh as far as the tines would go.

He roared in fury and Sophia grabbed her glass, heavy with water, and threw it at his face.

He blocked it with his arm and then lunged for her.

Sophia screamed and tried to jump backwards, around the table to keep a barrier between them, but two of the women who'd been hovering along the wall moved into her path to block her.

Travis collided with all of them, knocking them to the floor.

The next thing Sophia knew, she was being dragged off the floor by a brutal hand around her throat.

Ow. God! Couldn't breathe— Couldn't—

Once Sophia was on her feet, Travis finally let go of her throat, only to grab her by her arm.

He jerked her back around the table and shoved her facedown on it like he had the other woman.

His grip disappeared for a moment and Sophia scrambled to get up. But the next second he was back, jamming her face sideways onto the glass shards that littered the tablecloth.

Sophia was right beside the other woman, so close she could hear the pained little whimpers the woman was obviously trying to stifle.

"You wanted to stab me with this?" Travis shouted, spittle spraying Sophia's cheek as he leaned over her from behind.

"I think its time to return to the lesson I was trying to teach you." He lifted Sophia's face and then slammed it into the table again. "Actions. Have. Consequences."

Then he took the broken stemware and jammed it into the weeping woman's throat. The spray of arterial blood covered Sophia's face and mouth as she screamed in horror.

CHAPTER TWENTY-SEVEN

ERIC

Four Days Later

The first thing Eric thought when they yanked the black bag off his head was, *oh fuck, this isn't the Omni.*

"Dad!"

Eric's head jerked up as Travis dragged Sophia into the room. It was dark in the foyer that opened to a grand sitting room. Where the hell were they? It definitely wasn't the downtown hotel. When Jagger gained consciousness, they'd questioned him extensively about where Travis had been holding Sophia. The Omni made sense. It was where the former President used to live.

All their plans had hinged on this going down at the Omni.

What the fuck were they going to do now?

"No, Dad," Sophia cried, "why did you come?"

"Soph, it's okay. I'm here now. It's all gonna be okay." He tried to take a step toward her but the two guards holding him kept him in place.

Oh Jesus, his little Sophia. He felt kicked in the gut even just looking at her. She had bruises and cuts on her face.

"You said you wouldn't touch her!" he shouted at Travis, finally looking at the man standing behind her. It was so fucking stupid—he'd seen the video—but somehow, he couldn't actually believe that his best friend Arnie was really capable of hurting his little girl.

"I wouldn't have if she hadn't tried to stab me with my own glassware," Travis growled.

Eric could only shake his head in disbelief. "Let her go, Arnie. She doesn't have anything to do with this."

"Don't fucking call me that," Travis shouted, pulling out a gun and leveling it at Sophia's temple.

Eric's knees almost buckled. "Ok, ok, I'm sorry. Travis, President Travis, please. Please. I'm sorry. I'm here. Within the allotted time. So please. I'm here to trade myself for her. Take me instead. Please."

Travis just laughed. "Always so heroic. So willing to sacrifice yourself. That was your problem, wasn't it? You always had to come off as the Boy Scout. God forbid anyone think you were an actual flesh and blood man. You had to be perfect. Such a nice wholesome, American upbringing. Then of course you pick the perfect girl to marry, pop out a kid, then go selflessly off to serve your country."

"What do you want from me?" Eric would have thrown his hands in the air if they weren't tied behind his back. "I just did what I thought was right."

Travis shook his head bitterly. "You loved the way people looked at you. And you looked down on me every day of my life for not being as perfect as you."

"What the—"

"At first you tricked me. I thought you saw me as an equal. You invited me into your home. Shared your room with me. Fuck, you even shared your clothes and spent all your time with me. You called me your brother. It wasn't until college that I realized I'd been just another charity case to you."

"What the fuck are you talking about? We *were* brothers."

Travis scoffed. "Maybe. At least till I got inconvenient. You made a new family and didn't have any more time for me."

Was this really what he'd— "I got *married*," Eric said incredulously. "That's how it works. There's the family you grow up with and then you get married, and yeah sometimes there's a little bit of added distance, but I never shut you out. Jesus, Arnie, you're Sophia's godfather." Eric's voice almost broke on the words, watching the man he'd once loved as a brother holding a gun on his daughter.

But maybe if he could just keep him talking, reminding him of the old times—maybe it would be enough time for Drea's men to infiltrate the city through the old abandoned underground tunnels they'd dug out. It was why he'd waited almost the full five days to come, even though it killed him—to give them time to finish digging them out.

But you aren't at the Omni. There won't be anyone banging down the doors or coming to save the day.

Eric *had* to try to talk his way out of this.

"I loved and trusted you enough to want you to look after my daughter if something happened to me. You were my family. I was closer to you than my own parents. And when we shipped out together for basic, we were closer than ever."

"Yeah, for as long as that lasted. But then I started getting promoted ahead of you and you couldn't stand it."

Eric's mouth dropped open. "What the fuck are you talking about?"

"After our first tour when I got promoted and moved out of Africa, you think I don't know you turned down the chance to come with me?"

Eric looked down, but just for a moment. "I knew you were stealing cashes of weapons from supply and selling them to locals. I didn't want to be a part of it."

"So you chose your precious morality over your so-called *brother.* How convenient. Let's tell the truth, though. You just couldn't stand that for once in our lives, *I* was the one being promoted while you were being overlooked. Because *I* was willing to do what was required to play the game. I always had the survival skills you lacked."

He was fucking delusional. He thought Eric had been jealous? No,

Eric just had a little thing called a moral compass. He knew if he'd gone with Arnie back then, Arnie would have wanted to draw him into the smuggling operations and Eric figured the best way to avoid confrontation was just to stay behind in Africa for his second tour.

Not that putting off the eventual confrontation helped much.

It just made it all the worse that day when everything came to a head.

"And then again," Travis said, "you had another chance to come with me in San Antonio after I broke you out of that prison transport. I gave you a second chance. You had the opportunity to choose your *brother*, but you couldn't stand to see me as your equal. You were only ever happy when I was under your bootheel."

"That's not fucking true and you know it," Eric growled, fighting futilely against the guards holding him. "I loved you. But I couldn't stand by while you hurt innocent people."

"Oh bull *shit*," Travis said, taking a step forward and shoving Sophia forward with him. "You think I don't know about all the people you hurt and killed to protect *her*?"

Sophia's eyes shot to Eric's and he spoke quickly. "Not innocents. Never innocents."

"And who made you judge, jury, and executioner, huh? Fuck, you're such a hypocrite." Travis shook his head.

"Fine, I'm a hypocrite," Eric said. "Is that what you want? What do you want here? I'll do or say whatever you want. Just let her go."

"You think I want your fucking condescension? I'm the fucking President of the Republic of Texas, the last functioning Republic left in the United territories. I don't need *anything* from you. I fucking *won*. You're *nothing* to me. You're a mosquito and I'm a giant. I just wanted you to see that, once and for all."

"Because I've been running you like a marionette on strings for years, so you'll forgive me if I want to spend a minute or two boasting." Travis grinned. "When you reported on your superior officer for raping that villager, I encouraged him to flip the story and press charges against *you* so you'd be court-marshalled instead."

"Then I paid off officials at every step along the way back home. Xterminate was really hitting its stride and I thought it'd be a great opportunity for us to get back to the way we were. You know, how we'd been back in high school. But I knew a wife and kid would slow us down, so I called up the local militia whipping up riots in the area."

No. Eric reeled from all that he was hearing. "Arnie," Eric breathed out in one last attempt to stop him from what was coming, but Arnold Jason Travis finished just like Eric had been afraid he would.

"And I sent them straight to your house for some hot pussy."

"You fucking bastard, you killed my mother!" Sophia struggled in Travis's grip but shrieked when he pulled her arm back awkwardly behind her, immobilizing her.

"That's right," he shouted, looking Eric's way. "And I'm going to kill you, too, little girl, while your daddy watches. For once and for all, you're going to learn I'm not someone you can look down your perfect nose at."

"But you promised," Eric shouted. "If I came, you promised you'd let her go."

Travis laughed. "Don't you get it? I'm a god. And God can do whatever the fuck he wants. Now God's going to show you what it feels like to think you have family and then have it ripped away, right in front of your eyes."

"No!" he shouted right as Travis cocked the hammer and pressed the barrel of the gun even harder against Sophia's temple.

CHAPTER TWENTY-EIGHT

SOPHIA

For the past ten minutes, Sophia could only stand helplessly by as her father and Travis rehashed the past, growing more certain with every passing moment that neither she nor her father would walk out of this alive.

But no. Her father couldn't die. It couldn't have been for nothing. Wasn't that what she'd told Jagger? That she believed that life had meaning? Even *her* life?

But standing uselessly while Travis held a gun to her head, her presence having lured her father from safety into Travis's lair... it all had her questioning everything she'd ever believed.

She'd wanted to believe she was strong. She'd wanted to believe it *so hard*. But when it came down to it, here she was, a damsel in distress to the end.

She'd tried one last time to fight against Travis's hold when he revealed it was him who'd set the raping, killing mob on her mother, but he'd only bent her arms behind her back at such a painful angle that if she even twitched, pain screamed down her arm.

Then he taunted her father one last time, calling himself *God*.

"No!" her father screamed and the *click* of Travis cocking the hammer was as loud as if he'd fired it.

This was it.

She was about to die.

And no doubt her father soon after her.

By the same man who'd killed her mother.

It wasn't fucking fair.

And no one was coming to save them. Unless...

"Noooooooooo!" she shrieked, fury lighting every cell in her body as she wrenched her body downwards.

The *snap* of her arm breaking and the blinding pain only registered peripherally.

Gun.

She shot back up and hit the startled Travis in his elbow, knocking the gun from his hand. Then she dove for it.

She screamed in agony as she landed on her broken arm, but scrabbled for the gun with her good hand anyway. Her fingers closed around it and she swung around right as Travis's eyes widened and he held his hands up.

"You won't—"

She pulled the trigger.

Travis looked down at the red that began to blossom in the center of his chest. Sophia pulled the hammer back and shot him again. Then again.

And finally, finally, he staggered and fell to his knees, then he slumped to the floor.

Sophia immediately swung around and saw her dad was grappling with one of his guards. Dad must have kicked the guy in his nuts because the man was on the ground, clutching his privates with one hand—while reaching for his gun with the other.

Sophia didn't think. Couldn't think. She just ran forward and screamed, shooting him in the head right as he got a hand on his gun.

Then she pulled back the hammer one last time and aimed it at the head of the man still grappling with her dad.

"If you don't want your brains on the fucking wall, you'll untie him right this fucking second."

Both the man and her dad froze.

"Now!" Sophia shouted, the rush of adrenaline and terror and giddiness making her shake from head to toe.

The guard immediately did as she said and her dad took the man's gun.

"Dad!" she shouted, shooting at two other of Travis's personal guards who were running down the grand central staircase, no doubt at hearing the gunshots.

Her shots went wide in her panic, but her father took down one and then the other, *bang, bang*. When he turned back to the guard whose gun he'd taken, the man had his hands up.

"How many guards on the house?" her dad barked.

"Four inside," he pointed to the three on the ground and himself, his hand trembling, "four more on the perimeter, more at the gate."

Dad pointed at the walkie talkie at the guard's hip. "Tell them to stand down. You'll bring out Travis's body."

Then he turned to Sophia. She was still shaking. She wasn't sure she'd ever be able to stop. He grabbed her face, tears in his eyes. "You did good. You did so good, baby."

She smiled shakily and he nodded, pressing his forehead to hers. "I love you, Dad."

But then, they both heard coughing and sputtering.

Sophia looked over in shock to see that Travis. Wasn't. Dead.

Dad walked over to where he lay, and Sophia followed, feeling half in a trance. Her arm hurt. She had a feeling if everything wasn't so floaty and surreal, it would hurt a helluva lot more.

She'd shot him three times, but the bastard was still breathing. At least for the moment. The pool of blood around him grew bigger with every second and he wasn't so much breathing as heaving bloody gasps of air.

"Brother," Travis panted.

Her dad just looked down at the man impassively.

"I'm not your fucking brother." And then he put his boot on Travis's chest and shot him between the eyes.

Dad looked to the guard. "Take his body outside and make it known far and wide—Arnold Travis is dead."

CHAPTER TWENTY-NINE

FINN

Finn couldn't stop staring at Sophia where she lay in her hospital bed. She was sleeping but even in sleep, she was the most riveting sight he'd ever laid eyes on.

He wasn't alone, either. Mario stood on her other side, eyes locked on her sleeping face. Leo was on the couch behind him and Jagger was in another hospital bed beside Sophia's, also asleep.

They were in a real hospital, too. One with electricity and everything.

Drea's Army had taken Fort Worth. Finn still almost couldn't believe it. He, Mario, and Leo had joined the soldiers who'd snuck into the city through the old underground subway tunnels. They'd swarmed the Omni Hotel from the basement up and secured the building with far more ease than they'd expected.

And then they realized why—Travis wasn't there. And neither was Sophia.

Mario went nuts. He ran straight into the street and started fighting anyone and everyone. Drea had sent battalions to other key points in the city through the tunnels, so they weren't the only ones fighting, but still.

They'd intended to cut the head off the snake before engaging in battle, which would hopefully cut a third of Travis's forces since the mercenaries wouldn't fight if there was no one left to pay them.

But since the snake wasn't in the snake hole they thought, they were left fighting Travis's full force.

Not that it mattered to Mario, apparently. He didn't have any more idea where Sophia or Travis was than any of them, but he cut his way through the enemy as if he did. When he ran out of ammo, he used the giant machete he had sheathed at his back. Finn and Leo followed in his wake, doing their best to give the big man cover.

They were pinned down in an old parking garage when the soldiers they were fighting suddenly pulled back.

It took Mario grabbing one of the men before they all escaped and slamming him up against the wall to learn what was happening—at first it had just been a rumor but there were more and more eyewitness reports coming in, from the top brass, or well, whoever was left among the top brass—President Travis was *dead*. The mercenary soldiers had already pulled out and most commanders who were left were recalling their troops.

Finn learned later that General Drea took advantage of the confusion and had her entire force march on the capitol en masse.

But all Finn, Mario, and Leo had been concerned about at the time was finding where Travis's dead body everyone kept talking about had been last seen.

Mario grabbed another fleeing soldier and held him off his feet by his neck.

"Where's Travis? Where's the body?" Finn yelled.

"I don't know! Maybe the Mansion. He lives there, so maybe that's where he died? Or where they're holding the body?"

Mario shook the man and Finn demanded, "Where's the Mansion?"

"Just take this street that way about a mile, then turn left on 8th!" the man choked out. "I swear!"

Finn pointed his gun at the man's head. "Take us." The guy didn't need to know he'd run out of ammo fifteen minutes ago. It wasn't like Mario wasn't lethal enough anyway.

There was sporadic fighting all the way there but usually it was just gunfire in the distance. A couple of enemy soldiers saw Mario, gigantic and covered in blood, his huge machete at the ready and simply ran in the other direction.

And finally they came to the Mansion, surrounded by a big yard and a wrought iron fence.

Mario ran straight up to the door and banged on it. "Sophia! Sophia!"

Finn about passed out with relief when he saw Eric open it, gun in hand.

Mario shoved him out of the way. "Sophia?"

Finn hurried after him and almost fell to his knees when he saw her.

"Mario?" Her face was pale as she looked from Mario to Finn. "Finn?" She didn't look good. Well, fuck, she was beautiful, but her features were tight with pain and she held her arm awkwardly.

"Shit, Soph, are you hurt?"

"I'm fine. It's just my arm."

"I'll make it better," Mario said decisively, stepping back and then running up the grand staircase off the foyer.

"Mario," Leo called after him after kissing Sophia on the forehead. "Sorry about him."

"No, he's perfect," Sophia laughed, a tear running down her cheek as Leo ran after his brother.

"God, Soph, what happened?" Finn asked, pulling her into his arms but then freezing when she winced.

She leaned her head against his chest and breathed out like she was finally letting go of everything that ever troubled her. "It's over. That's all that matters."

Mario came back down five minutes later with a variety of pills. She took a couple that were for pain and when the fighting died down outside and they'd established coms with General Drea, Mario carried her to the hospital six blocks away.

That was two days ago and Finn could still barely believe it was true.

Had they all really survived? Was it over, for real?

Was Sophia actually *his*?

His to *keep*?

"Hey there stranger," she said, her voice a rasp as she blinked her eyes open.

"Water," Mario said, leaping to action and holding a cup with a straw to her lips.

She smiled at him and sipped obediently.

"Did I actually sleep any?" She looked back and forth between them. "Because I'd swear you two were in the exact same place when I fell asleep."

Finn smiled. "You've been out for a few hours. We were just enjoying the scenery."

She blushed and dropped her eyes.

"Hungry?" Mario asked.

Sophia blinked like she was thinking about it. "Maybe a little."

"I'll go get food." Mario immediately turned and rushed from the room. Sophia just shook her head at him.

She'd been in and out of it over the past two days. She'd had to have surgery for her arm. The doctors had to put a steel rod in, the fracture was so bad. She should have been screaming in pain when they'd found her two days ago.

But Sophia was always stronger than anyone gave her credit for.

Still.

"Soph, why did you leave like that?" Finn sat on the edge of her bed. "I would have gone with you. To the ends of the earth. Don't you know that?"

Her forehead scrunched with pain and she looked away. "No you wouldn't have. You would've tried to stop me."

"Soph, I—"

"Don't patronize me." Her eyes shot back to his. "Jagger was the only one who would do what I asked. And even he—" She broke off, looking over to the other hospital bed.

Finn's jaw clenched. "Because it was suicide, Soph. You walking in there like that. We could have come up with another plan—"

"There was no other plan," Sophia said obstinately. "The odds were against us. There was no other way to end it than to at least try to make a go for Travis. Even if it didn't work. I had to try." Sophia searched his eyes. "Please tell me you understand that I had to try. I did the only thing I could."

"But it shouldn't have been *you*!"

Her mouth dropped open and Finn could see that fuck, he'd hurt her. He was saying it all wrong. "Soph, I—"

"You making Sophia sad?"

Mario yanked Finn backwards by his shirt. Finn stumbled back so hard he almost ran into the wall.

"Mario, no!" Sophia cried, sitting up in bed, and then crying out again because she must have jolted her arm.

"Sophia!" Both Leo and Jagger woke with her name on their lips and Finn backed away. Her luminous green eyes were locked with his as he spun and left the room, the hospital door slamming behind him.

CHAPTER THIRTY

SOPHIA

Sophia was back home. Her *real* home.

Jacob's Well.

Drea and Dad had stayed in Fort Worth. They'd held actual *elections* for once and Drea had been elected President. It looked like they'd be there for awhile fixing the mess Travis had made of the Republic. Well, the guy before him hadn't done much better.

It was time to see what a woman could make of the country.

But meanwhile, Sophia was just glad to be home. With her family. Mario and Leo and Jagger and... and Finn.

They hadn't talked one on one since their argument at the hospital. It was stupid. She didn't even know really what they were fighting about. He was mad at her for leaving and going to try to take on Travis herself.

He didn't believe in her.

Okay, so maybe she did know what it was about. Her heart squeezed, the hurt still stinging as fresh as that day. He'd always see her as a helpless, spoiled kid who needed protecting.

She walked around her house—her new house. As a Marriage Raffle bride, she and her husbands had been given their own home. It was a cute little split level on the edge of town. The river was just down the hill. At night sometimes, when all was quiet, she could hear the rushing water.

In the month since they'd all been home, she'd been avidly cleaning and decorating—well, as much as she could with her arm in a cast.

The guys had taken to town life well. Mario and Leo had easily fallen into construction work and Jagger already had a bunch of trade contacts so he was working with Audrey's husband Clark who'd taken on Trade Secretary duties after Henry... well, after Henry died.

And Finn?

He'd gone back to his old job at the Scrapper Yard but it seemed like there was a perpetual storm cloud over his head.

He was always the first to excuse himself from dinner and the first out the door in the morning.

Because of her arm, she and her husbands hadn't done much more than kiss since they'd been home. They were all overcautious with her, much to her dismay.

But Finn barely even touched her.

She scrubbed mindlessly at a living room window—part of her efforts to clean the whole house top to bottom—thinking about everything that had happened when movement in the front yard caught her eye.

"Finn?" she said in surprise as he pushed open the front door.

He took his Scrapper gloves off and threw them to the foyer floor, then he stalked over to where she stood.

"I'm done with this bullshit. You're my wife."

He stomped over to her, grabbed her face, and kissed her.

She was so surprised, she couldn't help gasping and he took advantage of it, slipping his tongue between her parted lips.

When his tongue made contact with hers, it was like he'd made her come alive. *Boom.* Electricity zinged up her spine, up and down, from the top of her head to her toes and back up again.

Dear God, could she come just from a kiss?

She plastered her body to his, angling just the slightest to avoid her cast. But that was the only consideration she gave. She dropped the cloth she'd been scrubbing the window with and dug her fingers into Finn's hair.

He grabbed her ass and pulled her up and into him. He was hard. Rock hard. Feeling how she affected him made her groan into his mouth. Seriously, she was *thiiiiiis* close to coming. She lifted a leg around his hips and ground herself shamelessly on his shaft until oh— oh—

"*Ohhhhh!*" she cried.

Finn pulled back in surprise. "Holy— Did you just—?"

Sophia buried her face in his chest. Oh God, she was so embarrassed. She hadn't talked one on one to Finn in weeks and then the first time he so much as kissed her, she—

"Jesus, I love you, Soph," Finn chuckled, pulling her lips back to his and kissing her again.

It wasn't the first time he'd said it but... he hadn't said it since and that had been right after he'd almost died and she'd thought he just—

He stood up straighter, his erection still poking her. His eyes searched hers. "I'm done with the bullshit. I love you, Sophia. You know it was always you for me. I'm sorry if me not wanting you to go off and get yourself killed pisses you off. But if we'd had it to do all over again, even knowing what I do now about how everything turns out, and I'd had a chance to stop you, I would've."

She jerked back out of his arms. Or tried to. He held her fast.

"Just *listen* to me," he said, glaring down at her.

"I *love* you. I never had much in my life. And everyone I ever loved either left me or betrayed me or fuck, tried to fuckin' *sell* me. I never had much good in this world. And I never thought I'd have you."

He tugged her tighter against him, dropping his forehead to hers. "So I'm sorry, but no, I'm not sorry if once I got you, I wasn't willing to let you go. I woulda let the whole world burn. So maybe you were right to do what you did. Sneaking off like that. It about killed me waking up and finding you gone, but it all turned out okay. And if you promise you'll never leave me again, then maybe we can stop this fighting and be proper man and wife."

"Finn Knight." Sophia closed her eyes and nuzzled her cheek

against his, waves of relief and longing and frustration washing through her all at the same time. "I swear no one in my life has ever driven me as crazy as you."

"I'll take that as a compliment." She could feel him smiling against her lips and she just shook her head.

"You would."

"But I'm serious, Soph. Truce?"

She sighed and pulled back, looking him in the eye. His gaze was so earnest, pleading even. "I will never leave you, Finn. But I had to do what I did. You can't know what it was like," she swallowed, "my whole life, having everyone else sacrifice for me. It got so I was always playing a part—always being the happy, cheerful girl because how could I ever be anything different after people had *died* for me? How dare I ever be sad or depressed when I was alive and my mom was dead?"

"Soph, no—"

But Sophia just shook her head. "Going and doing what I did. I guess, I don't know—I thought it would balance the scales. Like I'd finally earn my right to be happy. Although really, I mostly just expected to die trying to kill Travis. But then at least I wouldn't have to feel ashamed and guilty all the time for living when others were dead."

Finn's face crumpled at her words and she touched his cheek, shaking her head again. "But afterwards, I realized it doesn't work like that. I did it—I was finally strong enough to take out the bad guy, but you know what?"

"It didn't bring my mom back. It didn't take back any of the sacrifices my dad made for me over the years. I don't know why I thought it would make me feel... less sad."

"And now I know that it wasn't just a mob that killed my mom. It was Travis who directed them to our house, and now he's dead. And that feels..." Sophia swallowed and then swallowed again but she couldn't keep the tears back. "It feels horrible. It all still feels horrible. I miss her so much."

"Oh, Soph," Finn said, drawing her face against his chest. "It's okay. It's okay to be sad about it. It's okay to cry and feel sad. Shit, cry as much as you need, all right?"

Sophia nodded, still crying. God, was it as simple as that? She needed permission to grieve her mother? She needed permission to say that it was okay not to be strong sometimes?

God, she'd spent so much of her life trying to prove she was strong to everyone—because the guilt and the grief got wrapped together until she just denied it all and pretended that she was okay, *always*. And beware anyone who tried to break down those barriers, even the tiniest bit. Namely, Finnigan Knight.

"I love you, you intrusive bastard," she laughed through her tears and kissed him, her good arm around his neck.

The front door pushing open had them both turning to look. Mario and Leo were walking through the door, Jagger on their heels.

"We're kissing again?" Jagger inquired.

"More than kissing," Sophia grinned. "We'll have to be careful, but take me upstairs, husbands."

A smile split Leo's face as he rubbed his hands together. "Yes, ma'am."

EPILOGUE

SOPHIA

Five Years Later

Sophia bit her lip as she looked in the mirror. "It's ridiculous to be anxious, right?" she said. "It's not like we haven't been together for years at this point."

"Don't be silly," Audrey said, "this is the wedding you always dreamed of and never got. Of course you want it to be perfect."

"Hey, stop moving," Vanessa said. "I still have to pin all these curls in place."

"Oh, sorry," Sophia said, trying to sit perfectly still.

She looked over at Audrey and Shay where they sat beside her at the little make up station they'd set up in a back room of the church. "Yeah, the first one was a little less than perfect. I thought Mario was gonna kill Jagger when he finally admitted it wasn't even legal."

That was six months ago. They were at the wedding for a new

Raffle wife and Sophia had been tearing up like she always did. Although this time it might have been from sheer exhaustion because she'd been up more than half the night with baby number *three* who was colicky and refused to sleep more than an hour and a half at a time.

Between baby Anna, wrastling the toddler *and* the four-year-old throughout the ceremony, Sophia had gotten home, broken into the secret stash of chocolate the guys had gotten her for her birthday, and had a proper meltdown.

Which was when Jagger told her, "I didn't realize until too late how important weddings were to you. But you can still have one. Here in Jacob's Well, I mean. With all your friends and your dad."

She'd looked up at him in confusion. "But we're already married."

Which was when his face had scrunched up and he'd taken a step back. "Well... *technically*..."

"What?" Sophia had swiped at her face. "Technically *what*?"

"Technically... that marriage back in Carlsbad might not have ever been... recorded anywhere. So it was never exactly... official."

Sophia lost her shit. She jumped up from the kitchen table. "Are you telling me," she'd all but shrieked, "that I have had three children," she got up in his face, "Out. Of. Wedlock?"

"No! I mean, sorta, yes. Ok no, I mean *no*." Jagger said, his hands held up in surrender as Mario growled and stepped forward. Jagger looked around in panic, but there was no one else to appeal to because the others were off tending to the kids to give Sophia a moment's peace.

"No," Jagger repeated, smiling at Sophia, "what I'm telling you is that you can still have the wedding of your dreams."

He was lucky that Shay had come around ringing the doorbell at that exact moment. And that the more Sophia thought about having a wedding, a *real* wedding, the more excited she'd gotten.

So here she was, on the fifth anniversary of her first 'wedding,' about to finally walk down the aisle in the church she'd dreamt about since she was a girl.

"Okay, finished," Vanessa said, standing back and holding her arms out with a flourish. Ever since her Vanessa's hair had grown back in, she'd become a connoisseur of cute hairstyles. Well, when she wasn't out spearing fish and the like.

"Oh Sophia," Shay breathed, standing up—which was a laborious enough task considering Shay was eight and a half months pregnant—and coming around to look at Sophia. "It's perfect. You're gorgeous."

Sophia stood up and turned around and Audrey held out a mirror to her. Sophia took it and her breath hitched. Her hair shone, a cascade of ringlets in an artful updo.

She turned around and beamed at Vanessa, hugging Shay to her at the same time. "It's beautiful."

Vanessa tucked a lock of her own hair behind her ear. "It's nothing. I'm glad I can help."

"Are you ready for the dress?" Audrey asked.

Was she ready for the dress? Was she ready for the *dress?* Sophia had been ready for the dress since she was seven and spent her allowance on an online subscription to *Wedding Weekly*.

Ten minutes later, the effect was complete.

The dress fit perfectly.

Shay had designed it. For several years now, she'd been turning her artist's eye towards fashion. She was a magician at piecing together old fabric into new clothes.

Sophia didn't know where Shay had found the uncut white organza to make the bottom of the dress from but *God*, it was gorgeous. Beyond gorgeous.

The top was done in lace and intricate beading and Sophia felt like a princess as she swirled in a circle.

After having three children in five years, taking the time to pamper herself and feel beautiful wasn't often at the top of her priorities list, so this felt even *more* special.

"I am *so* glad we made the guys make a pact that today was ladies day off," Vanessa laughed, flopping down in the chair Sophia had just vacated. "No mommy duties for a whole eight hours? We need to do this more often."

"Oh please," Audrey laughed, "the whole town'll be out for the wedding. The kids will be having a blast playing and the whole community will be watching them. I heard they're going all out for this wedding because you're like the official town daughter. Slaughtering extra pigs and breaking out the tequila and everything."

Sophia blushed. "They don't have to do that."

"Don't worry," Shay said. "It's not all about you. People love an excuse to relax and cut loose for a while." Then she dropped her head back, one hand on her protruding stomach. "Tequila. I miss tequila!"

"Awww, soon enough," Vanessa said, reaching over and patting Shay on the shoulder. Then she looked at Sophia. "Plus we're celebrating the good harvest. The new irrigation system they finished installing made such a difference. Plus the cattle herd's doing well. It's just good to feel like for once we aren't scrabbling to survive. Everyone feels it."

It wasn't just Jacob's Well, either.

Things were looking up all across The New Republic of Texas. Political stability and strong leadership had paved the path for strong intercountry trading routes to be set up.

Last time Sophia had talked to Dad, he and Drea were even thinking of sending emissaries to Mexico to see about establishing trade relations with their former enemies.

Speaking of Dad... Sophia frowned at her reflection in the mirror.

"What's wrong?" Shay asked, obviously noticing Sophia's change in mood.

"Any sign of them?" Sophia couldn't help looking toward the door.

"Not since we last checked," Audrey said, standing up. "But I'll go ask Nix to—"

"No, no, it's fine," Sophia said. Nix was the Commander of Jacob's Well now that her dad lived in Fort Worth and Nix he would be busy with all the activities planned for the day, plus the kids. "Anyway, Dad told me in his telegram a few days ago they had that urgent situation come up and that he might not be able to make it."

Being the First Husband to the President of the Republic kept Dad constantly busy.

"You know he *really* wanted to be here," Audrey said.

Sophia nodded, knowing it was true. If there was any way at all Dad could have been here, he would have. Whatever had come up, it must have been important. And Sophia understood, she really did.

Dad had his own life with Drea and they did important work that kept the entire country safe.

But sometimes... sometimes Sophia just missed her dad. Today of all days. Because as she looked at herself in the mirror, she was also powerfully reminded that her mom wasn't here either.

A rap came at the door.

Sophia swung around. Had Dad made it after all?

But then she heard the wail of a baby's cry as Audrey hurried to the door and opened it a crack.

"Nix."

"Sorry babe, but Emmy's been wailing her poor head off—"

"Yeah Mom. Baby misses you," said their four-and-a-half-year-old little boy, Max, bulldozing between Nix's legs and into the room.

"She says you been in here too long and she wants you to come out and play."

Nix lifted a heavy eyebrow at his son, which pulled the scar on the left side of his face taut.

"Actually, Max, I think baby sister is just saying she's hungry," Nix said, passing the baby off to Audrey. He leaned in. "Sorry, gorgeous. I tried to give you as much time as I could. I'll take her again after she's fed."

"It's fine," Sophia said. "We're all done in here."

Nix looked her way for the first time and a wide smile broke across his face while Audrey slid down her shirt and freed a breast to start feeding their five-month-old daughter.

"Well look at you." Nix walked over and gave Sophia a one-armed hug, careful not to muss her dress and landing a kiss on the side of her head.

"When did you go and grow up on me, pipsqueak?"

Sophia scoffed. "Uh, maybe about three kids ago?"

"Nah," Nix said, but then his smile sobered a little. "You remind me of my kid sister, you know that? Always have. And I'm proud of you. Your dad is, too."

"Damn you," Sophia said, smacking him hard on the chest. "Don't make me cry. You'll mess up my eye makeup."

Then she gave him a big hug. "Thanks for walking me down the aisle in his stead."

"Man," Nix said, "you have no idea how much willpower it's taking not to give you a noogie right now and mess up all this pretty hair."

Sophia pulled back and glared at him. "You do and you die."

Nix chuckled and Max jumped up and down. "Yes! Attack Daddy! Attack Daddy!"

Then Max ran with a roar and flung himself into Nix's legs.

"Oh yeah, little man?" Nix hoisted his son in the air and swung him around until he shrieked and giggled.

Then Nix held him over his forearm like he was a football and gave his bottom an affectionate swat.

"All right kiddo, let's go find one of your other dads so I can come back and walk Auntie Sophia down the aisle."

"Lemme down!" the boy squirmed.

"What's that?" Nix asked. "You want to go *up?*"

He lifted Max up onto his shoulders.

"No!" Max giggle-shrieked. "I said *down*, Daddy!"

"Oh, you want to go *around?*" Nix spun in a circle as he headed for the door.

"Daddy!"

"He's so good with him," Sophia grinned as the door closed behind them.

Audrey nodded, caressing her daughter's head as she continued to breastfeed. "I know. But with Emmy it's too funny, it's like Nix has forgotten how to take care of babies. He's always scared of breaking her. He carries her around like she's a porcelain doll."

"Oh my God, Logan was like that, but with *me* when I was pregnant," Vanessa said. "When the twins actually came, we were all too exhausted to waste too much time on more than the basic worries. Were they breathing? Okay, then we were good."

Sophia laughed. "Right? How did people before The Fall even *do* it without five or six parents to share the load? We take turns on who wakes up which nights with the kids and I *still* felt like a zombie the year Elle and Val were both under two."

Audrey shook her head. "I literally can't fathom doing it with fewer than at least four parents and even that would be pushing it."

A knock came at the door.

"That'll be Nix," Audrey said, looking to Sophia. "You ready, honey?"

Sophia pasted on a bright smile. Even if Dad wasn't there, she was still marrying the loves of her life today, surrounded by her friends and loved ones.

Vanessa reached up to fiddle with Sophia's hair one last time while Shay waddled over to get the door.

"Okay, Nix, you can let them know we're ready," Shay started saying as she opened the door wide.

And then they all froze.

Because standing on the other side of the door was Sophia's Dad, with Drea on his arm.

"Dad!" Sophia screeched, pulling away from Vanessa and sprinting across the room to fling herself into his arms.

"Sweetheart." He wrapped his strong arms around her and lifted her up off the ground.

Sophia pulled away, biting back tears, her throat thick. "You made it," she managed to choke out.

"Wouldn't miss it for the world," Drea said softly from beside them.

Sophia pulled away from her dad and hugged Drea just as hard, eliciting a little *oof* of surprise from Drea.

Over the years, things had more than mellowed between them. Sophia would go so far as to say that they were genuine friends now. Not that they had tons of time to hang out, what with Drea being President and all, but they saw each other often enough, and always had a good time when they did.

Sophia pulled back and looked Drea in the eye, squeezing her hands.

Thank you, she mouthed.

Drea just waved her off.

The bells rang out and Sophia grinned around at all of them. It was perfect. It was finally *perfect*.

Still holding onto one of Drea's hands, she clasped her dad's with the other.

"Let's go get me married!"

"I now pronounce you husbands and wife." Pastor Jonas announced. "You may kiss the bride!"

"Ew," said Shay's older son, Matthew, said loudly from the front row.

"Look the other way, boy," Jagger said before grabbing Sophia, dipping her backwards, and kissing her deep.

Swoon.

Every time.

Every. Time.

It didn't matter how many children she had or how many years passed, Jagger's hunger always felt like that day before she'd gone into Fort Worth. As if Jagger was kissing her like both their lives depended on it.

His tongue tangled with hers, a battle for dominance that she loved to let him win.

She gave herself to the kiss, to *him*, the man she'd now *finally* made vows to.

His eyes had shone as he'd made his vows in return, going off script almost immediately.

"I, Jagger Kincaid, do vow to love, honor, and trust this woman who was an oasis in the desert to me, who brought me life when I was a corpse walking and didn't even realize it, who gave me meaning, and a purpose, and a family, and I fucking love you, little dove, and I swear I will till my dying breath."

When Jagger finally, *finally*, let her up from the kiss, his dark eyes locked on her green ones, she felt so full up, she couldn't imagine a more perfect moment.

But then came Leo, a sparkle in his eyes, kissing and whispering an inside joke in her ear before nibbling on her earlobe in a way he knew made her giggle before passing her onto his brother Mario.

Mario held her face solemnly as he carefully repeated, word for word, exactly what Pastor Jonas said.

His language was stilted and Sophia knew that being under the spotlight here up in front of everyone made him beyond uncomfortable, but his eyes and his actions had always had far more to say than words ever could:

I will love you loyally.

I will love you completely.

I will love you always.

So those were the words she gave back to him.

His eyes were fierce with promise as he leaned down and pressed a simple kiss to her lips. She knew his intense passion would erupt tonight in the bedroom when he finally unleashed himself and a shudder went down her spine in anticipation.

Audrey's Clan had volunteered to babysit so for once, they'd have the house all to themselves for the whole weekend.

Finn had already declared that they were determined to put another baby in her this weekend.

Some of the other women had begun investigating birth control methods but not Sophia.

She wanted a house bursting with children, full of noise and laughter, and yes, children's screams and shouting, too.

She wanted it all. She wanted life, in every shape and color and sound.

Ever since she'd made the determination to stop living as if the only emotion she was allowed to feel was cheerful and happy, life had become more… interesting there for a while.

It was an adjustment. But so was living with four men. And their first daughter, Ella, had come only eleven months into their marriage.

There were growing pains, Sophia wouldn't lie.

But the same could be said for the entire nation trying to put itself back together after civil war, no matter how brief.

Finn finally stepped up and clasped Sophia's hand and warmth flooded her.

Here, of course, was the number one reason she'd been able to get through it all.

Her husbands. And yes, maybe Finn in particular.

Because while Jagger commanded her passions in a way that no one else could, and Leo made her laugh, and Mario gave her safety, loyalty, and love, it was Finn who'd been her first.

His vows said it all.

"It was always you for me, Soph."

And as his warm, familiar mouth closed on hers, she felt what she'd always felt with Finn.

A sense of coming *home*.

His kiss was long and sweet and lingering… and cut short by a loud shout from the front row.

"Shay!" Jonas called anxiously, pushing between Finn and Sophia.

Sophia swung to look and saw Shay holding her stomach, her features pinched in pain, and as Jonas got to her and Charlie and Gabriel helped her to her feet, Sophia could see a pool of water on the pew where Shay had been sitting and soaking the bottom of her dress.

"Mama!" Shay's daughter cried.

"It's okay, Nicky," Shay said, obviously breathing easier after the contraction passed. "Mama's just about to have your baby brother or sister."

Shay's husbands and women from the community hurried to Shay's side and helped her as she began waddling toward the back door of the church.

Shay paused and said something to Jonas who was holding her arm. He turned around hurriedly.

"We officially welcome Clan Kincaid to the community! Barbeque will be ready in fifteen. We're off to bring a human into the world!"

Cheers and clapping erupted from all around the church. Sophia laughed as everybody got to their feet. Almost immediately squirming little bodies jumped down from the pews and made a beeline for the doors to go play, parents shouting and hurrying after.

"I should go be with Shay," Sophia said, staring at the door all the women had gone through.

"She'll be fine, little dove," Jagger said, coming up and circling his arms around her from behind. He kissed the back of her neck. "And it's not every day I get to marry a woman as fine as you."

"But the barbeque—"

"Will be going on all night," Finn interrupted, taking her hand again. "I say we start this honeymoon early and send someone out for food later. Just think, for once we won't have to worry about rushing or being interrupted by the pitter patter of little feet or Anna waking up in the middle of the night."

Finn moved to her front, sandwiching her in between him and Jagger.

Sophia could feel both of them, hot and hard against her as the last of the church emptied out.

Leo and Mario came close, until she was boxed in on all four sides.

Just the way she loved it best.

"Well what are we waiting for?" she asked a little breathlessly. "Let's go get this honeymoon started."

EPILOGUE II

ERIC

Eric bounced his one-year-old granddaughter in his arms as he and Drea walked out of the church. The Vasquez Clan had two little ones near the ages of little Ella and Val, Sophia's other two daughters, and offered to look after them since Audrey needed to go with Shay.

Eric glanced over his shoulder at his daughter, surrounded by her four husbands.

"I still can't believe my little girl is big enough to have little girls of her own."

Drea smiled at him. "You're only forty-six. Hardly ancient."

Eric shrugged, then kissed his baby granddaughter's head. "I don't know. Sometimes I feel twice that."

"Don't we all. But look at this." Drea pointed at the lawn outside the church packed with people chatting and laughing, kids running around and getting underfoot. Eric got what she meant. It could have been any Pre-Fall church picnic.

"You did this," Drea said, sliding an arm around Eric's waist.

"Hardly," Eric scoffed. Was she serious? "No, babe, I'm pretty sure *you* did this. We'd all still be hiding in a cave somewhere if you hadn't stepped up and taken leadership of the country."

Drea laughed. "How about we just agree that we're both kickass and leave it at that?"

"Who's kickass?" Garrett asked as he, Jonathan, David, and Billy came up behind them. Eric and Drea had taken the fastest car they had, an old two-seater Camaro in order to get here on time. The others had followed in a bus and must have just arrived.

"Clan Valentine, naturally," Drea said, turning to them and welcoming each with a quick kiss.

"Fuck yeah we kick ass," Garrett said. "Did you see how quick those Hell's Hollow's assholes folded once we started putting pressure on them to cut out the slave trading?"

Drea sighed. "At least out in the open. They'll just go black market with it and we'll have to work even harder ferreting them out."

"Still," David said. "It's a win that all over the Republic law and order is becoming the norm and not the exception."

Drea smiled and Eric was glad as always for David's cool head. Eric couldn't always manage the same equanimity that the other man seemed to be able to keep, especially when it came to their wife.

Then Drea looked around at them anxiously. "Do you think Kylie's okay? Did you check at the telegraph office to see if we've gotten any word from her yet?"

"I checked," Billy said. "No word yet, but I'm sure she's fine."

Drea nodded, jaw hardening as she looked out on the happy crowd.

"I'm sure she's fine, though," Billy repeated. "We only just left her yesterday afternoon and they had to get all the way to Colorado."

They'd parted with Kylie at the northern border, them going one way, and Kylie going another.

She was being taken away by an emissary of the Queen of Colorado who'd appeared out of the blue and requested a meeting with President Drea Valentine.

That was the urgent business they'd had to attend to. Terrible timing, but there was no way they could say, hey, sorry, would you mind waiting a week while we jot down to Central Texas South to see our daughter get married, then we'll get back to your emissary who's attempting to make first contact after well over a decade?

No, they'd sped up to the north and met with the woman and the small security force she'd travelled with.

The Queen of Colorado wanted to meet face to face with Drea, the emissary said. She was inviting Drea to come visit Artemisia, what used to be called Denver.

Saying no would not only mean missing out on the opportunity to see what had previously been a closed land, it could be taken as an insult.

Or so Drea had said. Repeatedly.

Drea had wanted to go herself but finally Eric and the others were able to talk her out of it. It was simply too dangerous for the President of the country to walk sight-unseen into a potentially volatile situation.

So they compromised. They'd send an ambassador first. And considering that Colorado was apparently a matriarchy now, it needed to be a woman.

Kylie and Drea had first become friends when they lived in the bachelorette house in Jacob's Well, and Kylie moved up to Fort Worth to help Drea with administrative tasks when she became President. Over the years, Kylie had become more and more invaluable.

There was no one Drea trusted more to represent her.

Kylie had said yes when Drea presented the possibility of going without even batting an eye.

At the time, Eric had pulled Drea aside. "How is this any different from what Sophia did?" he'd asked. "Heading into New Mexico because men lured her there with false promises of truce and trade?"

"It's different because ever since we learned from Jagger what really happened during the war there, we've worked to independently verify all he said about the Queen of Colorado." Drea said it all patiently but Eric had been able to see the worry lines in her forehead, too. Who was she trying to convince? Him, or herself? "And everything the Queen's emissary said matches up to the intel our spies have gathered."

Still, Eric had overheard the conversation Drea'd had with Kylie. "I won't lie. This could be dangerous. We have no idea what you'll be walking into. I'm not ordering you to do this as your President. It's up to you."

"Of course I'm going," Kylie said without even missing a beat. "This is too big an opportunity."

"But you really need to think—"

"I'm ready, Drea. I'm ready to do something that matters. You know I've felt like I'm just spinning my wheels for years. After Justin, I just—"

"That guy was an asshole," Drea interjected.

There was silence for a moment and Eric knew he should pull back from the door. He hadn't meant to eavesdrop. But then Kylie went on.

"I can do this, Drea. Give me the chance to prove I can."

Eric had backed away after that but next thing he knew, Drea and Kylie were coming out of the room and it was settled. Kylie was going as their ambassador.

So that was that. Kylie had left with the emissary two days ago and they'd been on the road ever since.

Baby Anna started fussing on Eric's shoulder and Drea reached for her. "Who's a good girl? That's right, *you are*." Then she blew a strawberry on the baby's belly, eliciting little shrieking giggles.

Eric could only stare. Jesus, didn't she know she tore at his heart when she did things like that? Or really, all the time. She was just so fucking beautiful and strong and— and *stubborn*. But fuck if he didn't love her for it.

"That's a good look on you, Mrs. V," Ross from Clan Washington came up and said... or was it Riordan. Eric never had been able to tell the twins apart. "You ever think about popping out one of your own?"

"Riordan," said the other twin, coming up and smacking his brother on the back of the head. "Jesus, that's not something you ask a lady. Especially the *President*."

"What?" Riordan said. "It's all anybody talks about around here. I swear, they should change the name of this place from Jacob's Well to Baby's Well for as many kids the women are having all the time."

Eric worried Drea would be upset but she just smiled easily, taking it all in stride. They talked about kids sometimes, but she wasn't sure she wanted any. She'd gotten a fresh IUD a year ago from a haul from an old medical facility Scrappers had found. She said that if she did want to think about kids, it would be after she was through with her term in office, and none of them was sure when that would be.

Should the nation stick to the max eight-year term the old United States had? Or was a ten-year term more realistic to get the state of the nation to a more stable place before passing the baton off to someone else? Either way, they were in no rush. Drea was only thirty-one.

"Well it's good to hear the women of Jacob's Well are doing their part to repopulate the country."

"We're not supposed to say," Riordan leaned in, eyes gleaming, "But Vanessa's preggers again."

"Riordan!" Ross smacked him again. "You know she doesn't want people knowing yet."

"I can't help it, man." He looked back to Eric and Drea. "We're gonna have another girl. I can *feel* it."

"You're gonna feel my fist in your face if you don't learn to keep your mouth shut," Ross muttered.

"Oh really?" Riordan jumped on his brother, tackling him to the ground. They rolled around, wrestling and grappling.

A group quickly gathered, townsfolk clapping and whistling and cheering for one brother or the other.

"Glad to see nothing changes around here," Drea said affectionately, stepping back.

One brother pinned the other, crowing, "Say uncle! I'm not letting you up until you say uncle."

"Never!"

"Say it!"

"Good Lord," said Logan, walking over with a plate full of barbeque in one hand and holding their daughter's hand with his other. The little girl was also holding onto her twin sister's hand. "What are these two on about now?"

The two twin girls, Tara and Natalie, started jumping up and down, shouting, "Wrestle! Wrestle!" except they couldn't say their 'r's very well, so it came out sounding like, 'Westle! Westle!'

The pinned brother looked over to the girls. "Come rescue me, girls. Come rescue Daddy!"

Logan let go of his daughter's hand and both twin girls went and threw themselves on top of where their twin fathers piled on the ground.

"Oh, he's got me," Ross said, pretending to be incapacitated.

"Say Uncle!" cried the girl.

"Uncle, Uncle," the big man said, smacking the ground. Then he flipped around and grabbed one of the girls up, tickling her mercilessly.

Riordan grabbed the other girl and did the same.

"God I love coming home," Drea said, nuzzling close to Eric's side as the boys continued to tussle on the ground, the shrieks and giggles coming even louder.

"Oh yeah?" Eric looked over at her in surprise and saw her face was relaxed and happy.

"Reminds me what it's all for," she said.

They shared an intimate gaze for a long moment. Eric had never felt so goddamned full as he did right now, the sun shining down from above, his family around him, his daughter happily married. This was the shit happily ever afters were made of.

"Why we standing around here, woman?" Garrett smacked Drea on the ass. "Let's go get us some barbeque before it's all gone!"

"Oh you're gonna regret that," Drea shouted, turning and taking off after Garrett.

Eric laughed and followed after them, patting his baby granddaughter on the back as he went.

Want to read an EXCLUSIVE, FREE 45 page novelette, *Their Honeymoon*, about Audrey and her Clan's honeymoon that is available only to my newsletter subscribers, along with news about upcoming releases, sales, exclusive giveaways, and more?

Get *Their Honeymoon* by visiting BookHip.com/QHCQDM

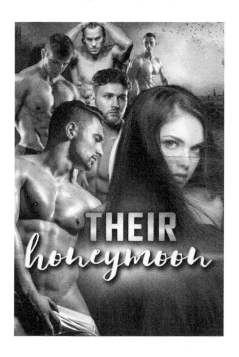

Have you missed any of the books in the
Marriage Raffle Series?

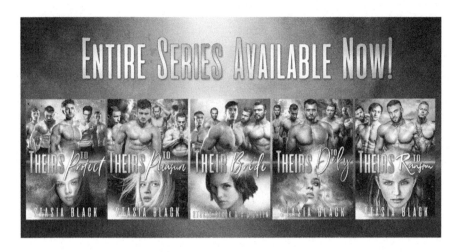

MARRIAGE RAFFLE SERIES
Theirs to Protect
Theirs to Pleasure
Their Bride
Theirs to Defy
Theirs to Ransom

A NOTE FROM THE AUTHOR

Just wanted to let everyone know that while the series proper is finished, there will be one more book coming that follows Kylie's adventures into Colorado, but I'm taking a break from this series for a bit to write some other ideas that have been burning to get out :) I do anticipate writing Kylie's book, HIS ONE AND ONLY, probably before the end of the year. As you might be able to tell from the title, it won't be a Revere Harem, but a strictly one on one M/F.

ALSO BY STASIA BLACK

MARRIAGE RAFFLE SERIES

Theirs to Protect

Theirs to Pleasure

Their Bride

Theirs to Defy

Theirs to Ransom

BREAK SO SOFT SERIES

Cut So Deep

Break So Soft

Hurt So Good

STUD RANCH STANDALONE SERIES

The Virgin and the Beast: a Beauty and the Beast Tale (prequel)

Hunter: a Snow White Romance

The Virgin Next Door: a Ménage Romance

ACKNOWLEDGMENTS

First round of thanks goes to Lee Savino who kept my spirits up during the process of writing this book and was just phone call away during several breakdowns. So much <3

Huge thanks to Aimee Bowyer for a SUPER fast beta turnaround on this one. It was a bit of a rough go but as always I find your feedback invaluable. *Hugs*

Thanks to Melissa Pascoe, you gorgeous lady, you, keeping my social media straight and helping me stay on top of things, thank you!

A bajillion thanks to Jennifer R! Or lol, not sure how you prefer to be named, but you know who you are, you insanely talented goddess who have made my life SO much more sane since you came on board. THANK YOU!

And to my hubby who never reads these but always deserves so much damn thanks. I'm staring at you right now as I write this, gorgeous, and I love you so fucking much, you nerdy genius, you. I don't feel like *me* without you, that's how intertwined we've got over the years. Now if both our lives would just slow down a *tad* so we could see each other's faces again on the regular. Sound like a plan? *mwah sexy*

ABOUT THE AUTHOR

STASIA BLACK grew up in Texas, recently spent a freezing five-year stint in Minnesota, and now is happily planted in sunny California, which she will never, ever leave.

She loves writing, reading, listening to podcasts, and has recently taken up biking after a twenty-year sabbatical (and has the bumps and bruises to prove it). She lives with her own personal cheerleader, aka, her handsome husband, and their teenage son. Wow. Typing that makes her feel old. And writing about herself in the third person makes her feel a little like a nutjob, but ahem! Where were we?

Stasia's drawn to romantic stories that don't take the easy way out. She wants to see beneath people's veneer and poke into their dark places, their twisted motives, and their deepest desires. Basically, she wants to create characters that make readers alternately laugh, cry ugly tears, want to toss their kindles across the room, and then declare they have a new FBB (forever book boyfriend).

Join Stasia's Facebook Group for Readers for access to deleted scenes, to chat with me and other fans and also get access to exclusive giveaways:
https://www.facebook.com/groups/StasiasBabes/

Made in the USA
Las Vegas, NV
17 February 2021